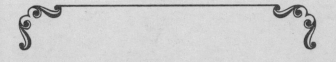

The duke found he did not like the way her hands left his shoulders. He took them in his and placed them back in their original position.

Without her permission, his left arm moved gently around Henrietta's waist. His right hand, shaking ever so slightly, came up to tilt her face up to his. He muttered something unintelligible, then slowly lowered his mouth to hers.

The touch of her lips was a delicious sensation that raced through his bloodstream. As Henrietta swayed against him, Giles fought down the need to deepen the embrace, then gave up the struggle. He pressed her tightly against his chest and lost himself in the sweet warmth of her mouth. . . .

A CRIME OF MANNERS

Rosemary Stevens

FAWCETT CREST • NEW YORK

With love for my family—
J.T., Rachel and Tommy

and

With special thanks to:
Jerry Lynn Smith, Cynthia Holt and
Melissa Lynn Jones

A Fawcett Crest Book
Published by Ballantine Books

http://www.randomhouse.com

ISBN 0-449-22457-0

Manufactured in the United States of America

First Edition: May 1996

10 9 8 7 6 5 4 3 2 1

Chapter One

Giles Vayne, the eighth Duke of Winterton, dismissed his valet and prepared to retire for the night. Climbing into his massive four-poster bed, he was about to blow out the candle when he heard his deceased father's voice.

"You must marry. Produce an heir. Your duty. A suitable gel. Honor to Vayne."

"Devil take that bird," the duke muttered as he threw the bedclothes back and crossed the room. He picked up a cover and angrily threw it over the large birdcage standing in the corner, effectively stopping the parrot before the bird could deliver himself of the rest of the oft-repeated lecture.

The occupant of the cage let out a loud squawk of protest at this Turkish treatment but shortly settled down to rest. A gray bird with red tail feathers, the parrot was an adept mimic who had lived with the previous duke for ten years. He could expound at length in the old duke's voice on that man's favorite subject: what Giles owed his family name.

The duke, weary, but now too agitated to sleep, poured himself a brandy from the tray left by Tyler, his valet. He wondered, not for the first time, if any other man was plagued with parental dictates from beyond the grave by a member of the avian family.

His father, a controlling, hardened aristocrat, had died the previous March in a fox-hunting accident, leaving the dukedom to his only son. According to the terms of the seventh Duke of Winterton's will, Giles was to take especial care of his beloved pet, Sir Polly Grey—the "Sir" was only a courtesy title, the old duke having knighted the bird himself.

For reasons that had become all too clear to Giles, the parrot was to be given houseroom in his bedchamber until the event of Giles's marriage.

Practically speaking, there was no way for this edict to be enforced, but Giles was a loyal son and, what's more, had a strong sense of duty. Sir Polly Grey, therefore, resided with Giles in London at the duke's town house in Park Lane, or as such was the case at present, the ducal estate, Perrywood, in Sussex.

His father would have been pleased to see the effect the bird's repeated nagging was having on Giles.

In his nightshirt, the duke sat with his brandy by the glowing fire, and considered the matter. The Season would begin in one month. He should at least look over this year's crop of hopefuls, he mused. He knew what was due his name, and it was time, perhaps past time, at the great age of two and thirty, to set up his nursery.

He ran a long-fingered hand through his dark hair. While any rich duke was reputedly attractive, Giles's easy elegance, strong air of command, and pleasing, if austere, countenance would draw the ladies whatever his position in Society.

Just then, a look of disdain marred his handsome face. What an odious task lay before him, he thought cynically. How could he possibly agree to leg-shackle himself to one of the simpering young misses who, hoping to acquire his title and fortune, used every wile and ploy imaginable to draw themselves to his attention? He much preferred the jaded charms of the sophisticated ladies of the ton or the demireps, who could satisfy his baser needs without unwanted entanglements.

Unfortunately, he believed Sir Polly Grey was right. He must go to London and find a beautiful girl of impeccable family, one with a fortune that could be added to his own; a miss who excelled in all the ladylike accomplishments, capable of gracing his table and bearing him fine sons. If she didn't bore him to death first.

The thoughts of breeding turned the duke's mind to a different crop of eligibles. The new foals at Squire Lanford's. Everyone knew the squire bred superb Thoroughbreds to be trained for racing at Newmarket. As a member of the Jockey Club, the organization that governed the horse-racing society known as the Turf, the duke had a keen interest in horseflesh. Perhaps he would allow himself the diversion of breaking his journey to London at the squire's.

His mind set, the duke returned to his bed.

On the other side of the room, Sir Polly Grey let out a satisfied cluck and fell asleep.

Three days later, at Squire Lanford's estate in the village of Hamilton Cross, Miss Henrietta Lanford went about her morning duties. She was clad in a drab round gown, her dark brown hair pulled back and held with a fraying ribbon.

She entered the hot kitchen in the back of the house and inhaled the spicy aromas.

Engaged in mixing a pudding, Cook, a gray-haired woman in a large mobcap, eyed Henrietta fondly. "Did ye enjoy the rolls on yer breakfast tray, Miss Lanford?" Mrs. Battersby asked, a knowing twinkle in her eyes.

Mrs. Battersby had been Cook at Squire Lanford's for as long as Henrietta could remember. "You know very well I did," Henrietta replied in mock reproach, her hands on her hips. "It was quite unkind of you to place three of my favorites within temptation's reach. I shall grow fat."

"Faugh," Mrs. Battersby snorted, straightening her apron over her own ample girth. " 'Tis a wonder you don't perish away to nothing, so little you eat."

The two women spent an amicable hour together planning the week's menus. At nineteen, the squire's daughter already possessed four years' experience in overseeing the domestic aspects of running her family home. Her mother showed no interest in such things.

Both of Henrietta's parents were horse-mad. When the midwife presented Mrs. Lanford with her baby daughter, the squire's wife found herself somewhat surprised and confused about what to do with an infant, her knowledge of the young confined to that of the breed with four legs.

Henrietta was brought up by her governess, Biddles, who'd left the Lanford home last year to take care of her sickly mother. Being of an overly romantical nature, as ill-favored spinsters are apt to be, she'd left behind an extensive supply of Minerva Press novels, hoping the books would provide Henrietta with a much different view of men than the one her horse-mad father and the dull local boys presented.

Henrietta was ordinarily a practical girl with a clever mind and a good nature. Biddles would have been shocked to see a dreamy side of the young lady's personality emerge after spending a winter of long evenings curled up with those novels. For Henrietta increasingly spent her time dreaming of falling in love.

This morning was no exception. After dealing with Cook, Henrietta threw a heavy, hooded cloak over her gown, protected her hands with a pair of woolen gloves, and took herself off to her beloved garden. Armed with shears and workbasket, she could daydream the morning away.

The freezing winter was turning into a frigid spring. She shivered in the crisp air, sniffing appreciatively at the not unpleasing smell of woodsmoke and damp earth. Henrietta soon forgot the cold as she cleared away dead twigs and leaves. She was lost in her favorite daydream.

In her imagination, *he* would be tall, dark-haired, and ride a large, white horse. She pictured herself strolling through a meadow on a sunny summer day, wearing a flowing pale gown of gossamer material. Her infuriatingly straight hair curled around her head like a halo. *He* would come charging through the woods into the meadow and rein his horse to a sudden stop at the sight of her beauty. Swinging down from his saddle, he would say he was a Prince from a Faraway Land. He'd beg her to tell him the name of the maiden standing before him who had captured his heart. The Fantasy Henrietta would coo a seductive reply, upon which the raven-haired god would be so overcome, he would . . .

"Miss Lanford, Miss Lanford! Ain't ye hearing me then?" The little housemaid tugged impatiently at Henrietta's sleeve.

"What?" The Practical Henrietta blinked. "Oh, Megan, whatever is it?"

"I been trying to tell ye but couldn't get ye to mind. Cook's all in a lather as we've an unexpected guest for nuncheon."

Henrietta stared at the red-haired maid in confusion. "A guest? Pray, who could it be?"

"I'm not rightly sure, miss. Alls I know is that Cook said I was to find ye right away. She said ye should be present at table."

The news of the Duke of Winterton's arrival had spread through the house with alarming speed. It wasn't often that members of the haute ton lingered for a meal at the squire's once they concluded their business. Not that the squire and his wife were in any way toad eaters. They simply had no conversation at all other than horse talk, which could be wearing to even the most devoted of Newmarket followers.

Her curiosity aroused, Henrietta entered the house through the kitchen, handing Megan her cloak and gloves. Having no time to waste, she hurriedly washed her hands and barely glanced at her untidy reflection in the looking glass she passed in the hall. It seemed her parents and their guest were already seated in the small dining room.

Henrietta checked as she crossed the threshold into the room, staring fixedly at the stranger rising to stand at his place at the table. Here he was at last! The hero of her daydream come to life.

Tall, with an athletic build, he was immaculately dressed. The snug fit of his blue morning coat must have been his tailor's proudest moment. His buff pantaloons had the effect of leaving little to the imagination, while at the same time allowing that imagination to roam. He wore his black hair longer than the current fashion dictated, and his eyes were a cool gray.

Never, outside her imagination, had Henrietta seen a more impressive, handsome man. Discomposed, she blushed. As he mockingly returned her stare, her gaze dropped to the carpet and she moved toward her chair.

The duke stood by his place, his cultivated air of boredom masking his surprise. The Lanfords had made no mention of a daughter during the morning's inspection of the squire's foals.

He saw a petite young girl in an unappealing gown. Confined at the neck, her dark hair fell in a straight mass down her back. Across her forehead were longish strands of hair which she brushed to one side in what he recognized was a nervous gesture. He caught a glimpse of large blue eyes and a small mouth before the color rose in her cheeks and she lowered her head.

The thought crossed his mind to be on his guard in case the Lanfords were using this opportunity to throw their daughter at his head. He'd certainly had every trick played on him by matchmaking mamas since he'd come of age.

Squire and Mrs. Lanford were taken aback as well at their daughter's presence. So wrapped up were they in the world of the Turf, they often forgot her existence.

The stocky squire was the first to recover and effected the introductions.

The duke responded to Henrietta's curtsy with a brief bow and sat down, hardly waiting for her to be seated.

Granite-faced Mrs. Lanford smiled at the duke, revealing a mouth full of large teeth. She resumed the conversation, saying with conviction, "I do not hold by the popular belief of trainers, Your Grace, who keep horses in overheated stables without any fresh air."

"Indeed." Squire Lanford took the reins of the conversation. "I have an article published in the *Sporting Magazine* detailing my abhorrence of the practices of some trainers. Purges, sweats . . ."

Nodding to a servant holding a plate of cold meats, Henrietta heard her father's voice drone on. She was used to turning her mind off once he got started on the subject of his precious horses. She had heard all his theories before, and could recite most by rote.

She toyed with her food, all the while covertly studying the duke from under her lashes. Biting her lip in vexation, she found herself wishing desperately that she were wearing her best gown.

Henrietta's knowledge of fashions was limited to the few fashion plates that occasionally circulated in the village. Still, she did not need the current issue of *La Belle Assemblée* to know the picture she presented at the moment was not the first impression she would have wished to present.

The duke's attention, however, appeared taken up by his host. As the minutes went by, Henrietta found herself becoming cross with him for not including her in the conversation. She remained silent, though, knowing it would be most improper for her to speak to the duke without his first addressing her.

The Practical Henrietta's mind lectured that Papa was hardly letting the duke speak a word, so how was he to show any interest, polite as it could only be, in herself?

The Fantasy Henrietta began weaving a rosy dream in which the handsome duke saw beyond her countrified appearance and gazed longingly into her eyes. Miss Lanford, he would say, I am blinded by your beauty. Come away with me and be my duchess.

It was at the straining point in these ruminations that the duke did, indeed, turn to Henrietta.

"Do you share your parents' love of horses, Miss Lanford?" he asked in a tone of complete indifference.

Giles could hardly have chosen a worse opening remark, innocent as its intention may have been, if he tried.

Over the years, Henrietta had resented her mother and father's preoccupation with their stables. In time, with Biddles's affection and guidance, she'd accepted her situation and come to realize her parents loved her in their way. Deep inside, though, she really didn't think much of herself. And she'd certainly never acquired her family's obsession with horseflesh.

"No," she replied with deceptive calm as her temper rose. Pique cause her to condemn even her own sweet mare. "I find them nasty, smelly beasts."

The squire glared at his daughter, his face turning an unusual shade of purple as he sputtered, "See here now!"

But he got no further, because Winterton, sensing an oncoming familial scene he had no desire to witness, smoothly interjected, "Do you go to London for the Season, Miss Lanford?"

Henrietta opened her mouth to say she had no such plans, when Mrs. Lanford answered matter-of-factly, "Yes, Your Grace, Henrietta will make her come-out this year."

Both husband and daughter looked at her as if she were touched in her upperworks.

Before either could refute her claim, the duke spoke again, looking down his nose at Henrietta. "You will, no doubt, enjoy the amusements London has to offer, Miss Lanford. And one can hardly detect the scent of horse*flesh*, I assure you," he ended satirically.

Henrietta's cheeks flamed from a mixture of annoyance at herself for making such a silly remark and the duke's insolence at reminding her of it.

After a few moments, Winterton rose from the table. "I fear I must take my leave of you so I may continue my own journey to Town." He raised a hand in an imperious gesture. "Pray do not trouble yourselves to see me out. I thank you for your hospitality."

"The foal will be well taken care of, Your Grace," Squire Lanford said, rising from his seat.

"I have no doubt of it, Mr. Lanford." The duke made his bow. "Mrs. Lanford, Miss Lanford, I bid you good day."

The Duke of Winterton's traveling carriage waited outside. It was followed by a fourgon, heavy with trunks that Tyler presided over with haughty majesty.

When the duke entered and gave the order, the carriage moved off. Leaning back against the comfortable squabs, he considered his morning. Certain the colt he'd selected would someday win at Newmarket wearing his colors, he felt a sense of satisfaction.

He thought of the squire and Mrs. Lanford unfavorably, condemning them as hopelessly provincial, although he had enjoyed examining the stables with the bluff squire.

A bump in the road brought a protesting squawk

from the other occupant of the carriage. Placed on the seat opposite the duke, Sir Polly Grey, sequestered in his own covered travel cage, was unhappy with the ride.

In the distinctive voice of the old duke he grumbled, "Giles. A suitable gel. Marriage."

Giles ignored the bird and wondered idly if the unworldly, artless Miss Henrietta Lanford would have suitors when she went to London. Perhaps with enough Town bronze and that rather charming blush she might be lucky and attract a well-to-do landowner.

Thankfully, her parents had done nothing to push the girl forward, nothing to bring her to his attention. Just the opposite looked to be the way of things. With a wry twist of his lips, Giles recalled the squire's reaction when Miss Lanford maligned horses. Obviously she took second place to the cattle in her family's affections.

No doubt he would not meet her again as they would hardly be moving in the same circles in Town. He flicked the memory of the chit from his mind.

The second the duke had quit the room, an excited Henrietta rounded on her mother. "Mama! Pray tell me at once if it is true I am to go to London."

The squire's jowls quivered with indignation. "Yes, Mrs. Lanford. Tell us how are we supposed to take our leave of three mares ready to foal in the next fortnight to go roistering up to Town! You know very well I cannot abide London at any time, and the thought of doing the pretty to a pack of high-in-the-instep fools discussing politics, gambling on cards, while my dear horses . . . It is not to be borne, madam!"

Mrs. Lanford had experienced the uncomfortable feeling a mother has when she realizes she has somehow been remiss in her parental role. The Duke of Winterton's presence reminded her forcibly that it was past time her daughter had a husband. Not that she considered Henrietta capable of attracting someone of the Duke's rank and standing in Society.

"Of course, *we* will not go to Town, Mr. Lanford. What a chuckleheaded notion. Henrietta will go to my sister in London, Lady Fuddlesby. Clara is very much of the bon ton and received everywhere. Keeps a town house in Grosvenor Square. Count on it, she will find our gel a suitable husband."

"London . . . a husband," Henrietta uttered faintly. The Fantasy Henrietta's thoughts rushed ahead to a courtship filled with romantic nights beneath a glowing moon, poems written in her honor, beautifully decorated ballrooms where *he* would twirl her round and round in his arms in that shocking dance, the waltz.

Still unmollified, the squire asked, "Are you not thinking of the expense, Mrs. Lanford? Why, I could expand the stables, improve on the lower pasture. . . ."

For once, Mrs. Lanford's ambitions were solely for her daughter. "Nonsense. It will be horribly dear, naturally, for Clara will need funds for Henrietta to have a complete new wardrobe, pin money, and oh, any number of costly things. And a decent dowry must be offered. But you are not thinking, Mr. Lanford! It is our *duty* to see our daughter married well."

There was no argument to that statement. The

squire heaved a great sigh and said, "Yes, I suppose you're right, m'dear. Well, it's off to Town you go then, Henrietta. See that you know what is owed us after all the care we have given you over the years." Wagging a finger at his daughter, the squire admonished, "If you play your cards right, you might just snare a gentleman from the Four in Hand Club."

With this speech, the squire considered his duty done and took himself off to sit in front of the library fire with a copy of *Pick's Racing Calendar*. Mrs. Lanford went to her desk to write Lady Fuddlesby that she was to bring out her niece, and Henrietta floated up the stairs to her bedchamber to dream about her imaginary beau who now wore the Duke of Winterton's face.

Several days later, at Lady Fuddlesby's town house in Grosvenor Square, a cat walked up the stairs with a letter clamped in his jaw. He was an unusual-looking animal. Stark white with a black tail, he had a wedge of black that extended across his eyes, quite like a domino mask.

A push with his shoulder opened Lady Fuddlesby's bedchamber door, always left ajar for just this purpose. He swaggered across the room to where the lady, seated at her toilet table, applied rouge with a light hand to her round cheeks.

The soft pink of the cosmetic matched the decor of her ladyship's apartments. Most of the gowns in her wardrobe were of that same hue, pink being her favorite and most becoming color.

Unlike her horse-mad sister, Lady Fuddlesby was all that was feminine. She could lay claim to great beauty in her youth and, despite the addition of thirty unwanted pounds, was still attractive at three and fifty.

"Oh, my dearest Knight, whatever have you there?" she asked, eyeing the parchment now dented with fang marks.

Knight in Masked Armour, for that was his full name, stood on his hind legs and dropped the missive in Lady Fuddlesby's plump lap.

Breaking the seal, she said, "A letter from my younger sister. How singular! One wonders how she found the time away from her horses."

Lady Fuddlesby perused the lines, clucking her tongue and emitting an occasional gasp. Knight sat at her feet in a patch of afternoon sunlight, his tail twitching with interest.

"Oh dear, oh dear. We are to have company, Knight. My niece, Henrietta. You have never met her, for she has spent her life isolated in the country, the poor dear. Goodness, she may arrive tomorrow!"

Perhaps in understanding of this bit of intelligence, and loath to share Lady Fuddlesby's attentions with anyone, Knight turned his whiskers down. It had just been the two of them these past five years, unless one counted a house full of servants. Viscount Fuddlesby had died of an apoplexy one evening at White's, over a particularly unfortunate hand of cards.

At the viscount's death, Lady Fuddlesby had been obliged to pay off his excessive gambling debts. While she was left with the town house, and a sufficient but not large income, she found the cost of living in London and being in Society to be exorbitant. A more clever woman might have managed well, but while Lady Fuddlesby had a kind heart, she was somewhat lacking in judgment when it came to practicalities and economies.

"Well, it seems my sister has made a mull of it. I shall be obliged to introduce the gel to Society and find her a husband. Oh dear, oh dear, I do hope she's in looks. It does make finding an eligible *parti* easier if one has beauty, especially when one is a mere squire's daughter."

A furrow appeared in Lady Fuddlesby's brow. "I daresay I shall come about, Knight. After all, a handsome draft on Mr. Lanford's bank is included, so we needn't worry the cost, and oh, I am sure Henrietta is a delight since her mama deplores her lack of interest in horses. It will be quite as if I had a child of my own."

At these last words, a reproachful meow came from Knight's throat.

"Oh! Forgive me, my darling boy," Lady Fuddlesby cried. She reached down to scratch behind Knight's ears, bringing an expression of intense contentment to his masked face.

Lady Fuddlesby straightened in her chair. In her mind she began to go over the upcoming Season's list of eligibles. She did not get far in these musings before the Duke of Winterton's name cried out in her brain.

No! Flying much too high, she thought. Still, how wonderful it would be, after all these years.

Clara had made her come-out the same year as Lady Matilda Danvers. They both had been drawn to the seventh Duke of Winterton. Matilda had won him, though, since she had been an earl's daughter, while Clara was only a plain miss.

Forgetting almost thirty years of a comfortable marriage to Viscount Fuddlesby, Lady Fuddlesby grew agitated at the memory of her defeat.

How gratifying it would be if she could bring about a match between her niece and the present Duke of Winterton. Perhaps she would send him a card, asking him to call . . . but she would have to see the girl first and be sure she dressed in the first stare of fashion, and . . .

"Oh, Knight," Lady Fuddlesby said, pressing her fingers to her temples, "I fear I am bringing on one of my headaches with all this thinking."

Knight sauntered over to her ladyship's bed, jumped up on the pink coverlet, turned round clockwise three times, lay down, and closed his eyes.

"My dear boy," Lady Fuddlesby crooned as she crossed the room and prepared to lie down next to the sleeping cat, "you always know what to do. A nap, of course, is just the thing to put me to rights."

Chapter Two

It is a sad fact that not all journeys to London go as smoothly as that of the Duke of Winterton and Sir Polly Grey.

Henrietta, with Megan along to lend her consequence, set out from home on a sunny, if cold, March day. There was no one to see them off except Cook. Mrs. Lanford was already down at the stables with the squire, feeling her part in her daughter's removal to Town was complete after writing to Lady Fuddlesby.

In keeping with the fickle English weather, on the second day of their travels the skies clouded and snow began to fall. At first it fell in thick white flakes that melted as they reached the ground. By late afternoon the wind picked up and the snow changed to a swirling mass that obscured the view from the windows of the squire's traveling coach.

"Do but look, miss." Megan's eyes were round with fright. "I wonder how Ben can see where he's drivin' us."

Henrietta wondered the same thing but was not about to voice her fears in front of the maid. "I am certain we shall be perfectly safe, Megan."

Henrietta could see her breath in front of her when she spoke, the cold having claimed the interior of the coach. Both girls were dressed warmly and wrapped in carriage rugs. Henrietta wore a dark blue wool pelisse over an old-fashioned gown of paler blue. Her hair was tucked up under a matching bonnet that framed her face.

As the women stared out at the storm, the coach pulled to the side of the road and stopped. Henrietta saw Ben's ruddy face at the window and she lowered the glass, letting in a gust of snow.

"I can't go on much further, miss. The snow's not buildin' up deep on the roads yet, but I can barely see as far as the horses' heads. I know of an inn up ahead and that's where we're goin', with your permission," he said, tugging a forelock.

"I shall be grateful if you can get us there, Ben," Henrietta said, shivering.

The coach set off again, and a short time later Megan exclaimed, "I can make out some lights. I'm that glad, miss, as I can hardly feel my feet from the cold."

They pulled up in front of an establishment that proclaimed itself to be the Pig and Thistle. Several carriages were in the yard, other travelers lured by the promise of relief from the elements. When Ben came back to help her down, Henrietta made note of an especially fine coach with a crest on its door. Ben went to see to the horses and avail himself of some gin and hot food while Henrietta, Megan behind her, went inside.

The warmth of the inn was almost painful to Henrietta's numb hands and feet. Looking inside to the crowded coffee room, she could see a large, welcoming fire burning brightly. The atmosphere was as festive as the gathering of people under a common adversity can be. The fact that everyone was drinking heavily added to the air of gaiety.

She stepped up to the counter and briskly addressed the wiry landlord. "Good afternoon. I require a room for myself and my maid for the night."

"I've no rooms left 'cause of the storm," he said sternly, looking at her provincial pelisse with disdain.

Henrietta could scarcely believe her ears. What on earth were they to do?

Across the coffee room, Viscount Baddick sat with Mr. Andrew Snively. Mr. Snively was one of those creatures just on the fringe of Society. His acceptance came chiefly from the fact he was cheerfully willing to sit down at the green baize with anyone. As he was an addicted gamester, winning or losing was rarely of consequence to him. He was not above stealing to support his pleasures when his funds were low; the lure of an elderly aunt's jewel box had precipitated his journey to her country house.

"What brings you to the country, Baddick?" he asked, idly toying with his brandy glass. "Surely all the women in Town haven't closed their legs to you?"

Viscount Baddick amused himself with Mr. Snively's company because they were both stuck at the inn. In Town, while he would never give Snively the cut direct, he sought his company infrequently since the viscount rarely gambled on cards. Women were the viscount's vice.

"Indeed not," Lord Baddick replied with a half grin. "I simply felt the need for some country air and have been at my estate."

"Rusticating? Now, which lady could have sent you out of Town?" Mr. Snively wondered aloud. "The demireps or even those bored widows you favor wouldn't kick up any dust over a broken promise or an abrupt leave-taking."

Lord Baddick heaved a bored sigh. "I have developed the most awful ennui, Snively. Challenge is what I crave." He leaned forward confidingly, a gleam coming into his hazel eyes. "I find a *fresh* conquest more exhilarating."

A frown appeared between Mr. Snively's brows. "You can't mean a young virgin!" At the viscount's answering smile, Mr. Snively warned, "You'd best have a care. Else an avenging father or brother will come after you with a set of dueling pistols."

Lord Baddick tossed off his brandy. "I am accounted an excellent shot," he lied. Quite the coward, he took the greatest of pains to be certain no woman he bedded had anyone to call him to account.

"Do you remember a quiet little thing named Lady Honoria Farrow?" the viscount asked in the manner of one about to impart some titillating information.

"Vaguely." Mr. Snively paused, then remembered. "Yes, in Town with her widowed mama for her second Season." Mr. Snively's eyes widened as the truth struck him. "Never say you . . ."

Lord Baddick's eyes shone with an unholy light. He leaned forward and lowered his voice. "You would be amazed, Andrew, how very simple it was. I was careful with my pursuit under the watchful eyes of the tabbies of the ton. I managed to inveigle an invitation to her home in the country for the holidays. A few promises—girls are so stupid, you know—and she gave me a delectable present on Christmas Eve." Lord Baddick concluded this lurid tale with an evil grin.

Mr. Snively laughed appreciatively, but even one with morals as low as his inwardly shuddered for the ruined girl.

Lord Baddick failed to mention how wide he had been forced to open his purse to quiet the crying girl and her outraged mama. Being extremely rich, this was no hardship. But it had been a near thing. He did not like the look in Lady Farrow's eye as he took his leave, hence his prudent stay in the country. He was only now returning to London.

As he glanced up, Lord Baddick's attention was caught by a young girl in apparent distress, exchanging words with the landlord. "See you in Town, Snively," he said dismissively before rising and walking across the room to investigate how he might turn the situation to his advantage.

Henrietta stood before the counter glaring at the landlord in outrage. "You are going to turn us out into this weather and you say there is no other hostelry nearby?" she demanded, anger bringing color to her cheeks.

The landlord appeared unmoved, but before he could reply, a gentleman placed a number of gold coins in front of him, saying, "A room for the lady."

Suddenly the landlord was all-obliging. "No, miss, I would never do such a thing. I have just the room for ye and yer maid. I'll have the missus make it ready."

"Do go to the kitchens, Megan, and get yourself something hot to drink and eat. I will see you upstairs," Henrietta instructed in a low voice. She waited until Megan bobbed a curtsy and hurried away, before turning to her rescuer.

This fashionably dressed gentleman was surely the owner of the coach with the crest she had seen outside. He was tall and golden-haired, and his hazel eyes studied her with a frank and open look. He wore a bottle-green coat with gold buttons over doeskin breeches and glossy black Hessian boots.

Before she could say a word, he held up a hand in a forestalling gesture. "I beg your indulgence for a moment, my lady. I am aware that we have yet to be introduced and I have been, one might say, presumptuous. Observing your plight from the warmth of the coffee room, I could not, in good conscience, have allowed you and your maid to be put out in such horrid weather. You would not have my reputation as a gentleman called into question over so paltry a matter as an exchange of names. I am Baddick, by the way." A disarming smile ended this gallant speech.

Henrietta did not know where to look. He had called her "my lady," mistaking her station in life.

For once, the Practical Henrietta and the Fantasy Henrietta were in complete agreement. Lord Baddick was most attractive and had indeed behaved as a gentleman. His easy manner persuaded her there was no harm in him. It was true he had saved her from an unthinkable situation and deserved her gratitude.

She dropped a curtsy. "You are most kind, my lord. I am Miss Henrietta Lanford of Hamilton Cross. I am on my way to London and this dreadful storm halted my progress."

Lord Baddick bowed. "Your servant, Miss Lanford. What a happy coincidence! I, too, am on my way to Town after taking care of estate business. But please, allow me to escort you into the coffee room. I am persuaded you must be hungry after your ordeal, and I would see you comfortable by the fire."

She hesitated only a moment before permitting him to lead her to a small table. He had them served with a game pie, vegetables, potatoes, apricot tartlets, and wine.

Henrietta removed her gloves and began to eat. She was famished, having eaten nothing since breakfast. Soon, feeling relaxed from food, wine, and Lord Baddick's polite conversation, she dropped her guard, and the two continued talking easily on a variety of subjects.

While smoothly keeping up his end of the conversation, the viscount's mind raced. This gullible dab of a little thing was exactly the sort he craved. Furthermore, he recalled purchasing a racehorse from Squire Lanford some three years past. Although the viscount would never acknowledge it, his own ill management of the horse resulted in the animal's poor performance at the racetrack. Lord Baddick had returned the horse to the squire, who'd given him a jaw-me-dead over the horse's condition. The angry squire had gone so far as to declare Lord Baddick was the sort of man who would *shoot* a fox.

Twirling the brandy in his glass, the viscount decided the seduction of Miss Lanford would have the added bonus of serving as a small measure of revenge against the squire. "Are you to make your come-out this Season, Miss Lanford? If so, I must have your promise to save a dance for me. Otherwise, with your fresh beauty and becoming manners, I fear I shall be quite cut out."

This piece of flattery was offered in such a good-natured, friendly way, it could not possibly offend. It was a heady experience for Henrietta to command the sole attention of an exquisitely dressed and well-bred man of the world.

"Yes, I am to stay with my aunt, Lady Fuddlesby. And after your service to me today, my lord, you may have your pick of dances." She giggled at him sleepily as she had drunk more wine than she was accustomed to taking.

Lord Baddick smiled tenderly into her eyes. "I own myself the luckiest of men."

Better and better, he thought. Really, this was a temptation he could not let pass him by. Lady Fuddlesby was of the bon ton, but a shatterbrain and an Original. She drove in the park with her cat on the seat beside her! His pulses quickened as a picture flashed in his mind of Miss Lanford underneath him in bed.

As the hour was late, Henrietta could not conceal a yawn.

Lord Baddick struck his chest with his hand. "I am the worst of men, Miss Lanford. Here I am keeping you to myself when you must be exhausted and only wishing for your bed. Should traveling be possible tomorrow and I not have the pleasure of seeing you before you leave, may I call on you in Town?"

"I should like it above all things," Henrietta assured him demurely.

They parted on the best of terms and Henrietta went upstairs to find her room. She opened the door on a comfortable chamber with chintz hangings on the bed and at the window. Megan was nearly asleep in a trundle bed, but rose to help her mistress out of her gown and into her nightdress before stoking the fire and going to sleep.

Henrietta pushed aside the curtains at the frosty window to look out. The storm was over and stars shone on the white landscape. It did not look as if a great deal of snow was on the ground, and it was likely they would get away tomorrow after all.

She thought about meeting Lord Baddick and smiled. Perhaps it had been fate. He was proper, but less austere than the rather intimidating Duke of Winterton. Lord Baddick seemed to think she would have many suitors in Town. Oh, she could not wait to reach London!

Hugging herself, she turned from the window to go to bed. Snuggling under the bedclothes, she fell into dreams in which the hero was alternately Lord Baddick and the Duke of Winterton.

Downstairs in the taproom, Lord Baddick drank heavily. It was all he could do to keep from climbing the stairs and trying his luck with the chit right then. But experience taught him not to rush his fences. He would enjoy the chase in Town.

Lord Baddick snickered to himself while endless possibilities for the young girl's seduction floated through his brandy-soaked brain.

At the moment, a serving maid was winking broadly at him as she leaned forward to refill his glass. Lord Baddick's lips curved into a grin.

Late the following afternoon, Lady Fuddlesby, attired in a rose-pink gown with only a few cat hairs on it, sat in the drawing room of her Grosvenor Square town house. Knight prowled about the room restlessly as if sensing his mistress's mood.

"Where can the girl be?" Lady Fuddlesby asked, her fingers twisting a lace handkerchief. "She should have been here yesterday. I cannot imagine what could have caused a delay."

The black and white cat wandered over to the tall windows and observed a light snow falling. He turned to look at Lady Fuddlesby, his tail tapping the windowpane.

"Oh! My dear boy. Of course, you have the right of it. Why, it might have been snowing quite dreadfully out in the country. Perhaps Henrietta was obliged to put up overnight at some damp inn."

Her ladyship's butler, Chuffley, appeared in the doorway. "His Grace, the Duke of Winterton, has called, my lady. Shall I show him in?"

Fiddlesticks! Lady Fuddlesby pressed her fingers to her temples, thoughts whirling in her head. "Yes . . . and bring tea, please, Chuffley," she managed.

"Oh dear, oh dear, Knight. What could bring him here now? He was not to come until after Henrietta arrived and I had her properly gowned," Lady Fuddlesby went on quite irrationally, forgetting the duke could not possibly be aware of the plans made for him, no less be prepared to fall in with them.

Knight had no answer but jumped to the fireplace mantel where he could observe his mistress and come to her aid if necessary.

The Duke of Winterton entered the room. He carried his hat and stick, indicating he would stay but a few minutes. His burgundy coat sat on his shoulders without a wrinkle. Fawn-colored pantaloons molded to his form, advising Lady Fuddlesby their owner possessed the best of legs. Black Hessian boots shone from a concoction about which other gentlemen's valets could only speculate.

"Lady Fuddlesby," he said, and bowed. Cool gray eyes looked at her questioningly.

"Your Grace, how kind of you to call," Lady Fuddlesby said, and curtsied. "Do sit beside me," she insisted, seating herself and patting a place next to her on the comfortable-looking brocade sofa. She had caught that icy look. While they frequented the same ton parties and had exchanged pleasantries, they were not precisely on calling terms. What was she going to offer as an excuse for asking him to call?

The duke sat down. Chuffley returned with a serving girl who settled a heavy silver tray on the table. Lady Fuddlesby busied herself with the tea things until the servants had gone.

She passed the duke a cup. "I know you must be wondering why I asked you to come," she said with charming frankness. "You must understand, after I saw you last week at the Alistairs' musicale, I felt most dreadful."

The duke looked at Lady Fuddlesby. A puzzled frown appeared between his brows.

Then, momentarily distracted, his attention was caught by two green eyes, belonging to a rather fat-about-the-middle cat, staring at him menacingly from the fireplace mantel.

"You see," Lady Fuddlesby went on improvising, "I knew your dear father when we were both young. And I realized that since his untimely death last year I have been remiss in offering you my deepest condolences. I could not rest until I received your forgiveness for my shockingly bad manners," she ended, feeling well pleased with herself at this farrago of lies. Not that Lady Fuddlesby made a practice of dissembling. It was just that on this occasion a small stretching of the truth was necessary.

Giles felt amused. He had heard her ladyship was jinglebrained, and it followed she would fall prey to contrition for imagined slights at this late date.

He chastised himself for being on his guard against this innocent lady when he arrived. But deuce take it! Hardly a moment's peace had been awarded him since he set up residence at his town house in Park Lane two weeks ago. Mamas and their marriageable daughters called on the flimsiest of excuses until he instructed his butler he was not at home to anyone. As ladies jockeyed ruthlessly for position, riding in the park at the fashionable hour resulted in several near carriage collisions. It seemed everywhere he went young misses were thrown at him like oranges at a bad actor at the playhouse. After a week of this, he was driven to the end of his tether by the antics of a Lady Betina Peabody.

This plain, young miss had the silly idea she could compromise herself and force him to marry her. Her plans no doubt included arranging her scrawny body across his bed. She'd tried to gain access to his town house by bribing a servant. The duke's servants were loyal and she failed. Persistent, if foolish, she attempted to get in by climbing up a trellis to a window. When her gown caught, she fell, breaking her arm.

Disgusted, the duke considered going back to his estate, but Sir Polly Grey knew his duty, and the old duke's voice brought Giles back to his mission.

Despite the fact he was in Town looking over suitable marriage prospects, he dropped a word in Lady Alistair's ear at her musicale that he was content in his bachelor state. She could be counted on to spread this gossip through the ton, much good as it would do. Meanwhile, he adopted an even more unapproachable demeanor.

Certainly, though, caution was not called for with Lady Fuddlesby, a sweet, if hubble-bubbled, creature. "Thank you, my lady. Please be assured I would forgive you if there was anything to forgive."

The duke smiled at her, and Lady Fuddlesby found herself thinking how like his father he was in looks. In character, though, the old duke was always the hardened aristocrat, while this man seemed to possess an understanding beneath his arrogant exterior his father had never developed.

Winterton raised his teacup, preparing to drink, saw a cat hair floating in the liquid, and put the cup down. He said, "I recall my father speaking of you in affectionate terms, my lady. Yes, do not look surprised. It seems in his youth he enjoyed your company immeasurably."

At these words, Lady Fuddlesby's resolve strengthened, and she was more determined than ever to promote a match between the duke and her niece.

For his part, the duke was simply enjoying a pleasant conversation away from marriageable females with one of his father's old friends.

It was unfortunate, when the duke and Lady Fuddlesby were feeling much in charity with one another, that a commotion could be heard coming from the hall below. The sound of voices grew louder. Lady Fuddlesby rose and the duke followed suit as they looked expectantly toward the doorway.

Coming up the stairs, Chuffley, normally the epitome of the English butler, wore an expression of discomfort about his puffy features.

An excited Henrietta followed on his heels. London enthralled her from her first glimpse out the glass of the squire's traveling coach. Snow was falling, making the city seem a magical place where anything could happen to a young girl on her first visit from the country. The noise, the press of carriages, the lights glowing from windows of tall, thin town houses, were all so different from the country. A giddy anticipation of the treats in store infected her.

She entered Lady Fuddlesby's house in awe of its

size. She didn't know what she expected, but nothing this grand, to be sure.

The butler and Henrietta reached the entrance to the drawing room. Chuffley announced, "Miss Henrietta Lanford, my lady. She *would* come right up," he added by way of explanation for this disturbance.

Henrietta walked into the room and shied like a colt at the sight of the Duke of Winterton. Biting her lip in vexation, for the second time in as many weeks she was sorry she had not taken care of her appearance before rushing into a room. A telltale blush heated her cheeks.

At Henrietta's hurly-burly entrance, a look of dismay crossed Lady Fuddlesby's face. In an audible undertone she said to herself, "Oh dear, and I did want him to see her looking her best."

Winterton turned sharply to look at Lady Fuddlesby, but the lady's attention was on her niece.

"My dear girl, I am so glad you are here," her ladyship said nervously as she stared at Henrietta's disheveled appearance. "I wondered what could have kept you since I expected you yesterday, but I thought the snow . . ." Lady Fuddlesby's voice trailed off feebly, and she twisted her hands together in agitation.

The duke's face was a study in frozen hauteur.

Gazing at him wide-eyed, Henrietta failed to notice his chilly demeanor.

Lady Fuddlesby, looking from Henrietta's infatuated expression to the duke's stiff countenance, sputtered a question. "Have you met before, perhaps?"

Not bothering to answer, Winterton abruptly seized his hat and stick and said, "Lady Fuddlesby,

Miss Lanford, I see I must leave you to one another." He bowed and left before either of the two ladies could utter a word.

With the duke departing so soon after her arrival, Henrietta felt her spirits deflate. He was more handsome than she remembered, and she longed to talk with him as she had with Lord Baddick. There was a difference in the two men, she thought slowly. Lord Baddick was friendly where the Duke of Winterton was reserved. He was probably just that way with people he did not know well, she reasoned.

Lady Fuddlesby came to Henrietta, taking both her hands in an affectionate squeeze. "I know I am a poor hostess, my dear, but I cannot wait another minute before I hear all about your previous meeting with the Duke of Winterton."

Henrietta studied her aunt, liking what she saw. Lady Fuddlesby's light brown hair was styled attractively to complement her rather round face. Pale blue eyes held a kindness and an interest her own mother's lacked.

"Well, my lady, there is not much to tell. His Grace came to inspect Papa's horses and stayed to nuncheon. I was only in his company a short while before he took his leave."

But long enough to have her affections engaged, divined Lady Fuddlesby. What miss would not be attracted to the duke? she mused, picturing his manly legs.

Knight chose this moment to jump down from the mantel and rub against Henrietta's skirts.

"La, you have a cat!" Henrietta exclaimed delightedly, and bent to stroke his back. "I adore cats. We have barn cats at home, but Mama would never allow them in the house. Pray, what is his name?"

"Knight in Masked Armour, my dear, but simply called Knight. He is very wise and not at all an ordinary feline."

The cat fell down onto his side with a thud and rolled over on his back to allow Henrietta's gentle hand access to his oversized belly. All the while he purred loudly, his eyes crossed in bliss.

"Oh, my dear, abandon that wretched fellow and come upstairs and get settled. I do hope you may be pleased with your bedchamber. And we have much to accomplish before the Denbys' ball next week."

"A ball," Henrietta breathed, and lapsed into her dreams as she prepared to follow her aunt.

Lady Fuddlesby, leading the way, took each step with a growing feeling of confidence. She was sure the girl would be a beauty once fashionably turned out. Perhaps any damage done today by the Duke of Winterton's seeing her prematurely was not so very great after all.

Meanwhile, the duke walked down the steps to the hall in Lady Fuddlesby's town house, convinced he had been tricked again. Miss Lanford, a green country girl if ever he saw one, was Lady Fuddlesby's niece. Obviously the lady was to sponsor her come-out. He would be seeing the chit frequently. They would, after all, be going about in the same circles. Since Lady Fuddlesby expected her earlier in the week, it further stood to reason the lady's request for him to call did indeed have matchmaking implications. Her careless mumbling confirmed it.

The duke strode out the front door and down the stone steps, roughly pulling on his driving gloves.

Lord Kramer, a pretentious dandy the duke did not choose to count among his close associates, hailed him. "T'faith, Duke. Stealing a march on the rest of us, eh?"

"Whatever can you mean, Kramer?"

"Well, 'tis all over Town Lady Fuddlesby is to push off her niece this Season."

Why did I not hear of this? the duke thought, irate. He wished Lord Kramer at the devil. "Miss Lanford is in Town for the Season," he ground out.

"Did you meet the gel or not?" Lord Kramer persisted.

The duke's patience was tried beyond all endurance. Through a red haze of anger he added Miss Henrietta Lanford to the list of unsuitable girls thrown at him. He remembered her horse-mad parents. He remembered she moved with a coltlike awkwardness. He remembered her long, straight hair, and some imp in his mind conjured up a resemblance to a horse's tail. Unconfined strands, lying across her forehead, became a forelock.

"I have seen the girl, and my opinion is that Squire and Mrs. Lanford would do better to give her a Season at Newmarket rather than London." With this crashing insult, the duke moved past an openmouthed Lord Kramer, climbed up into his phaeton, raised his whip, and drove off at a smart pace.

Lord Kramer, stunned at his good fortune, took himself gleefully off to his club to repeat the duke's words to all his friends.

Chapter Three

The next morning, Miss Henrietta Lanford was blissfully unaware of the scurrilous gossip circulating about her through the ton. She breakfasted and then returned to her bedchamber, accompanied by an appreciative Knight.

"Tell me, sir, are you well pleased with yourself?" Henrietta asked, amused. She stood with her hands on her hips while she gazed down at the shameless beggar.

Knight sat at her feet using a well-licked paw to clean around his whiskers and his black mask. He stopped for a moment to cast her a feline grin. Apparently deciding he would relax his strict rule against houseguests in the generous Miss Lanford's case, he companionably resumed his washing.

Henrietta chuckled and said, "Yes, I am most grateful to you for sharing that rather large breakfast Mrs. Pottsworth prepared. Judging from the fact that it is nigh on eleven o'clock, and Lady Fuddlesby has not left her room, I assume you are not accustomed to early-morning sustenance."

Henrietta left Knight to his ministrations and seated herself at the Queen Anne desk. It was time she composed a short note to her parents to send back with Megan.

A scratching at the door interrupted her. A

middle-aged woman with sallow skin and dark hair glided into the room. Henrietta noticed she held a copy of *La Belle Assemblée*.

Curtsying, the woman spoke with a hint of a French accent. "Good morning, Mees Lanford. I am Felice, her ladyship's maid. I thought you might enjoy looking at the fashion plates."

This was said while Felice's sharp eyes darted over every detail of Henrietta's appearance. Henrietta suddenly felt quite lacking with her unstyled hair and her dowdy sage-green wool gown.

"*Bon,*" Felice declared. "Your figure ees slight, but gratifyingly feminine. A diamond in the rough rather than, how do you English say, a Diamond of the First Water?"

"Thank you, Felice. Everyone here is so kind." Henrietta accepted the magazine and glanced at it uncertainly. "I confess to an ignorance of all the different styles and what to wear when. Her ladyship spoke of your talents with hair and dress." She hesitated before continuing, "I hope you can spare time away from your many duties to advise me."

Felice seemed satisfied. "Of course, mees. It will be a pleasure to be of service."

Just then, Knight left the room stiff-tailed, to take up his bird-watching post downstairs at the drawing room window. He and Felice did not get along, there being a disagreement over the shedding of cat hairs on Lady Fuddlesby's gowns.

Felice crossed to the wardrobe and began a critical inspection of Henrietta's gowns. She clucked her tongue at the wardrobe's meager contents and then said, "Her ladyship arranged for Monsieur Cheveux to come and cut your hair. When that ees done, we will need the whole new wardrobe for you."

Henrietta looked down at the elegant costumes portrayed in the magazine and reluctantly agreed. Nothing she brought from home would do in fashionable London. She touched an apprehensive hand to her hair and wondered what the hairdresser would have in mind for her.

When her ladyship awoke, Felice hurried along to help her with her morning toilette. Henrietta was left to fall into a fulfilling dream in which, dressed in an ensemble out of *La Belle Assemblée*, she bewitched the Duke of Winterton.

Later, Lady Fuddlesby entered the room accompanied by Monsieur Cheveux. He lifted a strand of his new client's hair, groaned, and let it drop from his fingers.

While his scissors deftly clipped away inches, Henrietta watched in the glass nervously. But Monsieur Cheveux used the curling tongs to coax her hair into a feminine topknot of soft ringlets with wispy curls framing her face.

Lady Fuddlesby, watching the process patiently, beamed at the transformation. "My dear, now I can see that your eyes are quite the loveliest shade of deep blue."

Henrietta demurred at the compliment, but felt a rush of gratitude to her aunt. No one had ever said her eyes were pretty.

The following afternoon saw the arrival of Lady Fuddlesby's favorite modiste. To satisfy a loyal client, Madame Dupre brought two gowns, already made up and needing only minor adjustments, as well as their accessories and a large selection of fabrics and trimmings.

Henrietta was flushed with happiness and nigh exhausted by the time Madame Dupre, Lady Fuddlesby, and Felice were finished placing fabrics against her skin, discussing at length the most suitable colors and styles, and declaring how she would outshine every other young lady.

And so it was a fashionable Henrietta, accompanied by Lady Fuddlesby and Felice, who went out into the London streets for the first time the next day. Although it was chilly, the sun shone and a blustery wind blew as the ladies shopped their way down Bond Street.

Henrietta realized the meaning of the Duke of Winterton's cynical remark when he told her she would not be able to detect the scent of horse*flesh* in the city streets. Indeed, she thought, horseflesh would be preferable to what she was smelling. She raised a perfumed handkerchief to her nose when the wind brought a fresh assault of unpleasant odors.

They stopped in front of a shop window where Lady Fuddlesby admired a bonnet, its price shown on a discreet card nearby. She shook her head after a moment and they moved on.

Henrietta chanced to look up and saw Lord Baddick approaching. A smile of welcome quickly lit her face.

"Well met, Miss Lanford, Lady Fuddlesby," he said, and sketched a bow to the ladies. Had she not stood with Lady Fuddlesby, Lord Baddick would not have recognized the new Henrietta. As it was, his pulses quickened as he took in the richness of her dark green velvet pelisse worn with a dashing hat of green velvet trimmed with sealskin. Her blue eyes sparkled under a charming array of curls. She looked fresh and unspoiled. How he would love to be the one to . . .

"Lord Baddick! How glad I am to see you. Do you know my aunt, Lady Fuddlesby?"

Lord Baddick saw Miss Lanford was flattered by his obvious interest. He took care to address Lady Fuddlesby with an equal amount of attentiveness. He was rewarded when she seemed as delighted as her niece.

Lady Fuddlesby was not well acquainted with the viscount, but was told of his helpful intervention at the Pig and Thistle, and so was prepared to like him. Tales of his disreputable treatment of women were not at all well spread among the ton and had not reached her ears.

"Lord Baddick, I must add my thanks for your timely assistance to my niece on the road to London," Lady Fuddlesby said graciously. She wanted the Duke of Winterton for Henrietta but was not so caper-witted as to discourage the attentions of a handsome, rich viscount. If nothing else, Lord Baddick's attentions might serve to make Winterton jealous, her ladyship judged.

"My lady, I assure you I consider myself the most fortunate of men to have had the pleasure of meeting Miss Lanford. If I was of any small service to her, it can only gladden my heart."

He bestowed a teasing glance on Henrietta, then continued speaking to Lady Fuddlesby. "I must tell you, Miss Lanford has promised to save me a dance, and I will hold her to that promise with your permission, ma'am. Do you go to the Denbys' ball?"

Lady Fuddlesby answered affirmatively to both his questions. After more pleasantries were exchanged, Lord Baddick went on his way, eager for the opportunity to further his schemes for Henrietta's seduction.

Henrietta felt the uneasiness about her upcoming first ball lessen with the knowledge the friendly Lord Baddick would be there to dance with. She could not help but wonder if the Duke of Winterton would attend and solicit her hand. A shiver of anticipation ran up her spine at the thought.

As they resumed their shopping, Lady Fuddlesby chirped, "Mark my words, gentlemen will be about you, my darling girl, like flies around the jam pot."

Smiling at her aunt, Henrietta hoped she might be correct at least where two gentlemen were concerned.

Only Felice wore a worried frown.

At the Duke of Winterton's town house in Park Lane, Giles was being helped by Tyler into a morning coat of darkest blue superfine. Tyler was a short, slim man with an arrogance almost as great as the duke's. Because the duke was considered a leader of fashion, the valet never let his master out of the house looking anything less than perfectly groomed and attired. Tyler secretly imagined a rivalry between himself and Robinson, Beau Brummell's man.

Sir Polly Grey, looking quite comfortable in his large cage, munched a piece of unbuttered bread. Butter upset his delicate system. His black eyes glittered when Giles stood ready to go out. The bird paused in his eating, and he garbled in the old duke's voice, "Vayne. Marriage. A suitable gel."

The duke scowled at the parrot and set out on his way to meet his godfather, Colonel Owen Colchester. Having gone to Oxford with Giles's father, Colonel Colchester was a longtime family friend. He had sent round a note announcing his arrival in Town and his retirement after a life spent in the army. He begged Giles to wait on him at his earliest convenience at Stephen's Hotel, the hostelry preferred by military men.

They had not seen each other since the old duke's funeral over a year ago, so the two men greeted each other with affection. The duke held a considerable amount of respect for his father's friend and, indeed, deemed him his own closest supporter. The colonel was the only person other than the duke's mother who got away with calling him "my boy."

"Well, sir, how does it feel to be a gentlemen of leisure?" the duke asked, the men seating themselves in two wing chairs close to the fire. The colonel was a tall, distinguished-looking, gray-haired gentleman with lively brown eyes. As he disdained the traditional military side-whiskers, his strong face was clean-shaven.

They conversed on several topics including the war and mutual acquaintances before the colonel got around to answering the duke's question.

"I tell you, my boy, I am at loose ends. My place in the country seems too docile for me right now. A little Town life is what I need to keep me from sinking into the doldrums." The colonel's beloved wife had died three years ago after a long struggle with the wasting disease. He still missed her sorely, and they had not been blessed with children.

"You must come and stay with me, sir. Plenty of room, you know. At least stay for the Season. I would be glad of your company."

The colonel accepted this welcome invitation promptly. He thought it would be an excellent opportunity for him to keep an eye on his godson. He shared the seventh Duke of Winterton's feelings regarding Giles's need to marry, although this belief in the colonel was not as violent as it had been in the old duke. More to the point, he sensed an unhappiness beneath Giles's air of fashionable boredom that troubled his fatherly nature.

After concluding arrangements for the colonel's removal to Park Lane, the duke continued to another call he was not as enthusiastic at making.

Matilda, Dowager Duchess of Winterton, kept her own town house in Berkeley Square, one of the best addresses in England. Lady Fuddlesby's old rival was enjoying her widowhood. A controlling sort of person, she'd spent her life crossing swords with her autocratic husband in a loveless marriage and now relished not having to deal with him or his detestable parrot.

Her mouth turned down at the corners, and her dark hair was flecked with gray, but she had a regal bearing.

At present she was entertaining Hester Eden, Countess of Mawbly, and the woman's daughter, Lady Clorinda Eden, in the Egyptian-styled drawing room. While the teacups were being passed around, the Duke of Winterton was announced.

Looking at the company, he drawled, "Perhaps I have called at a bad time, Mother?"

She answered him in a high, thin voice. "When was your company ever not wanted, Giles?" Although she was fond of her son, he proved as hard to control as his father, rankling Her Grace. She found Giles's single state vulgar and deplored the attention drawn to the family by it.

She looked to see Lady Mawbly's reaction to her son's entrance. The dowager suspected he was the reason Hester befriended her. A shrewd expression crossed her features while she thought with approval of Lady Mawbly's thinly veiled desire for a match between her daughter and Giles. Lady Mawbly's sole interests in life were her standing in Society and the acquisition of jewels. Clorinda was a suitable girl with a sizable dowry, and she excelled in all the ladylike accomplishments. She would do as the future duchess.

The duke dutifully kissed his mother's cheek and turned to the other ladies present. The dowager performed the introductions and he bowed low. Dismissing Lady Mawbly as a rabbity woman, wearing what must surely be the entire contents of her jewel box, he concentrated on the charms of her daughter.

He thought Lady Clorinda a Diamond of the First Water, sure to be the Season's Beauty. As Winterton scrutinized her, she sat in a calm and composed manner on a chair boasting of legs shaped like crocodile heads.

"Lady Clorinda, how fortunate we are to have you enliven our Season." He took in the glory of her emerald-colored eyes and golden curls. Her cleverly cut white muslin morning gown managed to reveal her seductive figure while remaining perfectly correct, intriguing him. Before he could rudely raise his quizzing glass to better inspect what was truly a magnificent bosom, the vision spoke.

"Thank you, Your Grace. I am pleased to make your acquaintance." Her voice was low and well modulated.

Deciding to stay longer than he initially planned, the duke sat on a remarkably uncomfortable backless sofa with serpents carved in the legs.

During the polite social conversation that followed, Lady Mawbly mentally rubbed her hands with glee. She could not have wished for a better opportunity for her Clorinda to meet His Grace! How clever she was, cultivating the dowager duchess's company instead of resorting to the machinations of other matchmaking mamas! But she dared not press her advantage. She waited for a break in the conversation and rose with a clattering of neck-laces.

"How the time does fly! Clorinda and I must be on our way. My husband, the earl, is in Town," she said as if her husband demanded every moment of her time. This was certainly not true as her lady-ship led her husband a dog's life, nagging him mer-cilessly. But Lady Mawbly was fond of punctuating her sentences with references to her husband's title because she was a mere baron's daughter before her marriage.

Clorinda took her leave of the duke and his mother with a quiet dignity. The minute the two la-dies reached the privacy of their carriage she let loose her ire. "How can you be so stupid, Mama?" Clorinda hissed, stamping the tip of her parasol on the carriage floor for emphasis. "I was just about to ask the duke if he would be attending the Denbys' ball Friday, and what needs you do but jump up and make us leave," she finished disgustedly.

For underneath her soft-spoken, poised exterior was the soul of a shrew. Clorinda shared her moth-er's love of Society, and that, combined with a will-ful, selfish personality, made her determined to become Winterton's duchess.

"Calm down," Lady Mawbly said soothingly, sens-ing one of her daughter's tantrums coming on and seeking to avert it. "Did you not mark the way His Grace never took his eyes from you? Why, you have enslaved him already, my pet. I am certain he will be at the Denbys' and will rush to secure two dances with you." She went on in this manner the entire way back to their town house before Clorinda was pacified.

Meanwhile, the duke commented to his mama

that Lady Clorinda was a pretty-behaved girl, raising his mother's hopes that he might marry after all.

Later, he found himself comparing Lady Clorinda
with Miss Henrietta Lanford, then wondered why,
when such a comparison left Miss Lanford the clear
loser, the thought disturbed him.

He chided himself for unfairly comparing the
two. Miss Lanford could not measure up to Lady
Clorinda in any way. She was unsuitable for the
title of duchess, being a mere squire's daughter.
Lady Clorinda, on the other hand, was an earl's
daughter. God put one in one's station in life and
expected one not to step below it when choosing a
mate. This was his father's philosophy, and Giles
told himself he shared it.

He certainly did not spare a thought for the effect his careless words to Lord Kramer comparing
Miss Lanford to a horse might have on her life, for
he had quite forgotten them.

The night of the Denbys' ball seemed an eternity
away and then it was upon them. Felice kept busy
assisting first Lady Fuddlesby, then Henrietta.

Trying to sit still while Felice arranged her hair,
Henrietta felt her nerves stretched to the breaking
point. She struggled for composure while her mind
dwelled on the Duke of Winterton. Surely he would
attend the ball. Would he find her new hairstyle
and fine gown pleasing? Would he dance with her?

"Mees, you must stop the fidgeting or I cannot do
my work," Felice admonished.

At last it was time to leave. It was never far to go
anywhere in the West End. Henrietta and Lady
Fuddlesby could have easily walked to the Denbys'
town house in Hanover Square, but that would

have been a social disgrace equal to tying one's garters in public.

The two ladies stepped out into the wintry spring evening and entered Lady Fuddlesby's carriage.

The night was thick with fog. Henrietta thought London appeared more than ever a fairyland. She recalled her dreams were always set in misty scenes and felt herself a princess in the softness of her white silk gown. Pearls decorated the thin braids Felice had artfully wound through the curls in her dark hair. As befitted a young girl in her first Season, a pearl necklace and eardrops were her only jewelry.

Lady Fuddlesby, lovely in dark pink taffeta with diamonds flashing at her neck, recalled her own first ball and said, "Oh, my dear, this will truly be a night for you to remember all your life. And you look most becoming." She could hardly wait to see the Duke of Winterton's reaction to her niece. She would wager he had dismissed Henrietta as nothing out of the common way after that first ill-timed meeting. A smug smile curved her lips.

Henrietta blinked back sudden tears. "Thank you, my lady. I confess I was unable to eat a bite of the delicious dinner Mrs. Pottsworth prepared, being so beset with anticipation of this evening. I do hope I will not disappoint you. You have been so very kind." She reached over to clasp her gloved hand with her aunt's in an affectionate squeeze.

Lady Fuddlesby smiled warmly and then remembered a task that lay before her. "I must seek out Lady Cowper to secure your vouchers for Almack's. The opening ball is next Wednesday evening."

Lady Fuddlesby chose Lady Cowper to appeal to, as Countess Lieven and Princess Esterhazy were awfully high in the instep, and one never knew what they might take exception to. She never considered asking Mrs. Drummond-Burrell. Lady Fuddlesby shuddered, picturing that terrifying woman.

Their carriage fought its way through the press until they arrived at the Denbys'.

Walking into the imposing town house, Henrietta could hear the strains of music coming from the ballroom. Her stomach a tight knot, she stepped up to the threshold and stared.

The room was bright from the light of hundreds of candles. Hothouse flowers scented the air. Henrietta saw a crowd of people all dressed in their finery. The gentlemen, in dark evening dress, were a stark contrast to the ladies in their colorful gowns. Jewels caught the candlelight and glowed.

A quadrille commenced and Henrietta said a silent thank-you to Biddles for having insisted on a dancing teacher. She grasped the tip of her ivory fan tightly, hoping she would remember the steps of all the dances.

Lady Fuddlesby led her over to rows of gilt chairs placed against the wall for the chaperons and the unlucky ladies obliged to sit out a dance. While they were making their way, Henrietta saw quizzing glasses raised and felt heat rise to her cheeks at the scrutiny. Was this the treatment afforded any new face on the London scene? If so, she must need to endure it.

Lady Fuddlesby saw one of her friends and they went to sit by her. Lady Chatterton, a tiny, pale woman dressed in a scarlet gown, nodded at Henrietta's curtsy and proceeded to speak to Lady Fuddlesby with an anxious torrent of words whispered behind her fan.

To Henrietta, it seemed everyone in the room

looked at her rudely and talked behind their fans. She sat uncomfortably on her gilt chair wondering what on earth it all meant.

She was not to know the Duke of Winterton's cruel insult likening her to a horse had spread through the ton thanks to Lord Kramer. The aristocracy fell on their latest victim like a pack of hungry dogs on a fresh slab of meat.

Lady Fuddlesby, hearing the whole shocking story from Lady Chatterton, could only mutter in a dazed manner, "Oh dear, oh dear."

No one approached them until Lord Harrison, a hard-gaming dandy known to his intimates as "Hazard Harry," accepted a bet and minced across the room to stand in front of a stricken Lady Fuddlesby.

She ignored his bright yellow coat and high shirt points and introduced Henrietta.

" 'Pon rep, my lady, you must allow me to dance with Miss Lanford. She appears a *high-stepper*," Lord Harrison said, and sniggered.

Lady Fuddlesby's emotional state did not allow her to catch this witticism, and she only nodded permission for him to lead Henrietta in a set of country dances just forming.

Now everyone could plainly see Miss Lanford did not in any way resemble a horse. But the rich, marriageable Duke of Winterton was a social leader. If he said she looked like a horse, Society was prepared to follow his dictates.

Henrietta, awkwardly making her way through the dance, felt confused and miserable. Felice would never have let her out of the house if something were wrong with her appearance, so there must be another reason for all the sneering attention being given her. But what? She thought her partner a figure of fun. With his pockmarked face and hideous coat, he was nothing like the gentlemen she dreamed of dancing with.

Lord Harrison began to feel he made a mistake in accepting his friend's bet to dance with Miss Lanford. She was obviously a shy little thing and possessed quite attractive blue eyes, when he could see them. Miss Lanford kept them trained on the floor. His compassion did not extend to speaking with her, however. He had his social position to consider. All his friends knew he'd asked her for this dance in response to a bet. To be seen conversing with her would spoil the effect.

The dance ended and Lord Harrison, bowing mockingly low, returned Henrietta to Lady Fuddlesby.

Lady Fuddlesby was putting off the moment when she must tell her niece what had occurred, desperately hoping something would happen to alter matters.

Henrietta was praying she would suddenly become invisible. She turned to her aunt and in a small voice begged, "Please, my lady, something is amiss. You must tell me what I have done."

Lady Fuddlesby tried to keep a social smile pinned on her face. To show in front of the company how very upset she was would only add unnecessary fuel to the fire. So through a cheerful grin she said, "Someone said you were . . . well, not in looks."

"I do not understand," Henrietta responded, bewildered.

Lady Fuddlesby could not bring herself to repeat what the duke had said. "Well, dear, it is all quite horrid and so very untrue. Why, I never heard such a load of nonsense! What can have possessed the man to make such a corkbrained statement, I cannot say." Lady Fuddlesby would have babbled on but was cut off by her niece.

"My lady, I shall scream if you do not tell me at once what was said of me!"

"Oh, very well," Lady Fuddlesby said, resigned. "You are bound to hear it sometime, I imagine. But you know, my dear . . ." She stopped, quailing before the steely look in her niece's eyes. Then she went on in a rush. "It was a comparison someone made, quite unjustly. It was said your parents could do better giving you a Season in Newmarket rather than London. Implying you looked like a horse . . . which you do not! I am certain there is some explanation." As if to herself, she added, "Perhaps he was in his cups, although he had nothing but tea at my house."

Henrietta sat openmouthed, trying to assimilate her aunt's words. Then a suspicion too terrible to contemplate formed in her mind. She asked faintly, "Who? Who said this appalling thing?"

"Well." Lady Fuddlesby twisted her lace handkerchief to shreds. Tears came to her eyes, but she blinked them back before anyone could see them. "I am sad to say it was the Duke of Winterton."

Henrietta's eyes opened wide and she gripped the edges of her gilt chair until her hands whitened with the effort. She thought she could feel the very blood rushing through her veins. How could he? Why? How had she given him a disgust of her? And then as she remembered how she had dreamed about him, she reached a trembling hand up to cover her eyes in shame.

At that moment, the Duke of Winterton made his entrance into the ballroom with Colonel Colchester. Giles was the epitome of elegance in his indigo evening clothes. His cravat, tied in the Oriental with a diamond pin in its folds, rose from a snow-white waistcoat.

Colonel Colchester, looking stately, greeted an old army friend and in a matter of moments had the unsavory story.

At the same time, Lady Peabody hailed the duke. At her side was her daughter Betina, who blamed the duke for her broken arm, which hung in a sling.

"Your Grace," Lady Peabody said, simpering, "you are such a wit."

The duke's eyes half closed.

When this compliment brought no comment from the duke, Lady Peabody went on. " 'Tis vastly diverting . . . Miss Lanford, a Season at Newmarket." She and her daughter tittered, all the while shooting amused looks in Henrietta's direction.

The Duke of Winterton's eyes snapped open, and for the first time he recalled his ill-chosen words to Lord Kramer. He mentally cursed the fop for repeating them.

He managed to disengage himself from the pushing Lady Peabody and her foolish daughter. As he made his way to Colonel Colchester's side, his gaze roamed the room until he located where Miss Lanford sat. Then he stopped short and stared.

Good God! She was lovely. There was an air of innocence about her, making all the other women in the room look old and tired. What a pity, he thought, that she was only a squire's daughter. But a horse? No one should have taken his remarks seriously, he decided, absolving himself of any misdeed.

"Well, my boy, what are you going to do?" Colonel Colchester, now standing beside him, asked.

The duke leveled his quizzing glass at a passing lady, much to her delight. "Do? About what, dear sir?"

The colonel felt himself becoming irritated. The duke was too puffed up with his own consequence. "Giles!" Seeing he had the duke's attention, he went on. "Have you heard what is going around about little Miss Lanford?"

"Ah, yes. I declare it grows tiresome when one's every comment is spread about."

Colonel Colchester felt a desire to shout at his godson. He controlled himself with an effort and said, "What do you intend to do about it? Do not look at me in that bored way. Miss Lanford was pointed out to me, and we must walk over there to where she and that charming woman in pink are sitting. Behave like nothing has happened."

His godfather's outraged tone finally got through to the duke. He looked again at Miss Lanford and Lady Fuddlesby sitting with the chaperons, and his conscience smote him. He magnanimously decided to dance with the girl and later put it about his remarks were meant as a jest. He failed to understand what the great fuss was about. Anyone could see she was attractive.

Before he could respond to Colonel Colchester, that man spoke again. "I would have thought a man in your position would have a care about what he said in public." Playing his ace, he stated, "It is your *duty*, Giles, to turn the situation around and bring the girl into fashion with the social power you hold."

"Doing it too brown, Colonel. I have already decided to do just that. Only, the next dance is about to begin. Allow me to partner the girl first, then you may join us when I return her to Lady

Fuddlesby. In that way, we can all spend a few minutes in tedious social chatter ensuring the girl's success."

The duke took himself off, and the colonel looked in frustration at his retreating back. Even though the rank of duke deserved respect, someone needed to take Giles down a peg, he decided.

Over by the chaperons, Henrietta, engulfed in the familiar pain of rejection she often suffered at her parents' hands, stared at the floor. This was a different kind of rejection, she determined, and made worse by its being public. She wondered if one could die of mortification.

The Denbys' ball was a sad crush. Lady Denby had packed in as many of the ton as possible. People were standing at the edges of the ballroom talking and gossiping. As everyone realized the duke was walking in the direction of Miss Lanford, the room grew quiet for a moment, then fans fluttered and the dreadful whispering began again.

Henrietta asked herself what could have happened now and raised her head. The Duke of Winterton, looking heartbreakingly handsome, was making his way toward her.

He will not approach me, she thought wildly. But as it became evident she was indeed his goal, she quickly looked down at her lap, her heart pounding so hard, she thought it might burst from her chest.

At her side, Lady Fuddlesby saw salvation and whispered to her, "How good of him. He will set everything to rights."

Pain coursed through Henrietta anew, but now an intense surge of anger accompanied it. How dare he! How could he have the audacity to seek her out after what he said of her? Surely he knew what the consequences of his horrible words would be to her come-out. Why, the man had no more feeling than an old shoe!

The duke was almost to Henrietta's chair, his intention to speak with her obvious. Quiet descended on the gathering again as everyone waited in hushed expectancy.

Suddenly Henrietta knew she could not bear to exchange a single word with the beastly man. Hands at her sides, she grasped the little gilt chair she was sitting on and with a jerking movement turned the chair pointedly, presenting him with an excellent view of her back.

Sharply indrawn breaths and titters met her ears. Dimly she was aware of the duke turning and moving past her.

Next to her, Lady Fuddlesby moaned, "Oh dear, oh dear," and fanned herself vigorously.

Across the room, Colonel Colchester raised a hand to cover a smile.

Chapter Four

Impertinent baggage, the duke thought furiously, forgetting his part in the contretemps. This is what one got when one associated with persons of inferior rank.

The duke walked past Miss Lanford and directly over to where Lady Clorinda Eden stood with her mama, Lady Mawbly.

Lady Clorinda, a slight smile on her pink lips, looked positively enchanting in white satin. The bosom of her gown was cut down to the very limit of the amount of flesh she could show and remain a lady. She pointed at the duke with her breasts as he approached.

The duke's mood lightened at the vision of the creamy mounds before him. "Lady Mawbly, Lady Clorinda, you are looking exceptional this evening," he said smoothly, directing his gaze at the daughter and certainly not at the puce-attired Lady Mawbly. "May I hope, Lady Clorinda, you have a dance for me?"

Clorinda's golden curls and seductive bosom drew the attention of many young men, but she held her courtiers at bay, determined to dance with the duke.

"Yes, Your Grace, I shall be delighted." She

placed her gloved hand on his arm demurely, and they moved away, the perfect couple.

As often happens when anger is released in a childish action, Henrietta was now assailed by a wave of shame. Lady Fuddlesby magnified this feeling by repeatedly mumbling, "Ruined, we are quite ruined."

"My lady, I beg your pardon. I feel awful that your kindness to me has been repaid in this manner. Please forgive me," Henrietta beseeched, laying a hand on her aunt's arm.

"Oh dear, you cannot have done yourself any good by turning your back on the duke. I admit the provocation was great, but how we are to come about now, I cannot say," Lady Fuddlesby lamented, shaking her head.

"It occurs to me I have denied myself the knowledge of his intention in approaching me. I wonder if he meant to offer some sort of explanation for his behavior," Henrietta mused. One that would allow her to forgive him, so he might once again reign favored in her daydreams.

This jumble of emotions continued to war in Henrietta's petite bosom. She bit her lip at the sight of the duke and a beautiful blonde moving to take their places in a set forming on the dance floor.

Across the room was the famous leader of the ton, Beau Brummell. His hair was a light brown color and his expression disdainful. He wore no jewelry and was attired in faultless evening clothes. Gossip pronounced the tying of his cravat, which was starched to perfection, sometimes took two to three hours.

He was in conversation with his friend Lady Jersey, one of the patronesses of Almack's. She queried, "What do you think of the Duke of Winterton's remarks regarding Miss Lanford?"

Brummell artfully took a pinch of his favorite snuff, Martinique, from a beautifully ornamented snuffbox. He was annoyed by the duke's social power, jealous of anyone other than himself being able to lead Society. "It was in poor taste for Winterton to be cutting up a fetching young girl's hopes like that. Miss Lanford showed him, though. Courageous girl."

Seeming to come to a decision, he added, "I will step over and solicit her hand for the next dance. That will secure her place in Society. Excuse me, my lady." He bowed to Lady Jersey, who watched with interest while he made his way to Miss Lanford.

Lady Fuddlesby saw him coming. Not one to speak harshly to anyone, she was in the middle of a rare bumblebath that caused her to say, "Henrietta, it is Mr. Brummell. Do not make a goose of yourself!"

Even growing up in the country, Henrietta knew of Beau Brummell. She looked up in awe as the famous Beau stood before them, an amused look on his face. He'd heard Lady Fuddlesby's warning to Henrietta.

"Good evening, Lady Fuddlesby. I pray you and that delightful fellow Knight are in good health?" he asked pleasantly. Brummell loved animals, so he looked with fondness upon someone who doted on her cat as Lady Fuddlesby did.

"Oh, you are too kind, dear sir! We are both well. May I present my niece, Miss Henrietta Lanford?"

In a carrying voice Brummell replied, "Miss Lanford, I am delighted to make the acquaintance of such a refreshing example of English woman-hood. Would you honor me with this dance?"

Henrietta blushed to the roots of her hair. She rose and walked out onto the dance floor with Beau Brummell.

Their dance together caused yet another sensation. Observing Society's interest in Miss Lanford and the Duke of Winterton, Lady Denby felt happily her ball would be the talk of London for days.

Henrietta thought Mr. Brummell was very much the gentleman. He teased her with amusing stories about various members of the assembled company, putting her at ease. She did not know what inspired his generosity but was grateful to him for bestowing his attention on her, and performed her part in the dance with style.

When the dance was over, they promenaded around the room, and just as Brummell was leading her back to Lady Fuddlesby, Henrietta turned to look up at him, a solemn expression on her face. "Sir, I most sincerely thank you for your kindness."

Well pleased, Brummell spread it about Miss Lanford's charming face matched a charming disposition. Fickle Society grew convinced the Duke of Winterton had played some kind of mischievous trick on them, and Miss Lanford was quite justified in her set-down of him.

The duke observed Brummell and Miss Lanford's dance with a measure of relief. He felt the responsibility of bringing her into fashion lifted from his shoulders.

Now Henrietta did not lack for partners. Still smarting, she refused to look in the Duke of Winterton's direction. However, this resolve perversely made necessary a constant need to know his whereabouts, so she might look the other way.

While she began to wonder where Lord Baddick was, that gentleman entered the ballroom in happy ignorance of all that had transpired in his absence. He had spent the early part of the evening in the arms of a dashing young widow, Lady Hoare. Her appetite in the bedroom proved voracious and she had been loath to release him from her clutches.

Therefore, it was a somewhat weary Lord Baddick who hastened forward to Henrietta, at Lady Fuddlesby's side. "You are breathtaking this evening, Miss Lanford," he declared, raising her gloved hand to his lips. "I am come to claim my dance." He held out his arm to her and she accepted it, eyes sparkling up at him.

"With pleasure, my lord. I began to think you had forgotten your promise when you were so late in arriving."

"Never! I was delayed helping a friend in need."

Lord Baddick's presence and compliments did much to restore Henrietta's spirits. She would not care what the duke thought of her!

It was the supper dance and Henrietta, despite her resolve not to care two straws for the duke, felt compelled to fill Lord Baddick's sympathetic ears with the tale of the duke's perfidious behavior and Mr. Brummell's subsequent rescue.

Lord Baddick spoke passionately. "Shall I call Winterton out, Miss Lanford? You have only to say the word." He felt secure in making this rash statement, knowing Miss Lanford would never agree to it.

"Oh, no, my lord!" She swiftly denied him. But the Fantasy Henrietta indulged in a gratifying dream in which the two handsome men fought a duel over the slur to her name. Then she brought herself back to reality with a sharp self-admonition not to think of the duke as handsome after what he had done.

The dance ended and Lord Baddick led her to a place at one of the long tables in the supper room. He filled a plate for her and one for himself, then signaled a footman for champagne. Henrietta placed a little bit of everything from her plate on her fork, as was the custom. She had never tasted champagne and, sipping the wine cautiously, found it pleasing.

"Have you seen much of London since your shopping expedition?" asked Lord Baddick, making polite conversation while his hazel eyes stripped her naked. He noted with growing anticipation her innocence was in sharp contrast to the charms of Lady Hoare.

"No, Lady Fuddlesby and I have been busy with my wardrobe and have kept quite at home."

She glanced to the head of the table where the Duke of Winterton was seated next to the blonde he had been dancing with. It seemed to Henrietta the top half of the lady's gown was missing, it was cut so low. She then dropped her startled gaze back to her plate when her eyes met the duke's cool gaze regarding her steadily.

At the duke's end of the table, Clorinda's next dancing partner presented himself, much to the lady's annoyance, and took her away. Colonel Colchester seated himself next to his godson, looking after Clorinda with a faint air of distaste.

"My boy, you have still not given Miss Lanford your apology. I know she behaved a bit too spiritedly when you approached her, but can one blame her?"

"Good manners must always override one's emotions," Winterton replied stiffly, forgetting that when he'd vented his frustrations in front of Lord Kramer, he committed the very crime of manners he now claimed to deplore.

At his godfather's frown, he sighed with an air of resignation. "You are right, sir, in that the lady is due an apology, much as it rankles me. How was I to know that prancing fool Kramer would make a piece of work over nothing? And what is Miss Lanford doing with an ugly customer like Baddick?"

The colonel glanced down the table curiously. "Why, what's wrong with him?"

"It is not generally known, but I happen to be aware of Baddick's unsavory exploits when it comes to women." With a speculative look he continued, "I wonder that he has resorted to seducing virgins. There was a story going around after Christmas. I cannot bring it to mind and will have to inquire," the duke finished, and then wondered why he should concern himself with Miss Lanford's suitor.

Colonel Colchester rubbed his chin thoughtfully as he wondered the very same thing.

In the ballroom, Lord Baddick escorted Henrietta to Lady Fuddlesby, saying, "Miss Lanford, I beg you will promise me another dance." Then, dropping his voice, he discreetly whispered in her ear, "I wish I might have a thousand dances with you!"

Henrietta wondered why the feel of his breath on her ear did not affect her as ardently as such things always did the heroines in novels. She attributed this lack of feeling on her part to the unusual circumstances of the evening. "Yes, my lord," she replied, and curtsied.

Standing next to Lady Fuddlesby, Henrietta could hear her aunt speaking with Lady Cowper regarding vouchers for Almack's. "And Miss Lanford's mother's mother was ..."

Henrietta prevented herself from squirming under the skeptical Lady Cowper's stare.

When the duke and Colonel Colchester approached, Henrietta felt the familiar telltale blush heat her cheeks. Winterton's nearness let loose a riot of uncomfortable emotions in her.

The duke, cool and aloof, introduced his godfather. Colonel Colchester was happy to finally be presented to Lady Fuddlesby, whom he privately termed a sweet-looking treat.

Winterton studied the card dangling from Henrietta's wrist. "Miss Lanford, how fortunate I am to find you free for the next dance. I thought I might have to wait until next Wednesday night at Almack's to secure the pleasure of dancing with you," he finished, glancing meaningfully at Lady Cowper. That lady nodded her acquiescence, and a smothered exclamation of delight came from Lady Fuddlesby.

Annoyed at his high-handed intervention on her behalf with Lady Cowper and his examination of her dance card, Henrietta said in a falsely apologetic voice, "Your Grace, I fear the next dance is a waltz and I have not been granted permission to dance it."

The duke could hardly believe his ears. Was Miss Lanford trying to sidestep his invitation? No lady had ever been anything less than thrilled at his escort. He stood cold and austere.

Into the awkward silence that followed, Lady Cowper pronounced, "You have my approval, Miss Lanford."

Outwitted, Henrietta turned to Lady Fuddlesby, but she would get no help from that quarter since her ladyship's face was wreathed in smiles at the turn of events. Henrietta had no choice but to allow the duke to lead her to the dance floor.

Joining the other couples prepared to begin the dance, she said, hesitantly, "I feel I must warn you I have never performed the steps of the waltz, other than with my governess, Biddles. She would not allow my dancing master to instruct me, feeling it improper."

"That is quite all right, Miss Lanford, you are safe with me," he said condescendingly.

She let out an unladylike snort. "Yes, indeed, Your Grace, just think of how well you have treated me in the short time we have known one another."

The duke ignored this sally. He moved close to her, slipping a gloved hand around her waist while his other hand held hers in a firm grasp.

Henrietta suddenly had difficulty breathing. She felt tiny sparks of energy radiating from their clasped hands up her arm, and the place where the duke's hand touched her waist burned. Fighting an intolerable desire to arch herself into his arms, she instructed herself, uselessly, to no longer be attracted to the duke in light of his contemptible behavior.

Watching from the side of the dance floor, Lady Clorinda viciously pinched her mama's arm, wringing a yelp from Lady Mawbly. "I wanted the duke to dance the waltz with me," she whispered fiercely. "He has already drawn enough attention to that country nobody."

Jewels clinking, Lady Mawbly turned to her daughter and said, "I am certain he is only doing it to stop the gossip, my pet. Why, you have only to look at Miss Lanford's inadequate frame to know she could never compete with you."

Clorinda vainly acknowledged this truth and positioned her bosom in the duke's direction in case he chanced to look her way.

When the music began, the duke, at first slowly, then as he sensed Henrietta's growing confidence, expertly, led her through the steps. Soon she swirled around the room in his arms. She had done so before, in her imagination, but the feeling it evoked was not equal to the variety of foreign sensations her body was now experiencing here in actuality.

Really, thought the duke, Lady Fuddlesby has done wonders with the chit. And those eyes, he did not recall they were so very blue. Her tiny waist made one feel protective. He pressed his lips together at the thought of her earlier humiliation.

"Miss Lanford," he nobly began his apology, "I fear someone took a carelessly uttered word from me and used it to amuse his friends. I hope you have forgotten the matter."

The duke's words effectively broke the spell Henrietta had fallen under in his arms. All in that moment, she realized that the duke's demeanor did not imply a reserved nature as she had naively believed after their previous meetings. The Duke of Winterton suffered from an excess of conceit and pride!

"Was that intended as an apology, Your Grace?" she said. The eyes the duke had just been silently admiring now glittered. "If so, I find it sadly lacking."

The duke looked down his nose at the girl in his arms.

"Miss Lanford, allow me to impart a piece of brotherly advice. If you will be going about in Society, you must learn something of the conventions.

When a gentleman asks a lady to dance and then apologizes for an unpleasant occurrence, a lady accepts the apology graciously."

Henrietta chafed at the word "brotherly." Her feelings for him had not run along those lines. "It appears to me that a gentleman would take responsibility for his words and not try to foist the blame of their consequences onto someone else!" she lectured.

The duke gritted his teeth. With a sinking feeling, he realized she was correct. It was past bearing, but his sense of honor came to the fore.

"Very well, Miss Lanford, I own myself at fault and ask your forgiveness. My churlish words were spoken in anger without any forethought."

At her puzzled frown, he went on, his usual air of hauteur gone for the moment.

"You see, I have been pursued for my title and fortune this age by many ladies and their mamas. It appeared at our meeting at Lady Fuddlesby's this was once again the case. I grow weary of the game and directed my distaste at you unjustly."

He quietly uttered the words she realized she most wanted to hear. "The feminine beauty I see before me is the strongest argument that my regrettable comparison of you to a horse could not possibly be further from the truth." His gray eyes turned silver for a moment, and Henrietta caught her breath.

Her own pride made her lie, "You may be easy, Your Grace, in that I have entertained no notions of attracting your attentions."

He smiled indulgently at what he believed a patent falsehood. *Every* miss of marriageable age wished to attract his attention. "Then we shall forget the matter."

She began to think he might have some understanding after all.

This feeling was dashed by the duke's next words.

"I observe you have taken up with the Viscount Baddick. I feel it my duty to warn you he is not what he seems." He spoke in the commanding air one might use when addressing a child.

He felt Henrietta stiffen and then move to break from his grasp. He tightened his hold on her. "Oh no, Miss Lanford, you will not flare up and bring another scene upon our heads this evening."

"You are insufferable, sir," she responded with some heat. "I do not know what you can mean when you say I have 'taken up with' Lord Baddick. And I assure you, not that it is at all your concern, that *he* has behaved as a gentleman."

Henrietta ruined this biting speech by throwing her head back defiantly, causing them both to lose their footing. With a quickness on his feet that could be credited to regular efforts at Gentleman Jackson's, the duke adeptly righted them.

Fortunately for the two combatants, the dance ended. Winterton gladly escorted Henrietta back to Lady Fuddlesby. With a chilly bow, he took himself off to the cardroom for the rest of the evening, much to the dismay of several ladies present, not the least of whom was Lady Clorinda.

Lady Fuddlesby was enjoying a comfortable chat with Colonel Colchester. They shared the common circumstances of having both lost a spouse and been left with no children to comfort them.

The colonel was loath to leave her ladyship's agreeable company, but when he saw the glowering faces of the two people leaving the dance floor, he said, "Lady Fuddlesby, forgive me, but I think it prudent to excuse myself. May I have the honor of calling on you?"

Lady Fuddlesby favored him with a radiant smile. "Please do, sir." Watching him follow the duke into the cardroom, her ladyship fanned her warm cheeks and told herself she had far too many years in her dish to be thinking such indecent thoughts about a man she had just met.

A preoccupied Henrietta went through the motions with her dance partners the remainder of the evening. Several times she caught herself gazing toward the cardroom and brought herself severely to task at this folly.

Lord Baddick noticed her distraction during their second dance together, and his eyes narrowed while he contemplated the meaning of this behavior. He had not seen her pay any one gentleman particular attention, so he ruled out the possibility of a rival. Still, if necessary, he would accelerate his own plans for her future.

Later, when she lay sleeplessly in her bed, Henrietta recalled the words Lady Fuddlesby spoke in the carriage on the way to the Denbys', and silently agreed the night of her first ball would truly be a night to remember.

On the afternoon of the following day, Henrietta sat with Lady Fuddlesby in the drawing room.

"Oh, my dear, I daresay I am well pleased with your success at the Denbys' last evening." Lady Fuddlesby served as chaperon during the afternoon as several young men had come to call. Floral tributes stood in vases around the room, including a lavish arrangement from Beau Brummell, who had stopped by for a brief visit.

"Yes, my lady. After an inauspicious beginning,

the night proved enjoyable." Henrietta stabbed a needle into a piece of stitchery, reflecting that every one of her gallants paled in comparison to the Duke of Winterton. And Lord Baddick, she firmly reminded herself.

Henrietta had passed a troubled night. As dawn approached she had finally fallen asleep and directly into the Duke of Winterton's arms. They were dancing the waltz in an empty ballroom. When she opened her mouth to speak to him, all that came out was a horse's whinny. The duke threw his dark head back and laughed at her. She woke up abruptly, sitting up in bed breathing hard.

After another period of restless sleep, she dreamt of Lord Baddick. In the dream, when that gentleman lowered his head to kiss her, he suddenly changed into the Duke of Winterton. At the very moment the duke's lips were to meet Henrietta's, she awakened for the day, feeling unreasonably frustrated.

Neither of these gentlemen had put in an appearance yet. Henrietta concentrated on wishing for Lord Baddick's company but started nonetheless when Chuffley intoned, "Colonel Owen Colchester, my lady."

Henrietta fought down disappointment as the colonel entered the room alone.

The handsome military man eyed both ladies appreciatively. "Well, I own I must be the luckiest of men. To have London's two prettiest ladies all to myself!"

Henrietta smiled and then glanced at her aunt, noticing the faintest of blushes rise in her round face.

In his arms Colonel Colchester carried two bouquets. He handed one of creamy yellow roses to

Henrietta, saying, "With the Duke of Winterton's compliments, Miss Lanford."

Henrietta stood up, surprised and more uncertain than ever. "Please convey my thanks to His Grace, sir." She accepted the flowers and moved away to place them on a side table, biting her lip hard to prevent herself from asking why the duke had not accompanied his godfather on this call.

Colonel Colchester handed a beautiful bouquet of pink roses to Lady Fuddlesby. "I see these match your gown, my lady. May I hope the color pleases you?"

"Oh, yes indeed, colonel," Lady Fuddlesby replied with a coy smile, and reached for the roses.

At that moment Knight walked into the room and saw the stranger. A running leap brought him into Lady Fuddlesby's lap and sent the roses flying.

"Oh dear, oh dear, Knight! Mustn't do!" She gently waived the cat away. "I am sorry, Colonel Colchester. This is my precious boy, Knight in Masked Armour. Perhaps he saw someone he did not know and felt he needed to come to my defense. You see, he is very intelligent and protective."

She and the colonel bent to retrieve the fallen flowers. Colonel Colchester caught a look he could only interpret as a warning from the cat, who then jumped to the fireplace mantel where he observed the caller through slitted eyes.

Chuffley appeared in the doorway again and announced, "Viscount Baddick."

Lord Baddick entered the room carrying an enormous arrangement of wildflowers. He bowed. "Good afternoon, Lady Fuddlesby. Miss Lanford, I see you have received many floral tributes today, which does not at all surprise me. A lady of your beauty must be admired by many." He handed her the flowers, saying, "I hope my humble offering may find favor with you."

Henrietta accepted this latest bouquet graciously. "Thank you, sir. Have you met Colonel Colchester?" she asked.

The two men shook hands, and Lady Fuddlesby begged Lord Baddick to take a seat.

The colonel remembered the duke's dubious opinion of Lord Baddick and decided to study him closely. He would not have sweet Lady Fuddlesby upset by an unsavory suitor for her charge.

Unaware of the scrutiny he was under, Lord Baddick remained standing and said, "In truth, my lady, I have come in hopes I may persuade Miss Lanford to come driving with me. The day is unusually fine and I have an open carriage, so we may observe the proprieties."

Lady Fuddlesby saw Henrietta's eager look and gave her permission.

Henrietta hurried upstairs to change her dress.

Lord Baddick sat on a matching chair opposite the brocade sofa, and charmed the company with amusing *on dits* until Henrietta reappeared clad in a Clarence-blue velvet carriage dress. A matching velvet bonnet trimmed with white fur complemented her doll-like features.

They took their leave, and after he saw her seated comfortably in his carriage, Lord Baddick drove them toward Hyde Park. He did not waste any time before he began tightening his web of seduction.

"Miss Lanford, as beautiful as the blue sky is this afternoon, its color pales in comparison to your eyes."

Henrietta felt exhilarated, riding next to this fashionable gentleman who thought her attractive.

"Thank you, my lord. It is a glorious day, is it not? I am so happy you came to take me out!"

Encouraged by this artless assertion, Lord Baddick assumed a serious mien and confided, "I find your happiness to be of prime concern to me, Miss Lanford. I pray you do not find me overbold, but in the short time of our acquaintance I have felt drawn to you as I have to no other lady."

"You are too good, my lord," she said, feeling a thrill of purely feminine triumph.

They pulled into the gates of the park, and Lord Baddick was forced to concentrate on his driving. The street was quite crowded. It seemed everyone was taking advantage of the weather.

Henrietta and Lord Baddick were chatting amiably when the traffic became so thick, they were obliged to stop their progress altogether.

During this pause another open carriage, going in the opposite direction, came abreast. Henrietta was caught off guard by the sudden appearance of the man who had dominated her dreams the night before.

The Duke of Winterton found himself staring into the wide, innocent eyes of Miss Henrietta Lanford. When he saw she was escorted by that cur Baddick, he felt himself grow irritated.

He gave the couple a brief nod and continued to hold Miss Lanford's gaze lazily, through half-closed lids. "Lady Clorinda, allow me to present Miss Henrietta Lanford and Viscount Baddick," he drawled.

Henrietta murmured a greeting, believing the duke more masculine than ever in a dark gray coat, leather breeches, and top boots.

Her eyes shifted to his serene companion, the blonde she'd seen him with at the Denbys' ball. Today the lady was dressed in the thinnest of muslins.

Her bosom was accentuated by a short leaf-green spencer that just reached the high waist of her gown. A plumed bonnet sat atop her golden curls.

Henrietta did not notice Lord Baddick's reaction to the beauty. His eyes drank in the sensuality of Lady Clorinda's body while he managed to sweep a bow and hold the reins. He'd noticed her the evening before at the Denbys', and hasty inquiries had netted him the disappointing information that Lady Clorinda was well guarded by both her parents.

"Lady Clorinda, your servant," Lord Baddick said, thinking of the many ways he could enjoy serving her indeed.

Clorinda remembered how Miss Lanford had stolen her waltz with the duke. Always ready to enslave another suitor, she smiled at Lord Baddick blindingly.

Turning a contemptuous gaze to Henrietta, Lady Clorinda addressed the viscount. "How do you do, Lord Baddick? What sturdy-looking horses you have, my lord."

Henrietta blushed at the obvious reference to her humiliation the night before.

Sitting beside Clorinda, the duke could not see the mocking look in that lady's eyes and thus missed the implication.

Lord Baddick managed to suppress an appreciative chuckle before he disgraced himself in his prey's estimation. He merely said, "Thank you, my lady."

A break appeared in the traffic and the carriages parted.

All the glory of the day died for Henrietta. She could no longer deny she felt hopelessly drawn to the duke. And he would never return her regard. A bitter jealousy stirred inside her at the thought of Clorinda's sophisticated charms. She sighed, clasped her slender hands together in her lap, and stared at them.

Lord Baddick thought for the first time the silly chit sitting next to him might have formed a tendre for the Duke of Winterton, the proudest, most arrogant man in London! All to the good, he reasoned. When Winterton spurned Miss Lanford, she would be even more ripe for the plucking.

The duke escorted Clorinda to her home, maintaining a cordial conversation. He found the lady met all his qualifications for duchess, but determined to proceed slowly in order to be certain.

Returning to his town house in Park Lane, he retired to his dressing room, where Tyler prepared him for the evening ahead.

Really, thought Giles, it was his duty to try to dredge up the details of the story about Baddick that had circulated after Christmas. It would not do to have gullible Miss Lanford hoodwinked by that coxcomb. Tonight, at the Whitfords' rout, he would see what he could discover.

As if knowing his master's thoughts were of a mere squire's daughter, from the bedchamber adjacent to the dressing room Sir Polly Grey chastised in the seventh Duke of Winterton's voice, "A *suitable* gel, Giles!"

The duke looked with some annoyance into the other room where the bird hopped about his cage in an agitated fashion.

"Tyler, close the door," he commanded, in order to cut the parrot off from sight and hearing.

Of course, he told himself, he could have no interest other than an altruistic one in the girl. She was not of his station.

Chapter Five

"There will be no cards or dancing. We simply arrive, present ourselves to our hostess, and take our leave," Lady Fuddlesby said, explaining the night's entertainment.

Entering the Whitfords' rout and seeing the number of people fashionably crushed into the town house, Henrietta doubted it would prove simple.

"Pray, my lady, what is the point? It appears the Whitfords have placed a wager as to the number of people that will fit into their house!" Henrietta said, bewildered.

"My dear, the most fashionable routs are the ones deemed a dreadful squeeze. The purpose is to be *seen* in the company of the cream of Society," her aunt assured her.

They spent an hour making their way up a narrow staircase to an overheated drawing room. Lady Fuddlesby introduced Henrietta to the Whitfords, and then her ladyship disappeared into the mass of grandeur.

Henrietta felt likely to suffocate. She searched in vain for her aunt through the noisy aristocratic crowd. Her efforts were hampered by her petite stature.

All at once a sense of awareness washed over her.

Her back distinctly tingled. When the crowd pressed in on her, she struggled to turn and found herself crushed up against a stiff white cravat.

"Good evening, Miss Lanford," the Duke of Winterton drawled, his saturnine face inches from hers.

Henrietta looked up into his silvery eyes and blushed rosily. Every time she saw him she was startled anew at his elegance. Even in this crowd his presence was compelling.

"Your Grace," she murmured, trying to regain her composure. She attempted a curtsy, but at their close proximity this had the effect of sliding her upper body down the front of Winterton's coat. Shocked, she cut the movement off abruptly, trying to back away from him, her flush deepening to crimson.

"Are you enjoying yourself?" Amusement flickered in the eyes that met hers. Then he raised his dark head and surveyed the room. "Where is Lady Fuddlesby?" he asked with an air of authority.

"She is here, Your Grace."

"Where? You should not be left alone to cope with such a situation."

Henrietta felt herself become impatient at his insinuation. "I do not know precisely where her ladyship is. We were separated in this terrible crowd of people."

To underline her description, a rowdy young buck hurriedly making his way through the crush jostled her, and she fell forward. Winterton lifted his arms to keep her from falling, his hands grasping her shoulders.

Henrietta stood motionless, observing his features from this up-close vantage. He was devastatingly handsome. His black hair gleamed in the candlelight from good health rather than the use of pomatum. His mouth was firm with a cynical twist to it. His nose was long and aquiline.

Henrietta was interrupted from her perusal by the realization the duke was looking at her enigmatically.

Dropping his hands, he turned his attention to Lady Clorinda, suddenly at his elbow. With the lady's green eyes glaring at her, Henrietta's self-esteem smarted intolerably and she quickly turned away into the throng of people.

Oh, why must she make a cake of herself in front of him! She was angry at the duke's power over her emotions and decided to wait outside for her aunt where the chill of the evening might cool her burning cheeks.

It took just as long to fight her way down the stairs as it had to climb them earlier. At last she was outside, breathing deeply.

"Oh, my dear, there you are!" Lady Fuddlesby cried, coming out of the doorway with Colonel Colchester at her side. "Where did you run off to?"

Henrietta fought down frustration at this niffy-naffy question. "I am sorry, my lady. Somehow we were separated." Henrietta noticed the colonel and smiled at him warmly. "Hello, sir. I did not see you inside."

"I'm blessed if you could! What an infernal waste of time a rout is," the colonel said gruffly. "Will I have the pleasure of seeing you ladies in the more civilized atmosphere of Almack's tomorrow night?"

"Yes, indeed, sir, thanks in part to your godson's kind influence." Lady Fuddlesby smiled at him.

"He's a good fellow, my lady, despite the rare dustup the other night at the Denbys'."

"Do not give it another thought, dear sir. Henrietta and I have quite forgotten the incident. We realize gossip can turn the most innocent remark black."

Lady Fuddlesby did not notice Henrietta's sigh of exasperation.

The colonel took his leave after he made sure the ladies were safe in their carriage, and he could be of no further service to them that evening.

"Now, why are you up in the boughs over some silly party, my boy? No need to make a piece of work over nothing," Colonel Colchester stated to the duke.

They had returned from the rout separately, the duke having escorted Clorinda and Lady Mawbly home first. The colonel joined his godson in his bed-chamber for a brandy before the comfortable fire.

"I had not decided whether to attend the Peabodys' breakfast on Thursday," Winterton said reproachfully.

"But Lady Peabody said you were to come and begged me to accompany you. Didn't think it amiss to agree. Felt sorry for her poor little daughter standing there with a broken arm."

"Gammon! Do you know how her 'poor little daughter' came by that broken arm? I thought not," the duke continued grimly at the colonel's questioning look. "Betina tried to climb up the trellis outside this very window with the idea of compromising me."

The colonel's brown eyes twinkled merrily and he could not restrain a chuckle.

"Think it funny, do you?" the duke asked. Feeling harassed, he sprang out of his chair to pace the room. "I will choose the future Duchess of Winterton in my own good time. Without any conniving or help from anyone. I am well aware what is due my name. Marriage is a business contract, and I intend to enter into it only after weighing all my options. I will not have it forced upon me."

The colonel's smile faded from his lips. "Giles, it grieves me to hear you speak this way. It is true a man in your position can have his pick of the ladies by virtue of title and fortune. But the real advantage is that you marry for *love*," the older man finished, thinking fondly of his own dearly departed wife.

"Fustian! I think mutual rank, fortune, and, I grant you, a certain amicability are better foundations for marriage than love." The duke returned to his chair, sinking into its softness. He looked down into the fire, his dark mood intensifying when a vision of Miss Henrietta Lanford's face inexplicably appeared in the flames. "I will honor the commitment to the Peabodys, however, for it would be rude to cry off now."

In the corner of the room, Sir Polly Grey swung round and round on his perch giddily. "A gel with strong hips. Good for breeding!" he cackled in the seventh Duke of Winterton's voice.

The colonel was familiar with the parrot's pontifications and felt a strong desire to introduce the bird to a certain masked cat he knew who would lick his whiskers at the meeting.

He contented himself with saying, "Your views tell me you have never been in love, my boy. And you cannot use your parents' marriage as an example, for a colder relationship, I am hard-pressed to imagine."

The colonel rose wearily from his chair before the duke could contradict him. He retired to his bedchamber without imparting the information that later at the rout he had offered their escort to the Peabodys' breakfast to Lady Fuddlesby and Miss Lanford. Best wait until tomorrow to tell him, he decided.

Wednesday evening brought the opening night at Almack's. Standing in the entryway, Henrietta knew she looked her best, but it did little to calm her nerves. Her ball gown was palest silver gauze. Tiny silver stars embroidered the deep square neck. Long white gloves adorned her arms beneath the gown's puffed sleeves. A dainty tiara of diamonds and sapphires glimmered in her curls, Henrietta feeling nearly faint when Felice had brought the costly headpiece to her earlier.

Henrietta was still Society-shy from her experience at the Denbys' and feared making a social misstep in front of the powerful patronesses of Almack's, all of whom were out in force tonight.

She crossed through the hallowed portals of Almack's and gazed about, disappointed. "My lady, can this really be the place whose admission tickets are so coveted? Why, the dance floor resembles a roped-off farm pen!"

Attired in her customary pink, Lady Fuddlesby stood beside her. "My dear, you are no one if you cannot dance at Almack's! It does not matter the rooms are dreary and the refreshments insipid. We are here to be . . ." She ended with a question in her voice.

"I know, I know," Henrietta said, "to be *seen!*" She and her aunt shared a conspiratory smile.

Lord Baddick presented himself at Henrietta's side, bowing low to the ladies. She thought his golden hair and hazel eyes showed to advantage against the contrasting dark brown of his evening coat and breeches. As usual, he calmed her nerves with his reassuring presence and compliments.

"Miss Lanford, now that you are here, the stars are truly shining," Lord Baddick said, his warm gaze encompassing her beautiful gown. "You see I come to you immediately to claim my dances, drawn as a moth to the flame." He scribbled his name by a country dance and the waltz.

As the country dance commenced at that moment, Henrietta tripped off with a delighted Lord Baddick to take their places in the set.

Lady Fuddlesby stood watching them when, moments later, a party containing Lord and Lady Mawbly, Lady Clorinda, and Matilda, Dowager Duchess of Winterton, entered.

Greetings were exchanged and Lady Mawbly introduced her daughter to Lady Fuddlesby.

Henrietta's aunt remembered Clorinda dancing with the duke at the Denbys', and she studied the girl carefully. Her gown was a pale green miracle of spider gauze. Lady Fuddlesby pondered the wisdom of the sophisticated cut for a girl of Clorinda's tender years. In addition, a striking necklace of emeralds, unsuitable for a miss in her first Season, draped across her creamy skin. One large emerald teardrop dangled down to rest tantalizingly between her breasts. The girl's mouth formed a petulant pout while she surveyed the room, obviously searching for someone.

The Mawblys moved on, but Matilda lingered to speak to Lady Fuddlesby. "Clara, Hester says that is your niece dancing with Viscount Baddick. Quite a success for you if the gel can bring him up to the mark. A title, plenty of money, and good-looking, too."

Lady Fuddlesby chafed at her old rival's superior

tone. Her reference to the viscount's title brought to mind her own acquisition of a title upon her marriage to Viscount Fuddlesby. A fact she was sure Matilda meant to remind her of.

Furthermore, she did not like the implication of Matilda's arrival with the Mawblys. It implied Lady Clorinda had the dowager's stamp of approval for her son, and Lady Fuddlesby was not about to concede the field when it came to her niece's chances with the duke.

"Henrietta has her pick of suitors, Matilda. It is unfortunate you did not see her dancing with Mr. Brummell at the Denbys' ball."

Matilda raised an eyebrow.

Lady Fuddlesby heaved a sentimental sigh, saying, "I had tears in my eyes at the time."

Matilda turned away, and Lady Fuddlesby, feeling she had won a skirmish, went to sit by her good friend Lady Chatterton, whose pale face resembled that of a corpse.

Across the room, Lady Mawbly whispered to her husband, "That gown Clara Fuddlesby has on is the one she wore the night I first noticed her pink tourmaline ring. I want that ring, Mawbly!"

The Earl of Mawbly was a small, thin man with a perpetually hunted look about him. He was totally under the cat's paw between Lady Mawbly and Clorinda, living in fear of their nagging. He wanted nothing more than to closet himself in his library with his books.

Nervously he asked, "Does she have it on now, Lady Mawbly?" Hester's obsession with her title extended to insisting her husband address her by it.

"No, but it makes no difference. I want you to buy the ring off her for me! It is unthinkable I should not have a pink tourmaline in my collection," Lady Mawbly insisted.

As the country dance lasted thirty minutes, Lord Baddick still partnered Henrietta when the Duke of Winterton and Colonel Colchester arrived.

The duke saw Miss Lanford and the viscount, and resolved to find out what he could about Baddick immediately, having not had an opportunity to do so at the Whitfords' rout.

Colonel Colchester went to seek out an army acquaintance, and the duke hailed his friend Sir Thomas Martin. Sir Tommy was a tall, gangling young man with a prematurely balding head and an infectious grin.

"Hey, ho, are you dicked in the nob, Winterton? I mean," he explained at the haughty expression on the duke's face, "rather like putting a fox among the hounds, your coming to the Marriage Mart, ain't it?"

"An apt way of wording it," the duke replied, glancing around at the doglike faces of the hopefuls. "I need your help, Tommy."

"You can't mean you want me to marry!" Sir Tommy exclaimed, horrified. "That would only get one of them off your back anyway!"

"Are you foxed?" the duke asked his grinning friend. "Never mind, now listen. I need information about Baddick. There was a story going around right after Christmas. Can you recall it?"

Sir Tommy concentrated hard and was rewarded. "Bad business. Lady Honoria Farrow. Mousy little thing. Never stood a chance against Baddick's practiced charm. He followed her to her country house and got his leg over her on Christmas Eve. The mother went into strong convulsions, but Baddick's rich. Paid her off. Bragged about it, just to his intimates, mind you, but scandals tend to get around. This new game is to prey on innocent misses with only some female to guard 'em. Speaking of fresh young misses," he said, raising his quizzing glass, "who's the dasher in the silver gown?"

The duke followed his friend's gaze to Miss Lanford, her face flushed and her eyes sparkling up at Lord Baddick while they danced. "A green girl from the country, Tommy. A common squire's daughter."

"Maybe stooping too low for you, Your Grace," Sir Tommy said sarcastically, "but not me." Then, as his thoughts were never of a romantical nature for long—"Want to change your mind about being here and toddle off to White's?"

Young puppy, thought the duke, out of reason cross with his friend. "No, you go on. I have only just arrived and may meet you at the club later."

When Sir Tommy left, the duke's mind kept repeating his words, "innocent misses with only some female to guard 'em." Miss Lanford was in town with only Lady Fuddlesby to protect her. Filling in the rest of the scene left the duke with a cold feeling in the pit of his stomach.

He ran his long white fingers through his dark hair. Deuce take it! He had tried to warn the chit at the Denbys', but her temper had flared. He would apprise Lady Fuddlesby of the situation.

Winterton made his way over to her, ignoring any attempts by people he passed to hail him. Glancing back at the dancers, he realized he had but a few minutes while they promenaded before Miss Lanford might return to her chaperon.

Lady Fuddlesby looked up from her conversation with Lady Chatterton, pleasantly surprised at the

Duke of Winterton standing imperiously in front of her.

"My lady, a word with you, please."

Puzzled, Lady Fuddlesby rose, and she and the duke stepped a few feet away. "Yes, Your Grace?"

"I feel it my duty to warn you about Lord Baddick, ma'am."

Jealous! He is jealous, thought Lady Fuddlesby. How delightful! He must have formed a tendre for Henrietta in spite of the apparent quarrel during their dance at the Denbys'.

At the moment, though, Lady Fuddlesby reflected she must humor Winterton because, like any gentleman, it would take the duke a while before he realized the real nature of his feelings. "Why, what can you mean? Lord Baddick's behavior is all that is proper."

"There are certain stories going around about him. I have reason to believe they are true." The duke found himself searching for the right words. He could not just tell this delicate lady that Baddick meant to take her niece to bed without the benefit of marriage lines. "You would be wise to cut the connection between Baddick and your niece."

Lady Fuddlesby gazed at him reproachfully. "Are those words not a trifle strong, Your Grace? You gentlemen are allowed your little peccadillos. Surely Lord Baddick is guilty of nothing more than that. Why, your own mother was speaking to me minutes ago about the suitability of a match between Henrietta and Lord Baddick."

She rapped him on the arm playfully with her fan. "Are you certain of your motives in telling me this, Winterton? Henrietta is a charming girl. . . ." Lady Fuddlesby trailed off with a knowing gleam in her eyes.

The Duke of Winterton stared down at her coldly. "You must be guided by me in this matter, my lady."

"Giles!"

It was unfortunate that Matilda chose this particular moment to accost her son. He turned a scowling face to her.

"Goodness, what has you in a pucker?" she asked, wondering what on earth her son could find to converse with Clara Fuddlesby about. "No matter, I want you to say hello to the Mawblys."

The duke bowed to Lady Fuddlesby and escorted his mother away, wishing a pox on all women.

Henrietta danced every dance, and during each of them found her gaze wandering to the duke. She wondered about his conversation with her aunt. She noticed him escorting an older woman and thought she could detect a family resemblance. His mother, she decided while trying to keep her toes from being trounced by a sweating, overweight baron.

She smiled with relief when Colonel Colchester solicited her hand. "I know I am an old man, Miss Lanford, but perhaps you will humor me. I would ask your lovely aunt to partner me, but I see I have left the matter too late," he said, frowning as Lady Fuddlesby clung to the arm of an elderly man. It was difficult to tell who was supporting whom.

Henrietta chuckled. "Sir, I accept your kind offer although it is lowering to be second best! And one could hardly call you old."

They moved out onto the floor, Colonel Colchester setting himself to please with humorous stories of his life, but both their minds were elsewhere.

Henrietta saw the duke dancing with Lady Clorinda. They seemed totally wrapped up in one another. Henrietta's gaze ran down the length of the duke, thinking him the most handsome man in the room in his claret evening coat and black breeches. She longed to be in his arms, swirling about the room to the strains of the music.

Colonel Colchester led her back to Lady Fuddlesby and claimed that lady's hand for the next dance, a waltz.

Lord Baddick, true to his word, partnered Henrietta. As they walked out onto the floor, Henrietta's eyes widened in dismay, and she had to prevent her mouth from falling open when she saw the duke preparing to dance with Clorinda again.

She was not the only one to notice this marked attention, and whispering reached a peak. Never had the wealthy, marriageable duke shown an interest in any miss on the lookout for a husband. Speculation regarding the relationship ran rampant. Two dandies immediately placed a bet on a betrothal announcement, rushing out the front door to record the wager in the betting book at White's.

Clorinda relished the sensation she and the duke were causing. Surely the title of Beauty of the Season was clearly hers. And if matters went as she planned, so would the title "duchess" be hers.

The emerald lying between Clorinda's breasts seemed to have hypnotized the duke. He was too mesmerized by the vision of her creamy mounds, practically popping out of their constraints right under his nose, to consider his behavior.

Another couple danced nearby. "Miss Lanford," Lord Baddick said, "twice I have told you your eyes are more beguiling than the sapphires in your tiara."

"You are funning, my lord," Henrietta managed. She tried to pull herself up from the dregs of misery. Disappointed, she judged the special feelings she experienced when the duke held her during their waltz were not repeated while she was in Lord Baddick's arms.

More important, it appeared Clorinda had won the duke. Or at least her charms had, Henrietta thought dejectedly.

Seeing Miss Lanford's reaction to Winterton and Clorinda, Lord Baddick decided to press his advantage. "No, my love, I am not funning. You possess the most beautiful eyes I have ever beheld." He was pleased to see he had her attention now.

"My lord, you must not address me so."

"My apologies if I have offended you, fairest one." His eyes burned with a zealous light. "You have me completely under your spell. I am yours to command."

All this flattery acted as a balm to Henrietta's bruised heart. She smiled at him weakly. "Then I command you to not hold me quite so closely, else we shall be disgraced."

When the dance was over, Henrietta felt unutterably weary. Lord Baddick led her over to a small sofa and she sat down gratefully. The viscount took himself off to find a glass of lemonade for her.

Henrietta sat staring at her lap, telling herself her depressed feeling was due to exhaustion from dancing all evening, but knowing it to be a lie.

When a gentleman sat beside her, she raised her blue eyes, expecting to meet hazel ones. Instead, a cool gray gaze rested on her.

"I came to ask you to dance, Miss Lanford, but I can see the effort would be too much for you. I will content myself with sitting the next dance out." The Duke of Winterton sat back, crossing his long legs.

Lord Baddick reappeared with Henrietta's lemonade.

"Ah, Baddick, thank you," the duke said dismissively, accepting the glass and passing it to Henrietta.

Struck speechless when confronted by the man she had just bitterly decided was lost to her, Henrietta felt her feminine defenses switch her pain to anger. How could he let almost the entire evening go by without approaching her, dance with that blond trollop twice, and then come and sit beside her in the most casual way?

Lord Baddick was not a flat. He saw the look of fury on Miss Lanford's face. Thinking things could not be going better, he bowed and moved away to the side of the room to watch.

"Miss Lanford, I want you to think of me in the light of an older brother," the duke began.

Henrietta thought, there was that hated phrase "brother"! She remembered he had used the term during their waltz at the Denbys' while reading her a lecture on the conventions.

Winterton continued, "It is not to be expected that a young girl from the country would recognize when a gentleman's intentions are not honorable. While I find it distasteful to bring the matter up once again, I feel it my duty to inform you my suspicions about Lord Baddick have proved correct. Do not encourage him."

Henrietta's eyes blazed and her fingers clutched the sticks of her fan. "You amaze me, Your Grace! Let me be sure I understand this. You would stand in the place of a brother to me. And as such, you do not wish me to continue enjoying the company of a handsome, kind gentleman? What right have you to meddle in my affairs?"

"He is not a 'kind gentleman,'" the duke said between his teeth, ignoring her question. "His intentions towards you are the very worst! Someone must protect the innocent from harm, and as Lady Fuddlesby does not appear up to the task—"

"Do not dare to insult my aunt!" Henrietta interrupted him, her fingers snapping the sticks of her fan. She felt her feelings at that moment could only be relieved by slapping his proud face. She controlled herself with an effort.

The duke felt like shaking her. "Miss Lanford! You are behaving like the veriest schoolgirl! You show a decided lack of judgment where Lord Baddick is concerned. I suggest you pattern yourself after one of the more pretty-behaved misses making their come-out, such as Lady Clorinda."

"As you wish, Your Grace," Henrietta replied obligingly. She stood up in front of him, grasped the bodice of her dress, and pulled it down as low as it would go without exposing her nipples. She thrust her bosom forward and gave him a court curtsy.

Her mocking expression met his astonished face before she turned and flounced away from him, leaving the duke to rise to his feet in a mixture of shock, fury, and some other emotion he could not give name to.

"Minx!" the Duke of Winterton shouted after her in the suddenly quiet room.

Lord Baddick's face broke out in a wolfish grin.

Colonel Colchester supported a swooning Lady Fuddlesby.

Mrs. Drummond-Burrell, the patroness of Almack's Lady Fuddlesby most feared, issued an edict to withdraw Miss Lanford's vouchers at once.

Chapter Six

Silence reigned in the carriage in which Lady Fuddlesby and Henrietta rode home from Almack's. The older woman was in shock and held a vinaigrette under her nose to prevent herself from collapsing.

Henrietta's anger had cooled, and she felt a heavy sense of remorse. The minute the footman helped her down, she picked up her skirts and hurried inside the town house, rushing up the stairs to her bedchamber. She struggled to hold back tears.

A startled Knight, coming into the hallway from the kitchens, ran after her.

Henrietta reached the privacy of her room gratefully. A fire had been lit, casting the room in a soft glow of light, so she did not bother with a candle.

Determined not to hurl herself across the bed and burst into tears dramatically, and not wishing for Felice's company, she busied herself with changing into her nightrail.

Laying the beautiful silver gown across the back of a chair, she bathed her face and arms in water left by a thoughtful housemaid. Keeping her mind firmly on the simple tasks, she unpinned her hair. After carefully laying the tiara aside, she climbed into bed.

Pulling the covers up to her chin, she settled onto

her side. Only then did the tears quietly begin to fall.

She did not see the moving hump under the bed-clothes and so jumped slightly when a masked fe-line face suddenly appeared from under the sheets in front of her face.

"Knight!" she cried, reaching out to hug his head close. He bore this indignity stoically, seeming to know the girl was upset.

Henrietta spent several minutes crying and hold-ing the cat to her. At last, with a slight hiccup, the tears ceased. She released Knight to reach over to a small nightstand for a handkerchief. After drying her eyes, she propped herself up with a pillow and addressed the cat.

"Knight, this evening I behaved just like the schoolgirl Winterton accused me of being. I embar-rassed myself and Lady Fuddlesby. Why must my foolish emotions take control whenever I see the duke?"

Knight listened sympathetically, unable to pro-vide an answer to the question.

"That is what all this daydreaming has gotten me. I keep imagining the duke holding me in affec-tion, when nothing could be further from the truth. But no more!" she resolved. "My days of spending time in dreams are over. After all, dreams are for children. The reality is, I must work hard to enjoy this Season my parents are giving me, and find a husband they will be glad to call son."

Her fingers folded and refolded a bit of pale blue coverlet while she continued. "The duke is drawn to Lady Clorinda. She is more beautiful than I and has more . . . assets," she concluded, thinking of her own petite figure. "I wish her the joy of him!" she declared, her chin coming up.

Knight raised a paw to the girl's face in support.

Henrietta scratched the cat's head before sinking down under the covers. "Lord Baddick thinks me well enough," she said, and yawned. "From now on, I shall ignore the stuffy duke and bestow all my attentions on Lord Baddick."

Henrietta had made this decision before, but felt determined this time. She remembered the duke's warning about Lord Baddick only hazily before she drifted off into an exhausted sleep.

Knight sensed the need for his presence was over and silently left the room. His mistress would also require his assistance.

Downstairs, Lady Fuddlesby had gone into the drawing room, an anxious Chuffley hovering behind her. "Shall I have tea served, my lady?"

"Yes, please, Chuffley," Lady Fuddlesby sniffled.

Chuffley hurried down to the hall and gave the order to a footman, then scurried to the door as the knocker sounded. Who in the world could be calling at this hour? he wondered.

Colonel Colchester thrust his hat and stick at the surprised butler and demanded, "Where is her ladyship?"

"I will ascertain if she is at home," Chuffley replied, awkwardly clutching the items in one hand and holding out a silver salver for the colonel's card.

"Blast it, man," the colonel snapped, pushing his way past the butler. He took the steps with a sprightliness uncommon for a man of his years, rightly assuming Lady Fuddlesby to be in the drawing room.

He came upon her quietly weeping. Crossing the room, he sat beside her on the brocade sofa. He took one of her gloved hands in his, and patted it reassuringly.

"Oh, dear sir!" Lady Fuddlesby cried, astonished at his arrival. She used the remains of a shredded lace handkerchief to dry her eyes.

"Now, now, my lady, you must calm yourself. I will not have you so distraught," the colonel said bracingly.

Chuffley entered with the tea tray, eyed the situation, and decided his mistress was safe. He retired, properly leaving the door open.

Colonel Colchester hesitated as he prepared to take over the pouring out of tea. "Would something stronger help?"

"No, thank you," Lady Fuddlesby replied, and attempted a weak smile. "I cannot say what might help matters after the doings of this night! But I should not burden you. . . ."

"Nonsense!" the colonel said roundly, passing her a filled cup. "Only consider. Miss Lanford and my godson's actions speak of passion between the two. Perhaps they do not realize it yet, but there can be no doubt a strong feeling exists between them."

"Yes, a strong feeling of dislike!" Lady Fuddlesby retorted miserably. She took a sip of tea and then set the cup down on the table. "And I did so have hopes . . ." She broke off, a tinge of pink coming into her cheeks.

The colonel squeezed her hand. "Wonderful!"

"But the difference in their stations . . . It would be flying too high for Henrietta," Lady Fuddlesby bemoaned.

"Stuff! Am I to believe you feel your niece, my godson, or anyone for that matter, should place such things above love?"

"They may not be in love."

"Yet. But I think there is every reason to believe that given a chance, they will find themselves well suited," Colonel Colchester said slowly.

"Whatever could they have fallen to brangling over?" Lady Fuddlesby wondered aloud. "Oh, but the scandal of their behavior!" Tears threatened again.

" 'Twill only be a nine days' wonder, my lady. You know it to be true!" he stated at her doubtful expression. "The worst that will happen is Miss Lanford's vouchers will be withdrawn, and she and the duke will be the subject of curious tittle-tattle. Then Society will find something else that will set their tongues wagging."

"I pray you have the right of it, Colonel. But what are we to do about our plans for the Peabodys' breakfast? You had generously offered the escort of yourself and His Grace. . . ."

"And we shall continue with those arrangements, my lady," the colonel stated firmly, hoping his doubts about convincing the duke to follow a scheme he at present knew nothing about, and doubtless would not be happy to hear of, did not show on his face. "To be seen arriving together will do much to stay the rumors."

"Thank you, dear sir. I do not know what I should have done tonight without your reassuring company." Lady Fuddlesby smiled at the colonel while they both rose, the colonel holding the lady's hand.

Knight arrived downstairs and entered the room. He saw the couple and vaulted to the top of the sofa next to them, hissing at Colonel Colchester.

"Knight! Goodness, what are you about!" Lady Fuddlesby asked the cat in surprise.

"Er, I shall take my leave now, my lady." The

colonel knew when to retreat. As he quit the room, he kept a wary eye on the hostile animal.

After the colonel left, an obviously angry Knight escorted her ladyship to her bedchamber. Lady Fuddlesby scolded her pet severely, if uselessly, until they both fell into a troubled sleep.

Henrietta slept late the next morning but did not feel refreshed upon awakening. She tried to banish the morose feeling weighing her down, but it was still present when she went downstairs and greeted her aunt in the breakfast room.

"Good morning, my lady," Henrietta began, eyes downcast. "I cannot think how to convey to you how terrible I feel about my disgraceful actions last night. I beg your forgiveness and give you my promise that from now on I shall be a perfect pattern of proper behavior."

Lady Fuddlesby rose from her chair and came to take Henrietta's hands in hers. "There, there, my darling girl. You are young, and youth must be allowed its mistakes. Of course I forgive you!"

Henrietta had to fight back the tears that formed in the back of her eyes at her aunt's show of kindness and understanding. Her own mother had never behaved thus. "Thank you," she managed.

They took their seats at the table, and Lady Fuddlesby poured a cup of chocolate for her niece and placed a roll on a plate for her. "Now, dear, you must eat something, for though we are invited to 'breakfast' at the Peabodys', a Society breakfast does not begin until three in the afternoon."

Henrietta drank some chocolate and asked, "Where do the Peabodys live?"

"Well, my dear, of course, they have a town house here in Mayfair, but they also have an estate in

Surrey where the gathering is being held," she explained in a light tone. Gathering her forces, she made her announcement. "Colonel Colchester has graciously offered the escort of himself and his godson. I am certain we will be conveyed in the greatest of comfort in the duke's carriage."

Lady Fuddlesby almost backed down at the stricken look in her niece's eyes but then relaxed when Henrietta brought herself under control.

"Drink your chocolate, my dear, and then we shall choose something fetching for you to wear. It always boosts one's courage when one knows one looks one's best," Lady Fuddlesby pronounced.

Lady Fuddlesby and Henrietta sat in the drawing room, both trying not to show how nervous they were while they waited for the gentlemen.

Henrietta wore a white muslin gown with a lilac spot. Her lilac pelisse was complemented by a chip straw bonnet decorated with matching lilac silk flowers and a small cluster of artificial grapes.

Chuffley announced the Duke of Winterton and Colonel Colchester.

Henrietta's gaze flew to the duke, but he was his usual self, cool and aloof. He wore a dark blue coat over a white waistcoat. Biscuit-colored pantaloons were tucked into his shiny black Hessian boots.

Colonel Colchester smiled comfortably at the ladies, his manner defying anyone to tell him his godson and Miss Lanford were the prime subjects of the rumormongers. He looked about the room expectantly. "Where is my friend Knight?"

Lady Fuddlesby, in a rose-colored gown with matching pelisse, replied with a little laugh, "Can you not feel his gaze boring into your back from the fireplace mantel?"

Knight sat perched on his favorite people-watching post. His tail swished dangerously close to a Sevres vase while he stared at the colonel, murder in his eyes.

Colonel Colchester turned around and addressed the cat. "I have brought you something, my brave soldier." He opened a bag he held and produced a dish. Removing the cover, the colonel walked slowly over to the cat. "You do like fresh lobster, don't you, Knight?"

Knight did indeed.

Colonel Colchester watched with satisfaction when he placed the dish on the floor, and the black and white cat jumped down from the mantel. Barely glancing at the gift-bearing colonel, the cat consumed the treat eagerly.

"Sir, what a shameless bribe! And so on target as well. Dear Knight never deigns to touch the ordinary fish head. He insists on table food, and I admit I indulge him," Lady Fuddlesby said, chuckling appreciatively.

Henrietta could not suppress a ripple of laughter and thought she detected a gleam of humor in the duke's eyes. The tension in the room seemed to lessen.

Colonel Colchester said, "Perhaps my unprincipled methods will serve to win him over. I do not wish to count him as my enemy," he finished, directing a look at Lady Fuddlesby that brought color to the lady's cheeks.

Winterton drawled, "If you ladies are ready, we should be on our way. I do not like to keep my cattle standing."

The party moved out to the duke's waiting closed carriage, which was as luxurious as Lady Fuddlesby predicted. A footman hurried to assist the ladies into the conveyance. Henrietta and Lady Fuddlesby sat on one side of the leather seats. To Henrietta's consternation, the duke sat opposite her, his long legs stretched out in front of him, brushing her skirts. The colonel sat across from Lady Fuddlesby.

When they moved off, the colonel and Lady Fuddlesby began a conversation about Knight. Lady Fuddlesby told the story of how she had rescued the dear little fellow, one day in the park when he was just a kitten, while he was being tortured by four small boys.

Only part of Henrietta's attention was on the discussion. The other part of her mind was busy commanding her body to relax and stop being assailed with unwanted feelings at Winterton's proximity. She had been mortified to learn he, along with his godfather, was to escort them to the breakfast. But she was astute enough by now to realize that it could only be advantageous to be seen in his company after the shameful doings of the previous evening. If only her heart would cease this useless longing!

For his part, the duke sat back, his lids half-closed, wishing he were elsewhere. He thought over the conversation he'd had with his godfather that morning.

The colonel had come to Giles's bedchamber to find him sitting up in bed reading the morning paper. "My boy, I have offered our escort to Lady Fuddlesby and Miss Lanford to the Peabodys' breakfast today." At the duke's disbelieving look, the colonel held up his hands in a defensive gesture. "It was done before the events of last night, and it would be unforgivable to withdraw the invitation at this late date."

The duke sighed and folded the newspaper.

"Lady Fuddlesby is a good woman, but her niece wants conduct."

"Miss Lanford is young, spirited, and learning her way. If her actions at Almack's did display a lapse from proper behavior, it can be no excuse for lowering your own standard for good manners," the colonel reminded him.

Sir Polly Grey paused in the middle of eating a breakfast of seeds and apricots to remark in the seventh Duke of Winterton's voice, "Good manners and good breeding."

The duke pointedly ignored the bird. He didn't want to think of the breach from his usual superb conduct when he had shouted "Minx" after Miss Lanford.

"Very well, sir, we will keep the commitment. But I hope you will refrain from putting me together with Miss Lanford in the future. I tried to do my duty by her, warning her of that loose screw Baddick, and she refused to listen. After today, I want nothing more to do with the girl. I am in Town to find a wife, if possible. And I need not tell you that when I marry, it will be to some lady of excellent birth. Not some blue-eyed chit from a horse farm."

Now, as the carriage bowled along, Winterton noticed the dark shadows underneath Miss Lanford's blue eyes. Guilty conscience kept her awake last night, he thought with satisfaction.

Then his attention was abruptly caught as an astonishing sight met his eyes. Outside the carriage window was Sir Polly Grey's frantic face. He flew alongside the glass, obviously trying to come to the notice of his master.

Winterton rapped his stick on the roof. "Hold hard," he shouted. Then he muttered, "That bird is a Bedlamite. What notion could he have taken into his feathered head now?"

When the carriage slowed to a stop, the duke threw open the door and swiftly jumped down, ignoring the startled exclamations of his fellow travelers.

Sir Polly Grey had been in the room during the duke's conversation with the colonel that morning. When Winterton had, for the first time, uttered the word "marry," the bird had opened his beak in an expectant manner.

The old duke, training the parrot to speak his lecture about his son's need to marry, had often rewarded the bird with the special treat of hothouse grapes when Sir Polly Grey had successfully repeated the phrases. Hence, oftentimes the old duke would say, "Yes, Sir Polly, Giles needs to *marry*," while offering the prized grapes.

Winterton, of course, not knowing of this ritual, had not produced any grapes after saying the word "marry" despite indignant, squawking protests from the parrot. Sir Polly Grey apparently decided to follow his master, anxious to get his treat.

It had been a simple matter to unlock his cage door. Indeed, he had done so often in the past when he wished to exercise his wings. From there, the window latch proved amusingly simple, and he had flown out high above the trees following the duke.

He had followed the carriage unobserved until the unexpectedly long flight grew tiring. They were well outside Town.

The duke, standing on the ground looking up toward the bird, held out his hand in the manner of a perch for Sir Polly Grey. He wondered how the parrot had managed to escape the confines of his cage and find a way out of the town house.

Fortunately, the grateful bird came to him at once and the two entered the carriage.

Winterton gave the office to move forward. There followed some confusion when Sir Polly Grey flew over to land on Henrietta's hat, pecking excitedly at the artificial grapes ornamenting it.

"Oh, Your Grace, he is beautiful!" Henrietta exclaimed. She let loose a trill of laughter while the duke quickly removed the parrot from her bonnet before harm could be done.

Blue eyes shining with pleasure, she asked excitedly, "Is he yours? Was he actually following us? May I hold him?"

"I suppose I must admit the scoundrel belongs to me. But I doubt if he will come to a stranger; these birds are known to be mistrustful. . . ." He trailed off as Henrietta held out her hand in imitation of the way the duke made a perch out of his hand, and Sir Polly Grey promptly hopped over.

Henrietta gasped with obvious enjoyment. "Oh, he is lighter than I thought he would be, but his claws are so strong! Do but look how very lovely he is!"

Lady Fuddlesby and the colonel added their admiring comments, but the duke's gaze was transfixed by the sight of the girl opposite him. She looked so fresh and innocent. Her delight in the bird charmed him. Her lips puckered while she tried to chirp back to the parrot, who was chattering bird nonsense. Shocking himself, the duke experienced a strong desire to kiss Miss Lanford's pink lips.

The colonel interrupted these unsettling thoughts. "Er, don't you think it might be wise to place some sort of covering on Miss Lanford's clothing, in case Sir Polly has to, er, well, we wouldn't want Miss Lanford's pelisse soiled. . . ."

"Yes, good idea," the duke replied. He pulled out his handkerchief, reached over, and spread it out on Henrietta's lap. Her wide blue eyes met his silvery gaze, and neither looked away. Long moments passed while the duke attempted to master an unfamiliar desire to protect and cherish Miss Lanford.

Henrietta desperately tried to discern the meaning behind the duke's eyes, which were now a stormy gray color. She felt a slender, delicate thread begin to form between them, and she gloried briefly in the shared moment.

Colonel Colchester observed the couple, and flashed Lady Fuddlesby a speaking look.

The spell was broken when suddenly the parrot saw the handkerchief and erupted into loud sounds of nose-blowing.

Everyone dissolved into whoops. Even the duke was laughing helplessly. When again in control of himself, he explained, "My father, who owned the bird for ten years, suffered from sneezing fits. Parrots have an excellent memory and they can produce sounds in their proper context. Hence, the use for a handkerchief was not lost on this intelligent fellow."

The remainder of the drive passed in congenial conversation about the amazing bird, although not once did Sir Polly Grey speak in the seventh Duke of Winterton's voice.

When they arrived at the Peabodys', the duke gave instructions to a servant regarding food for the parrot. "Some fruit will serve. I seem to recall he is especially fond of grapes."

The duke then charged his driver with securing some type of carton that might be used to transport Sir Polly Grey back to Park Lane in a borrowed gig.

The day was chilly, but the sun shone and there

was no wind. Long tables laid with white cloths and laden with food had been set up beside an ornamental lake. The duke bowed to Lady Peabody and Betina but avoided the vulgar pair.

The gathering was large. Society stared to see Miss Lanford and her aunt arrive, obviously in charity with the Duke of Winterton and his godfather after the scene at Almack's the night before.

Lady Clorinda was present with her parents. She relished the jealous looks cast at her by the ladies of the ton who felt she had snatched the matrimonial prize of the Season. Made confident by the duke's marked attentions paid to her at Almack's Clorinda barely held her fury in check when Winterton arrived at the Peabodys' with Miss Henrietta Lanford. Clorinda's face, however, was a beautiful mask as she tripped up to them dressed in the thinnest of muslins.

"Giles!" she cried happily, placing her hand on the duke's arm possessively. Then, seeming to realize the impropriety of this overly familiar behavior, she blushed adorably. "I meant to say, Your Grace, of course." Much fluttering of eyelashes and a thrusting chest accompanied this correction.

The duke felt somehow relieved to see Lady Clorinda despite her improper use of his name. Somewhere in his mind the voice of duty assured him that Lady Clorinda was of appropriate rank, and possessed a sizable fortune, not to mention her bosom. She was a suitable choice for his duchess. Another, quieter, voice said there was something about her that rang false. That Miss Henrietta Lanford was the true lady. But he had lived his life according to the dictates of his sense of duty, and old habits die hard.

To Henrietta's disgust, the duke smiled down at

Lady Clorinda, who promptly began an intimate conversation with him that required his full attention. Henrietta looked about the crowds for Lord Baddick.

The viscount saw Miss Lanford and disengaged himself from a flirtatious conversation with a recent widow. He hailed Henrietta, wondering if the time was right to put his plans into action.

"Miss Lanford, Lady Fuddlesby, your servant," he said, arriving to stand before the ladies and sketching a bow. "How enchanting you look in lilac, Miss Lanford! Won't you take my arm and walk with me a little?" Out of the corner of his eye, he caught a suspicious look from the Duke of Winterton and felt a qualm of unease. He dismissed it, believing the duke's interest would not be held by a mere squire's daughter.

As the party moved toward the food tables, Lord Baddick and Henrietta dropped back and followed at a leisurely pace. Holding out his arm for her, Lord Baddick saw with satisfaction the dark shadows underneath Henrietta's eyes. He began speaking in a low, comforting voice. "I could not rest last night, thinking of your humiliation at Winterton's hands. You, who are all that is innocent and good, should be protected from such as he."

Henrietta shuddered inwardly at the memory of her childish behavior at Almack's. "My lord," she said quietly, "you are most kind, but I beg you to speak of other matters."

Lord Baddick, secretly pleased his prey continued in a vulnerable state, placed his gloved hand over hers and squeezed it lightly. "Forgive me, fairest one. Believe that it is my greatest desire you should forget the entire incident. Allow me to obtain a plate of delicacies for you. Something to eat and drink will help restore your spirits." He led them to the table where people milled about, chatting and nibbling food.

Of its own volition, Henrietta's gaze sought the duke. He stood with Lady Clorinda and her parents, Lord and Lady Mawbly. Lady Fuddlesby and Colonel Colchester were nearby. As Lord Baddick selected foods from the table, Henrietta idly noticed Lord Mawbly break away from the little group and walk over to Lady Fuddlesby. A puzzled frown appeared between Henrietta's brows as Lord Mawbly and Lady Fuddlesby moved away to conduct a private conversation, and the duke stepped up to his godfather, taking the lady's place. Lord Baddick returned to her side, offering her a filled plate, and she turned her attention to him.

Across the lawn, Lady Fuddlesby waited for Lord Mawbly to state his business. She was impatient at this interruption from an affable conversation with the colonel.

"Lady Fuddlesby, thank you for sparing me a few moments of your time," Lord Mawbly began, his eyes darting back and forth, looking anywhere but at her. Lady Mawbly had not ceased her nagging about Lady Fuddlesby's pink tourmaline ring. The injustice of her not possessing such a stone was simply not to be borne. When she saw Lady Fuddlesby arrive, she demanded her husband accost the woman immediately and offer to buy the ring whatever the cost.

"Why, certainly, Lord Mawbly, but I confess I am at a loss to know what this is about," Lady Fuddlesby prompted with raised eyebrows.

Lord Mawbly bitterly addressed the ornamental lake. "You see, my wife loves jewels. Never has enough. Wants your ring, the pink tourmaline. Pay you whatever sum you name." He appeared relieved to get the request out, but this proved shortlived.

Lady Fuddlesby was taken aback. The pink tourmaline ring had been a gift from the late Viscount Fuddlesby. He brought it back for her from Russia after a diplomatic mission he undertook shortly after their marriage. It was a particular favorite of hers, being her well-loved pink color and holding sentimental value. The thought of it gracing Lady Mawbly's hand brought a moue of distaste to Lady Fuddlesby's lips.

"I am sorry to disappoint you, Lord Mawbly, but I could not part with it," Lady Fuddlesby informed him gently but firmly, then turned and walked away.

Lord Mawbly, in a panic, sought to prolong the moment he must tell Lady Mawbly of his failure. He slipped away toward the Peabodys' house in hopes of obtaining a few minutes' refuge from his wife.

Through narrowed eyes, Lady Mawbly watched him disappear. She and Clorinda stood near Henrietta and Lord Baddick, who were conversing over their plates.

Henrietta's proximity was not lost on Clorinda. When she saw Lord Baddick move to the end of the table to get some champagne from a footman, she seized the moment.

In a carrying voice she felt certain would reach Henrietta's ears she said, "Does Papa plan to be at home in the morning, Mama?" Before Lady Mawbly could answer, Clorinda winked at her, tilting her head slightly toward Henrietta, and continued, "I dearly hope so as the duke has an important question to ask of him." Maidenly giggles followed this lie.

Clorinda's words struck her target. Henrietta wished she had not eaten anything because she suddenly felt violently ill. So the duke was to marry Clorinda. She should not be surprised. She should not care. She would not begin to cry and bring yet another scene down upon her and her kind aunt's head.

Henrietta rushed the few steps over to Lord Baddick, placing a hand on his arm to gain his attention. "Please, my lord, I am feeling a bit faint. Would you take me away for a moment or two? A stroll, perhaps, might clear my head."

Lord Baddick exclaimed solicitously, "At once!" He removed the plate from her hand, setting it on the table. Observing the blank look in her eyes, he felt a thrill of power. Something had happened. 'Twas a shame he missed whatever it was, but no matter. He knew an opportunity when he saw one.

They walked in the opposite direction of the crowded tables toward a small copse of trees. The grass was soft under Henrietta's lilac slippers. Lord Baddick's arm felt safe and secure under her hand.

Henrietta felt cloaked in a sense of unreality. Her mind focused on the duke and Lady Clorinda. They would marry, have children. A mental image of the duke, holding a beautiful baby, brought a fresh twist to the icy knot in her stomach.

Lord Baddick walked them around to behind the screen of the trees. He turned to face her. "Miss Lanford . . . Henrietta, my love," he murmured, slipping an arm around her waist. He drew her close, bending his head down to hers.

Henrietta did not realize how isolated they were when they reached the other side of the trees away from the party. All she was conscious of was the pain in her heart. Lord Baddick's face looming over hers, about to kiss her, brought her sharply back to reality.

"My lord!" she exclaimed, stepping back outside his arms. "Indeed you must not!" She raised her hands to her flushed cheeks.

Lord Baddick seethed with rage. The little tease. He *would* have her. Like any other woman, she was most likely holding out for a marriage proposal. Well, he would not let a few meaningless words stand between him and his desire. He dropped down to one knee.

"Forgive me for rushing you, fairest one! Your beauty momentarily blinded me to the honor I must always show you." He reached up and grasped one of her hands, a look of adoration marking his features. "I know you do not yet return my love, but allow me the chance of earning that longed-for emotion. Will you be my wife?"

Henrietta blinked in astonishment. A proposal of marriage from this rich and handsome lord! Why, oh, why could it not be the Duke of Winterton? Giles. Her mind registered the duke's given name for the first time. But he was to marry Clorinda.

She looked down at the eager face of Lord Baddick. It was true she did not love him. But he was kind and he said he loved her. Perhaps in time she would come to love him. Her parents would be pleased. And she must marry! There was *no other life* for a gently bred female.

Trembling with the enormity of her decision,

Henrietta gently raised the hand Lord Baddick held until his lordship rose to his feet. She looked frankly into his hazel eyes and said, "Yes, my lord. I shall marry you."

Chapter Seven

Lord Baddick felt his pulses quicken in triumph. "Henrietta, you have made me the happiest of men!" He raised her gloved hand and placed a light kiss on it. He could hardly satisfy his lust at this cursed breakfast, so he would not frighten her. "But I am so dreadfully ashamed," he bemoaned, his eyes downcast.

"Why, what is amiss, my lord?"

Lord Baddick quickly lied. "I must beg Lady Fuddlesby's leave to pay my addresses to you, and I do not have the family betrothal ring with me in Town!" He looked at her longingly. "It is a large sapphire, surrounded by diamonds. A perfect match for your eyes."

"My lord, it does not matter. You may ask my aunt without producing a ring, and I am sure—"

Lord Baddick's mind raced. "Never! It would be an insult to you. I planned to offer you my escort to the Royal Italian Opera tonight. Catalani is to perform. I could leave Town for my estate the first of next week." This much was true, Lord Baddick thought, unwillingly remembering the suspicious look on the Duke of Winterton's face earlier. He thought bleakly he would probably have to rusticate again.

"I could be back at your side, with the ring, by

the end of next week. Oh, 'parting is such sweet sorrow,' fairest one!"

Henrietta really did not care one way or another about the ring, but if it mattered to this man she would one day call husband . . . "Very well, my lord. We will wait until you have returned with the ring to ask my aunt."

Lord Baddick grinned. "A secret betrothal, then?"

Her answering smile was bittersweet. How the old Fantasy Henrietta would have relished this! "Yes, a secret betrothal. But only until you return to Town."

He put his arm around her and gave her a friendly squeeze, as if they were children and had formed a secret pact.

They began walking back to the alfresco meal. No sooner had they rounded the copse of trees when they came face-to-face with a stony Duke of Winterton.

Henrietta shot him a startled look. "Your Grace!"

The duke eyed the pair grimly. "Miss Lanford," he said, his cold gray eyes on the viscount, "I wondered at your absence." His tone was relatively civil, but his jaw tensed. It appeared the girl had totally ignored his warnings about the blackguard.

Henrietta glared at the duke with burning, reproachful eyes. "It appears your 'brotherly' instincts are once again coming to the fore, Your Grace. I do not know what has given you fancies, but I assure you I am perfectly safe!"

Winterton's sharp gaze ran the length of her. As he addressed Henrietta, he turned his attention to Lord Baddick. Lazily he drawled, "I hope you may be right, Miss Lanford. I have no desire to visit Chalk Farm." He bowed mockingly before turning and walking leisurely back to the party.

Henrietta, caught up in her own anxieties, did not see Lord Baddick's complexion pale at the mention of the famous dueling grounds. She had no idea what Chalk Farm was. Confused, she asked, "Pray, my lord, what did the duke mean by not wanting to visit Chalk Farm?"

Seemingly interested in a small beetle on the path, Lord Baddick replied, "I neither know nor care. It may be one of his properties."

"But why should that have anything to do with me?"

Lord Baddick squashed the bug with the toe of his boot. "Bless me if I know. Perhaps Winterton's in his cups."

As they walked back to the others, Lord Baddick kept up a light flow of conversation regarding the Royal Italian Opera. No mention was made of the betrothal or plans for their wedded future, which would have alerted Henrietta that something was dreadfully wrong here, had she a tendre for Lord Baddick.

Instead she allowed herself to be diverted, her youthful enthusiasm growing at the prospect of her first opera. "Oh, my lord, I must ask my aunt if we may go! I would so love to hear the famous Catalani sing!"

They approached Lady Fuddlesby a few minutes later with the plan. She and Colonel Colchester were enjoying thin slices of Westphalian ham. The lady pronounced herself in alt at the prospect of hearing the diva. "Yes, we would be quite delighted to attend, Lord Baddick. How kind you are to offer your escort!"

Colonel Colchester's eyes narrowed. There was to be a reunion of several of his retired military friends that evening. He had committed himself to the festivity and could not draw back at this late time. While he did not like the idea of the ladies being alone with Baddick, he could see no way out of his obligation. "I would like to accompany you, Lady Fuddlesby, but fear I cannot." After a moment's consideration he added, "Perhaps I could meet you after the opera, and we could all enjoy a late supper at Grillon's."

The pleased ladies quickly agreed to this plan, and Colonel Colchester decided he had bested the viscount.

Lord Baddick felt he needed to go carefully when planning his next move. The duke and his godfather were proving to be a nuisance. "I shall call for you tonight at nine of the clock." He bowed and took his leave.

Watching his lordship's retreating back, Henrietta wished she could confide her betrothal to Lady Fuddlesby. But she suppressed the emotion when she remembered her promise to keep it a secret. There could be no harm in waiting a week, she reasoned.

Lady Fuddlesby looked at her with a decidedly matchmaking gleam in her eye. She leaned close to her niece and whispered encouragingly, "You see, my dear, did I not predict gentlemen would be about you like bees around a rose?"

"Something like that, Aunt," Henrietta said, and laughed. She impulsively leaned forward and placed a swift kiss on Lady Fuddlesby's rouged cheek. She did not like keeping secrets from this lady whom she had grown to love.

Straightening the bonnet Henrietta's kiss had displaced, Lady Fuddlesby allowed her mind to dwell on her desire for a match between her niece and the Duke of Winterton. She wished he were to escort them to the opera. She contented herself with thoughts of the charming events of the carriage ride and the duke's jolly little parrot. Colonel Colchester had the right of it. There was *something* between the duke and her niece. The way they had looked at one another when he had spread that handkerchief across her knees! And the situation continued to improve. Why, the two had not come to cuffs in one whole day!

Lady Fuddlesby beamed with pleasure. "Oh, my dear, do help me sneak a little of this wonderful ham home for Knight. He does so enjoy it!"

At the Royal Italian Opera that night, Henrietta's head hurt worse than she could ever remember. The pain began on the drive home from the Peabodys' in the duke's carriage. Unable to face conversing with him, she had feigned sleep the entire way. Once she was home, a nap eluded her. She lay upon her bed, unable to believe she was betrothed.

Had she been too hasty in accepting Lord Baddick? She stole a sidelong glance at him as he sat next to her in the opera box. What was she to wait for? a voice sneered in her mind. Did she expect the Duke of Winterton to suddenly cast Lady Clorinda aside, and change his brotherly feelings toward herself to that of the lover?

She could not appreciate the rather piercing voice of Madame Catalani. Many of the Nobility seemed to find each other a more interesting sight than the celebrated woman on stage.

Henrietta turned to Lady Fuddlesby, who sat on her other side. "Why are so many people raising their quizzing glasses to look around them, rather than at the singer?"

Her aunt pursed her lips in disapproval. "The purpose of coming to the opera, dear, is the same as going to any other entertainment, I fear. Thank heaven your reputation seems to be untarnished after the . . . lapse the other night at Almack's. People nodded to us most properly when we entered. I am certain word has gotten around about our arrival with the duke at the Peabodys', so everyone has written the . . . unpleasantness off as a mere peccadillo."

"I am glad we will suffer no embarrassment. But you mean Society comes to the opera to be *seen*?" Henrietta asked. "Just like at the rout or Almack's? Not to hear the music?"

"Oh, my dear, yes. It can be worse than tonight. Some of the gentlemen can be quite loud. Madame Catalani commands more respect than some other unfortunate divas who have graced that stage." Dropping her voice to a whisper, Lady Fuddlesby leaned close to Henrietta and discreetly pointed her fan. "Oh, do but look. The Duke of Winterton has arrived in his box with his mother."

Henrietta's gaze flew down the auditorium to where the duke was helping his mother to a chair. As she stared at his handsome, athletic figure, shown to perfection in impeccable evening dress, her heart jolted and her pulse pounded. Despite his maddening arrogance, Henrietta could not help dreaming of being crushed within his embrace. What would it be like to feel his arms around her? How would it feel to touch his face, his hair?

"Fairest one, are you feeling quite the thing? You are so pale."

Lord Baddick's voice, filled with concern, brought Henrietta sharply back to reality. These wayward thoughts of the duke were most improper, she chastised herself. Though no one but herself and Lord Baddick knew it, she was a betrothed lady. Her thoughts must only be for her future husband. She turned to look at him, managing a smile. "You are so perceptive. My head does ache frightfully, but do not concern yourself, my lord. I shall come about."

When Henrietta's disobedient gaze next found its way to the duke's box, she was dealt her punishment. Joining him and his mother were Lady Clorinda and Lord and Lady Mawbly. All over the theater, quizzing glasses rose when the lady assumed to be the future duchess arrived. Her golden beauty and voluptuous figure were most alluring in an aquamarine-colored opera dress.

A gentleman in a nearby box nearly fell to his death as he leaned forward to better appreciate the dress's neckline.

Henrietta sat back in her chair miserably. She fixed her gaze on the stage, but could hardly see because of the tears forming in her eyes.

Over in the Duke of Winterton's box, Giles greeted his guests, and then sat back to enjoy Catalani's performance. But almost at once, his gaze wandered unerringly to where Miss Henrietta Lanford sat with her aunt and—deuce take it!— Viscount Baddick. A shadow of anger swept across the duke's masculine face.

Then he wondered at the emotion. The girl was no concern of his. She was a mere squire's daughter, well below him in station. He had condescended by doing his duty and warning her about the cur. Now she would have to take care of herself. Had he not washed his hands of her after the contretemps at Almack's? What had possessed him to threaten Baddick with a duel over Miss Lanford

when he had found them together at the Peabodys'? He must have taken leave of his senses!

The Duke of Winterton covertly studied Miss
Lanford while she watched the stage. Her color
seemed high. He noticed her pale blue dress complemented her dark hair, which was braided into a
coronet. Her slender white neck seemed to beckon
him, begging for the touch of his lips—

"Giles!" Matilda, Dowager Duchess of Winterton,
hissed. "What are you gaping at?"

"Nothing, Mother. I do not gape." The annoyed
duke felt manipulated by both his parents. His
mother was the one who had invited the Mawblys
to join them at the opera. It was clear Lady
Clorinda had the dowager's approval for the position of the next duchess. The duke felt as if being
with Clorinda all afternoon at the breakfast had
been sufficient. While her beauty prevented her
from being a bore, the lady was beginning to appear somehow superficial. Her range of attractions
was perhaps limited, he mused.

As for his father, through his unholy vessel, Sir
Polly Grey, the deceased seventh Duke of Winterton lectured him incessantly on what was due his
name. Sometimes the duke felt as if he could cheerfully place his fingers around the parrot's meddle-
some throat and make it produce a sound similar to
the one coming from the lady's mouth onstage.

At the intermission, an incredibly strong desire
to speak with Miss Lanford again about Lord
Baddick gripped the duke. He argued with himself.
Then he chanced to look over and see Baddick place
a possessive hand over Miss Lanford's as they
spoke. A decidedly unpleasant picture of the viscount taking further liberties with Miss Lanford

presented itself in the duke's mind, catapulting him out of his box.

As the duke left the box without an explanation, Clorinda's green eyes lit with shock and anger. She wanted him to remain at her side so members of Society could come and pay their respects to the new couple. An alarming thought that the duke's interest in her was not as high as it should be crossed her mind. While her lips formed a pout, she glanced about her speculatively, reassured by the gratifying attention being given her by the young bucks in the pit. She sat back and chided herself for being silly. Of course Winterton wanted her.

Since Lady Fuddlesby had wandered away to visit friends, Henrietta and Lord Baddick were alone in their box, conversing in low tones about the performance. Henrietta's headache reached new proportions and she unconsciously rubbed her temples.

A brief knock preceded the Duke of Winterton's unexpected appearance. His voice was quiet, yet held an undertone of cold contempt. "I wish to speak with Miss Lanford, Baddick."

Lord Baddick rose to his feet and faced the duke. "She is right here at my side, Winterton." The viscount placed a slight emphasis on the word "my." "Go ahead and say what you will," he taunted.

Henrietta stood anxiously, not knowing how to react to the animosity she felt flowing between the two gentlemen now glaring at each other.

The duke's gray eyes were as cold as the North Sea. "I wish to be *private* with Miss Lanford. Take yourself off, Baddick."

Lord Baddick's voice was inflamed and belligerent. "No. I don't think I shall allow you to be private with my *fiancée*," he said from beneath his teeth. Instantly, as the words were out of his mouth, Lord Baddick regretted allowing the duke to goad him into this portentous slip of the tongue.

Henrietta gasped.

An odd twinge of disappointment squeezed the duke's heart. Through stiff lips he addressed a visibly trembling Henrietta. "You are betrothed?"

A sharp denial rose in Henrietta's throat. She pressed her gloved fingers across her mouth to prevent it from escaping. Controlling herself, she dropped her hand to her side. She answered calmly, with no lighting of her eyes, no smile of tenderness regarding her prospective nuptials. "Yes, Your Grace."

The Duke of Winterton searched Miss Lanford's face. "I wish you happy," he said at last. Without looking at Lord Baddick, the duke turned and left the box.

Afterward, Henrietta lost all sense of time until the final curtain on the opera fell.

While they made their way to his lordship's carriage, Lady Fuddlesby chattered. "We did so enjoy ourselves, Lord Baddick, did we not, Henrietta? We owe you our thanks, my lord."

"Yes, indeed we did," Henrietta replied, and then stumbled slightly. Lord Baddick's arm reached out to steady her before she could fall.

"Henrietta, whatever is the matter?" Lady Fuddlesby asked, alarmed.

Breathing deeply of the evening air to refresh herself, Henrietta confessed, "My lady, I am sorry to spoil our plans to join Colonel Colchester at Grillon's, but I have the most horrible headache. I must beg you to allow me to return home."

"Oh, my dear, but of course! One can hardly function with one's temples pounding. I know from experience the only thing for it is to lie upon one's bed until it passes!" Lady Fuddlesby said sympathetically. Turning to Lord Baddick, she announced, "We must take her home at once."

Lord Baddick, who had been thinking furiously ever since his careless admission of the betrothal in front of the duke, felt as though the Fates smiled upon him. What an absolutely splendid opportunity. He must take his pleasure this night and be gone to the country on the morrow. If ever asked, he would say both the duke and Miss Lanford were mistaken. He never offered marriage.

Arriving at his carriage, Lord Baddick helped the ladies inside. Once they were settled he said, "Lady Fuddlesby, allow me to take Miss Lanford back to Grosvenor Square after setting you down at Grillon's. I am persuaded that if Miss Lanford is merely to retire upon arriving home, there is no need for you to miss the pleasure of a late supper."

Before Lady Fuddlesby could protest, Henrietta quickly added, "Yes, dear Aunt, Lord Baddick is correct. You must not disappoint the colonel just because of my wretched head. Besides, if you return home with me, Colonel Colchester will be at Grillon's wondering what has become of us until you are able to send a messenger."

Lady Fuddlesby looked doubtful. "Thinking we would be quite late, I gave the servants the evening off, although Felice most likely is home. I would need to give you the key, Henrietta, for Felice is a terribly sound sleeper, and will never hear the knocker. You would need to go up to the attics and wake her to help take care of you." She did not mention her other concern, which was the impropriety of Lord Baddick and Henrietta driving from Grillon's to Grosvenor Square alone. Of course, since the evening was fine, Lord Baddick did have his open carriage, so it might answer. . . .

As if reading her thoughts, Lord Baddick reassured her. "My lady, you have my word as a gentleman no harm shall come to your niece. The conventions will be satisfied because I have my open carriage. I shall see Miss Lanford safely to the door, unlock it for her, and be on my way."

Lady Fuddlesby capitulated. "Very well, let us be off. But you must promise, my dear, to wake Felice the moment you arrive."

Henrietta nodded her agreement, and when they pulled away from the curb, her ladyship thought her niece looked very pale indeed. It was highly doubtful the viscount would be boorish enough to press his attentions on an ill girl, she told herself. And Lady Fuddlesby did so wish to be in the colonel's company. Her feelings for him were growing most affectionate, and she believed them returned by the handsome military man.

When the carriage pulled up in front of Grillon's, Lady Fuddlesby could see Colonel Colchester walking up to the entryway. Pulling a key out of her reticule, she handed it to Henrietta, and a last-minute wave of doubt struck her. Her brows drew together in concern. "You are certain, my dear, that you do not wish me to accompany you?"

"I am certain, ma'am. Please go and enjoy yourself." Henrietta managed a weak smile. She wished she could tell her she and Lord Baddick were engaged so her aunt might not worry.

Lord Baddick barely waited to see Lady Fuddlesby at Colonel Colchester's side before moving off toward what he anticipated would be a very invigorating end to the evening.

The drive to the town house passed quietly and

uneventfully. Lord Baddick did not wish to alarm his prey now that the moment had arrived.

At the door to the town house, Henrietta withdrew the key her aunt had given her. Lord Baddick took it from her cold fingers. "Here, allow me," he said, turning the lock. The door swung open. The viscount waved his hand toward the inside of the hall, motioning Henrietta to precede him.

"My lord, perhaps you should not come in," Henrietta began uncertainly as she crossed the doorway and turned to face him.

Lord Baddick obediently remained outside. "If you do not wish me to, then of course, I will not." He spoke softly while he cajoled, "My heart, we are betrothed. I beg a moment to be private with you. I have decided to leave for my estate in the morning so I may place my ring upon your lovely finger without any further delay." He grinned boyishly. "My mother will have questions for me about you, which I confess I know not the answers to. Can you not spare a few minutes for me?"

It did not seem an unreasonable request. "Very well, then." Henrietta stepped back so his lordship could enter.

She led him upstairs to the drawing room where candles were lit and a fire burned low. They stood near the hearth.

When Lord Baddick moved close to her, Henrietta abruptly felt herself become nervous. "You are so young and fresh, Henrietta. Where is the pain in your head?" he asked in a whisper. "I will ease it." His hazel eyes gazed intently into her blue ones.

To her dismay, when Henrietta tried to speak, her voice wavered. "There is no need. I am feeling a little better. What were the questions you wanted to ask?"

The viscount chuckled and delayed answering. A spark popped from a log in the fireplace next to them and Henrietta started. He smiled slowly at her. Reaching out, he captured a dark curl close to her face and wound it around his finger. "Have you ever been kissed before, my innocent?" His gaze moved from her hair and rested on her pink lips.

"My lord! Naturally I have not allowed anyone such a liberty." She was becoming increasingly uneasy under his scrutiny. She supposed he was within his rights to want a kiss from his fiancée.

She swallowed hard. Once they were married, he had a right to as many kisses as he wanted and much more. Although what that "more" might be, Henrietta had no idea. She only knew more than kisses were required to have babies. This aspect of marriage to Lord Baddick had not been considered, and her stomach clenched tightly.

Lord Baddick sensed her fear and it fed his desire. Moving his hand from where his fingers had been toying with the glossy curl, he held her head still and his mouth came down to hers.

At the last second, Henrietta twisted her face away from his and the wet kiss landed on her neck. His lordship did not seem overly concerned with this change in location, however, because he began kissing the slender white column with a frightening intensity.

Henrietta closed her eyes briefly to fight down a wave of fear and nausea. "You must help yourself to some claret while I fetch Felice," she said, panic such as she'd never known before causing her voice to shake. The Duke of Winterton's words suddenly rang in her head. *His intentions toward you are the very worst.*

"We do not need Felice for what we are going to

do, Henrietta." The viscount's voice sounded as if it were coming from far away, and his kisses moved to her bare shoulder.

How could she ever have thought she could marry him! Her hands came up to push at his strong shoulders, but his arm was a steel band around her waist. "No! You must not," she cried sharply. His hands seemed all over her, and then one made its way to her breast. She pulled away with all her might, hearing the sleeve of her dress tear. Without thinking, she drew back her hand and slapped his face.

They stood there, breathing hard, stunned. Then an evil look appeared across Lord Baddick's features. Henrietta felt as if a mask had dropped from his face and she was seeing the true man for the first time.

"Now, fairest one, that will not do at all," he stated furiously. Something in his posture reminded her of a wild animal about to spring on its prey. "You have tried my patience, you little vixen."

His voice and manner changed back into that of the charming gentleman. "Henrietta, accept your fate and be merry. You will enjoy yourself, I promise."

A sheer black fright swept through Henrietta. She opened her mouth and screamed.

Lord Baddick lunged for her, but the shock of that cultured voice in the middle of his barbaric attack caused Henrietta to feel a cold courage. She grabbed a brass candlestick off the fireplace mantel, stepped back, and hurled it at him with all her might. The viscount ducked, cursing all the while, and the heavy candlestick flew harmlessly over his head to smash one of the drawing room windows.

Henrietta turned to run, but the enraged Lord

Baddick caught her by her dress's skirt, causing them both to tumble to the floor.

At that moment Knight, his sleep disturbed by Henrietta's scream, raced into the room. He threw himself, needle-sharp claws extended, onto Lord Baddick's head. A bloodcurdling yell erupted from the viscount.

Henrietta scrambled to her feet, her heart pounding in her chest, and ran from the room.

While these horrible events transpired, the Duke of Winterton sat in a rented hack outside in the street in front of Lady Fuddlesby's town house, calling himself every kind of fool. Upon leaving the opera, he had ordered his astonished mother to make use of his carriage and driver to convey herself home.

Giles felt convinced there was something shilly-shallying about the "betrothal" between Miss Lanford and Baddick. When he had studied her face after Baddick's announcement, he could detect no joy. She did not love the viscount, he was certain. Why, then, had she agreed to marry him? Was it to obtain a title? In his experience most women married for a title or money or both. Somehow, though, he had not received the impression Miss Lanford was mercenary.

The fact of the matter, the duke decided, was that Baddick most likely had no intention of going through with the marriage. Giles shrewdly guessed the viscount had probably blurted out the information in anger when he had demanded to speak to Miss Lanford in private.

These deductions, and fear that it was all a ruse on Baddick's part to further a physical intimacy with Miss Lanford, motivated the duke to hire a hack and keep an eye on Lady Fuddlesby's town house. The ladies were in Baddick's care this evening, and he wanted to be certain they arrived home safely.

Now, as he sat watching the house, his white cravat gleaming in the darkness, he questioned his judgment and his sanity. What was this unfamiliar, protective feeling he felt for Miss Lanford? The blue-eyed squire's daughter was dominating his thoughts, causing him to behave in ways foreign to him. Never before had he cared one whit for the fate of any young miss.

Abruptly his attention was caught. Had that faint sound been a scream?

All at once one of the windows of Lady Fuddlesby's town house shattered. An icy dread washed over him, and the duke vaulted out of the hackney and raced up the front steps of the town house. The front door was mercifully unlocked. He flung it open, dashing into the hall in time to catch a breathless Henrietta, who rushed headlong down the stairs into his arms.

Chapter Eight

The Duke of Winterton's usual cool and aloof manner fled. As he held the trembling petite figure close in his arms, his mind registered her disheveled appearance. An acute wave of fear struck him.

"Miss Lanford! What happened? Where is Lady Fuddlesby?"

Henrietta did not want to speak or move from the security she felt in the circle of his arms. She desperately clung to him, burying her face in the soft cloth of his evening coat, feeling safe and protected from the monster upstairs.

Winterton decided the girl was in some sort of shock. Disordered thoughts whirled in his head. Where the deuce was everyone? No servants had appeared at the commotion.

"Miss Lanford, please, try to tell me what happened. Let me pour you a brandy to soothe your nerves, perhaps upstairs in the drawing room—"

"No!" Henrietta found her voice. "I fear he is still up there and . . . oh!" She broke off as sounds coming from the stairs reached them.

The duke gently put the girl aside and looked up the stairs at an incomprehensible sight.

Lord Baddick walked unsteadily down the first few steps. His face and neck were covered with bleeding cat scratches. Drops of blood spotted his white cravat. Knight had done his work well.

"Good God," the duke uttered. He vaguely heard Henrietta's whimper, for when the viscount's treachery became apparent, a red mist of rage rose before the Duke of Winterton's eyes.

In a second he was across the hall and up the stairs.

Lord Baddick recoiled in fright at this new threat. "The deed was not done!" he blurted to no avail.

The duke grabbed the viscount by the collar and planted him a facer. Baddick fell from the impact and rolled down the remaining stairs.

Winterton stripped off his jacket and tossed it carelessly aside. He hurried down the steps to where the viscount was attempting to rise. Before Baddick could accomplish this task, Winterton dragged him upright and began pummeling him with crushing blows.

Henrietta covered her mouth to keep from screaming. She watched wide-eyed, a part of her marveling at the strength, skill, and passion of the normally austere duke.

Suddenly she feared he would go too far. She started forward and cried out, "Stop! You must stop! You will kill him! He is not worth you, Giles!" Henrietta shouted, using the duke's first name in her agitation.

Winterton let the viscount drop to the floor, where he lay moaning in pain. "You will leave this house . . . return to your lodgings . . . pack, and be on your way out of England by dawn," the duke got out somewhat disjointedly as he steadied his breathing. "If you ever return, I shall kill you," he finished.

Lord Baddick could not stand, but managed to crawl his way out the front door.

Henrietta rushed to the duke, her hands coming up to rest on his shoulders. "Are you injured?" she asked, blue eyes wide with concern.

The duke's brain was in tumult. Since he was a lad, he had never engaged in fisticuffs outside of Gentleman Jackson's. His emotions were normally kept firmly in check. Never, before this evening, had he experienced such a wide scope of passions. And the cause of each and every one of them now stood anxiously before him, clutching the cambric shirt above his waistcoat. He could feel her fingers through the thin material.

"Oh, I do so thank you. You and Knight saved me from that satyr. I never imagined . . ." Henrietta trailed off as she noticed the duke seemed to be peering at her intently. His gaze dropped to her bare shoulder exposed by the torn dress. She lowered her hands and reached for the torn material, making a feeble attempt to cover herself.

The duke found he did not like the way her hands left his shoulders. He took them in his and placed them back in their original position.

Without his permission, his left arm moved gently around Henrietta's waist. His right hand, shaking ever so slightly, came up to tilt her face up to his. He muttered something unintelligible, then slowly he lowered his mouth to hers.

The touch of her lips was a delicious sensation that raced through his bloodstream. As Henrietta swayed against him, Giles fought down the need to deepen the embrace, then gave up the struggle. He pressed her tightly up against his chest and lost himself in the sweet warmth of her mouth.

Much too soon, the voices of Lady Fuddlesby and

Colonel Colchester approaching the front door reached his ears, hurtling him back to reality. The consequences of kissing Miss Lanford acted like a pitcher of cold water on his growing passion. He could not marry an untitled girl. His father would revolve in his grave. He owed the great name of Vayne more than a mere squire's daughter as his duchess.

Abruptly the duke thrust the girl away from him. His eyes glittered before he dropped his lids down halfway to conceal them. Once more correct and formal, he drawled, "Miss Lanford, I beg your forgiveness. I fear I am foxed."

Henrietta's nerves were overset, and this preposterous statement sent her over the edge. Bursting into tears, she turned and ran up the stairs. Lady Fuddlesby and Colonel Colchester opened the front door in time to see her go.

"Goodness! What has happened here? You are in your shirtsleeves, sir! My dear niece . . . oh!" Lady Fuddlesby sputtered before hurrying after Henrietta.

The duke walked over to where his coat lay crumpled on the floor and picked it up, absently thinking Tyler would turn in his notice when he saw it.

Colonel Colchester folded his arms across his chest. "Well, my boy, I am waiting for an explanation."

The duke ran his fingers through his hair. In a tired voice he said, "It is as I feared. Baddick tried to force himself on Miss Lanford. Between us, Lady Fuddlesby's chivalrous cat and I were able to prevent him from ravishing the girl. She is understandably suffering the vapors."

His godfather's eyes narrowed, studying the

younger man's strained countenance. He'd wager there was more to the story, and he was not a gamester. "I assume England will see no more of Viscount Baddick?"

At the duke's terse nod, the colonel was satisfied for the moment. No sense in trying to get anything out of Giles now. While his overall physical appearance gave no indication he had exerted himself unduly, his face was white and set. "We can do no more here, my boy. Best leave the ladies to themselves. There is a bottle of brandy, perhaps two, waiting for us at home."

Upstairs in her bedchamber, Henrietta finished telling her aunt almost all the evening's events. Disconcerted, she left out the part about the duke's kiss, her fingers coming to rest on her still-burning lips every so often. "So you see, Aunt, I am quite all right now. A good cry was all I needed to calm myself."

The ladies sat together at the edge of the bed. Lady Fuddlesby's arm was around her niece in a comforting hold. "Oh dear, oh dear, Henrietta, thank heaven the duke arrived when he did! Although one must wonder at the miracle of his timely intervention. I thought he was with his mama and the Mawblys. Well! I daresay I am grateful for whatever brought him here. And we will never have to see that dreadful man again!"

Henrietta turned her head away and stared down sightlessly at the blue coverlet. In a voice rich with bitterness she said, "Oh no, I am positive Winterton will be at whatever Society function I attend, ready to stand 'brother' to me."

"What?" Lady Fuddlesby exclaimed, rising to her feet. "Henrietta, have your wits gone begging? I meant that vile Lord Baddick. You told me the duke has sent him out of the country!" At her niece's nod, Lady Fuddlesby continued in a more subdued tone, "Now, my dear, as that wretched Felice has slept through this entire nightmare— and believe me, I intend to have a sharp word with that woman—I will help you into your nightdress myself. And I am so proud of my gallant Knight. Did I not tell you he is protective? That is why I named him Knight in Masked Armour, you know."

Lady Fuddlesby chattered on while helping her niece out of her torn gown and into a lace night-dress, tucking her under the coverlet and admonishing her to get a good night's rest as it would not do to have dark circles under her eyes. Her ladyship finally closed the door softly behind her.

Henrietta's mind sped her directly back to the duke's arms. The memory of his lips pressed to hers was pure and clear and made her shiver with an urgent need to repeat the experience.

Unbidden, Winterton's humiliating apology sounded in her brain, and her eyes closed in anguish. How could he express remorse at what had been, for her, a beautiful token of love?

Henrietta's eyes snapped open as the truth struck her like a hammerblow. She loved the Duke of Winterton!

Hard on the heels of this discovery came the crushing conviction he did not love her. Was he not all but betrothed to Lady Clorinda? Confusion caused a crease in her brow. Why had the duke kissed her if he was to marry Clorinda?

As she lay in the darkness, Henrietta felt achy and exhausted. How was she to bear the long remainder of the London Season? Could she not simply cut her parents' losses and go home to Hamilton Cross?

Settling onto her side, she realized the futility of running back to her parents. She must marry, and she was more likely to find a husband she could tolerate here in London. Not that it mattered whom she married when she could only love the duke.

Before sleep overtook her, a vision of a plain but kindly gentleman presented itself. One who would treat her considerately, not lecture her like a brother and then maddeningly kiss her like a lover.

Lady Fuddlesby's pink skirts rustled as she opened the door to her bedchamber. She had been downstairs supervising the returning servants while they secured the broken window in the drawing room. Satisfied the house was prepared for the night, Lady Fuddlesby sought her bed.

"There you are, my darling boy!" she exclaimed, observing Knight.

In the manner of one completely exhausted, the cat sprawled out on his back across the bed's pink coverlet. He opened one green eye in his black mask and looked at her.

"I am so proud of my precious, dearest Knight!" she reached out a hand to rub his oversized belly affectionately. "It is a good thing Henrietta and I smuggled you home some ham earlier today so your strength was up to fight that awful man."

Giving the cat a last scratch behind his ears, Lady Fuddlesby moved away to sit at her toilet table. Deep in thought, she began removing her earbobs as the cat on the bed lazily licked a spot on his shoulder.

"I hold myself responsible for what happened tonight, you know." Lady Fuddlesby's voice was low, and Knight ceased his ministrations to look at his mistress in surprise. "Now that Henrietta is with me, I stand in the place of her parents. It is my responsibility to see no harm comes to her. And only see how I have failed in my duty!" Tears gently fell down her ladyship's plump cheeks.

Knight crossed the room and jumped in her lap. He raised a tentative paw to her face, his whiskers twitching with concern.

Lady Fuddlesby's tears lessened and she hugged her pet close. A final pat seemed to reassure Knight she had control of herself. He left her lap to watch her from the floor.

Her ladyship sat with her fingers pressed to her temples, pondering the problem of her niece's Season. Events were not progressing quite as she would want. The Duke of Winterton and Henrietta were not betrothed, and if the duke was foolish enough to make Clorinda his duchess, Henrietta would have to settle for someone else. The girl needed an event that would show her in a good light. One where she might be the center of the admiring attention of many gentlemen.

At last Lady Fuddlesby clapped her hands together and said, "I know the very thing, Knight. We shall give a ball in Henrietta's honor! The poor dear looked moped to death tonight, and who could blame her? She needs something to look forward to, and every miss making her come-out should have her own ball."

Knight's tail twitched, as though he understood. The cat hated having groups of people in the house, not taking well to strangers. He was fond of Henrietta, and was grudgingly tolerant of Colonel Colchester now that the gentleman paid him homage with gastronomic treats. But crowds, even when they included his favorite people, were sure to aggravate him.

Oblivious to the cat's soon-to-be displeasure, Lady Fuddlesby continued planning. "We shall have masses of hothouse flowers, in pink perhaps, and an orchestra and champagne and lobster patties. . . ."

Green eyes brightened at the word "lobster."

Lady Fuddlesby's chatter stopped, and she sat with a suddenly troubled expression. "There is only one problem. I dare not ask the tradesmen for the large amount of credit I will need to do things properly. They have not pressed me before, but I cannot place myself in the position of being dunned."

She began removing the rest of her jewelry, and the difficulty perplexed her. Then she looked down at the pink tourmaline ring she was putting away in a small velvet box.

"Of course! I shall agree to sell this ring to Lord Mawbly. He offered to pay me whatever sum I named." A mental image of the odious Lady Mawbly wearing the ring caused Lady Fuddlesby to purse her lips. "I cannot like it, but it is the only thing that will answer. Henrietta *must* have her ball."

Lady Fuddlesby gazed at the ring fondly, not really seeing it, but instead seeing the Viscount Fuddlesby when he had given it to her all those years ago. Her eyes misted at the memory.

Then another memory intruded. That of her old friend Lady Lushington. The lady and her husband had left England for the continent long ago. Lord Lushington had a penchant for drinking and gaming, and his combination of the two had resulted in their reaching *point non plus*. Lady Fuddlesby remembered how, before the couple were forced to flee their creditors, Lord Lushington had often sold his wife's jewels, providing her with paste copies so she might still hold her head up amongst the ton.

Lady Fuddlesby thought she would enjoy having a paste copy of the pink tourmaline ring. Not to wear in company. Merely to keep and bring out on occasion to remind her of her husband's kindness.

But how did one go about these things? Surely she would be too embarrassed to make such a request of Rundell and Bridge, even if they did that sort of work, which she was not at all sure they did. Weren't these things handled by disreputable, smoky sorts?

Lady Fuddlesby's imagination conjured a picture of an odious, greasy man behind a counter in a dingy establishment. He was probably French.

Her ladyship's eyes opened wide. French! Felice! Felice would know how to go about having a paste copy made. Tomorrow she would charge the maid with the task. It was the least the woman could do after sleeping through the attack on Henrietta!

A scratch on the door signaled the arrival of a housemaid to help her ladyship into her night-dress. The girl made up the fire before leaving with instructions for Felice to present herself in her mistress's bedchamber the very moment her ladyship rang in the morning.

Lady Fuddlesby went to bed satisfied with her scheme.

With a cavernous yawn, Knight joined her, drifting off to sleep immediately to dream of lobster patties.

The next morning when the plan was put to her, a guilt-ridden Felice was only too happy to comply with her ladyship's request. She knew the very man who could do the work and would go to him without delay.

Lady Fuddlesby decided not to tell Henrietta her plans for the ball until after she had secured the paste ring, sold the genuine to Lord Mawbly, and received the money.

She almost changed her mind when she entered the small dining room for breakfast and saw a downcast Henrietta absently crumbling a piece of toast in her hand while staring out the window.

"Good morning, my dear," Lady Fuddlesby began cheerfully. "It looks perfectly lovely outside, does it not?"

Henrietta straightened in her chair and brushed the crumbs from her fingers over her plate. "Yes, my lady. I was just thinking that if I were in the country, I would go for a long walk."

Just the thing to encourage her to brood, thought Lady Fuddlesby. "Thank goodness London provides us with better amusements! You must change your gown and come with me this afternoon. Last night at the opera I told Lady Chatterton we would call on her today."

Henrietta sighed but made no comment, and her aunt talked lightly of what gown she should choose, the latest *on dits*, and what she and the colonel had partaken of at Grillon's.

That afternoon the warm breeze ruffled the skirts of Henrietta's soft yellow muslin gown when she stepped out of the carriage in front of Lady Chatterton's house in Curzon Street. She and her aunt, who was clad in a vibrant pink, were ushered into the gloomy drawing room by an ancient butler.

Sitting amongst the dark, massive furniture was tiny Lady Chatterton. Dressed in a gown of burnt orange, she clashed violently with the heavy deep purple draperies drawn against the sunlight. The effect of these colors against Lady Chatterton's corpselike skin was most alarming, but Henrietta noted her aunt seemed to find nothing amiss.

"Nelda, how are you today, dear? Is it not glorious outside?" Lady Fuddlesby asked blithely in spite of her hostess's obvious aversion to sunny weather. "You know my dear niece Henrietta, of course."

Lady Chatterton, who had witnessed her friend's charge's unbecoming behavior at the Denbys' ball and Almack's, but liked the girl nonetheless, greeted Henrietta warmly.

Turning back to Lady Fuddlesby, Lady Chatterton spoke in her rapid whispery voice, "Clara, I have a surprise for you. My nephew is here from the country. May I present Mr. Edmund Shire? Edmund, this is Lady Fuddlesby and her niece, Miss Lanford."

Henrietta observed the large man with the kind face bowing before them. He was tall and barrel-chested with a long Roman nose. He wore an olive-green coat, which looked more serviceable than fashionable, over dun-colored breeches. His hair was a nondescript brown and cut shorter than the current fashion.

The company sat around the tea tray and Lady Chatterton poured.

"I say, Miss Lanford," Mr. Shire said with interest, "you wouldn't happen to be related to Squire Lanford of Hamilton Cross, would you?"

"Why, yes, sir, he is my father," Henrietta answered, accepting a cup from Lady Chatterton.

"By George!" Mr. Shire responded, striking his knee with the palm of his hand and letting out a loud guffaw. "Your papa breeds the best Thoroughbreds in all England! I had the pleasure of visiting his stables once. Found myself amazed at the gentleman's knowledge of horses, a subject dear to my own heart."

Henrietta smiled at Mr. Shire's unchecked enthusiasms. "He would be happy to hear such compliments, sir, having devoted his life's work to perfecting the racehorse."

Mr. Shire looked over Henrietta's becoming appearance with obvious approval and beamed. He seemed much struck. "I say, Miss Lanford, I'd be vastly pleased to take you up behind my matched grays. Not the type of horseflesh you're used to, I fear, but a deuced fine team."

Henrietta's mind flashed a picture of a fine pair of gray eyes, but she quickly banished the vision.

With a torrent of words, Lady Chatterton jumped into this break in the conversation, saying proudly, "My nephew is a fine driver, Miss Lanford. You will not have to be afraid of overturning with him holding the ribbons. Why, if Edmund had a mind to, he could cut a dash in the Four in Hand Club! But he spends all his time finding ways to improve his lands."

"Is that so, Mr. Shire?" Henrietta asked with what she hoped was an appropriate show of interest.

Mr. Shire's complexion turned an uncomplementary shade of red. Clearing his throat, he said, "A man must know what's important in life, and keeping one's land in good heart is of primary concern to me. Can't abide these Town bucks spending their days in pursuit of one pleasure after another."

Lady Fuddlesby thought the easy-natured Mr. Shire was just what her niece needed at the moment to bring her out of the doldrums. Lady

Chatterton had quickly whispered an aside that her nephew had torn himself away from his estate in order to find a wife.

Unmoved from her determination to have the Duke of Winterton as a husband for her niece, Lady Fuddlesby reasoned it would do the duke no harm to see Henrietta on the arm of another. And if the duke did prove impossible, Mr. Shire was a country gentleman and rich. "Henrietta, I am persuaded some fresh air would be beneficial to you. Do accept Mr. Shire's kind offer. Lady Chatterton and I will wait here for you while you take a turn around the park."

Henrietta stole a glance at the clock on the mantel. She saw it was well before the fashionable hour and was gratified. Encountering the Duke of Winterton would be unlikely.

Then guilt at these wayward thoughts made her smile overbrightly at Mr. Shire. "I should like it above all things, sir."

Throughout the ride in the park, Mr. Shire proved himself to be considerate and undemanding company. Never did he treat her to an excess of civility or flowery compliments as Lord Baddick had. Nor was his manner puffed up with his own consequence as the duke's was. He was a levelheaded man; trickery or arrogance seemed foreign to his nature. Henrietta judged him an altogether suitable gentleman. She told herself he was not boring. It was only her persistent, unfair comparison of him to the Duke of Winterton that made him seem so.

When Mr. Shire returned her to Lady Fuddlesby and asked if he might call on her the next day, Henrietta smiled her acceptance with a determined cheerfulness.

Throughout the following days, Mr. Shire could frequently be seen at Lady Fuddlesby's town house in Grosvenor Square. He escorted the ladies to the playhouse, where he sat uncomfortably out of place while Henrietta watched the actors with enraptured concentration.

As the weather was sunny and warm, Mr. Shire took Henrietta for drives in his open carriage and for ices at Gunter's, where he sat awkwardly in his chair while he tried to enjoy the frivolous confection.

In between these outings, Henrietta would often curl up in the window seat of the morning room with an improving book. No more novels for her.

Even so, her mind would frequently drift off to memories of the Duke of Winterton's never-to-be-forgotten kiss. Her eyes closed, and once again she could feel the touch of his lips on hers. The strength of his strong shoulders underneath her hands. The clean, masculine smell of him.

She had not seen him save for a glimpse of him and Lady Clorinda in the park. No notice of their engagement appeared in the papers, and Henrietta wondered at it. A little voice in her head insisted there might still be hope, but Henrietta stamped down these thoughts. While Colonel Colchester continued to call on Lady Fuddlesby, the duke had remained absent.

In Park Lane, for his part the duke was becoming increasingly irritated with himself. He spent his days working out his frustrations at Gentleman Jackson's and dining with his godfather. He noted, a trifle guiltily, Colonel Colchester frequently wore a disapproving frown. The older man had tried to glean Giles's feelings regarding Miss Lanford and had been snapped at for his trouble.

Occasionally the duke escorted the fair Clorinda for a drive, but he found her charms now seemed overblown. Nevertheless, being seen in her company kept other misses at bay, so he did not cease his attention to her.

At night, a fever gripped his body. A fever for the sweet taste of Miss Lanford's innocent lips. The soft, soft feel of her skin.

As these thoughts took over his mind, the duke tossed restlessly in his bed. Matters were not helped by Sir Polly Grey's untimely utterance of a snippet of the old duke's marriage lecture. "Hips good for breeding," the parrot insisted.

Deuce take it! Perhaps he should acquire a mistress. Then he scowled horribly when this plan produced no real spark of interest or anticipation.

The duke had only seen Miss Lanford once in the park in the past week. A giant of a man had been driving her. Discreet inquiries gained Giles the knowledge Mr. Edmund Shire was a well-to-do landowner. Just the sort he had initially thought Miss Lanford would be lucky to attract when he met her at her parents' estate.

He decided he needed to see the girl again. Maybe this spell she had him under would disintegrate in the harsh face of reality. Lady Chatterton, Mr. Shire's aunt, was holding a musicale in two days' time. Giles was confident Miss Lanford would attend. Punching his pillow for the hundredth time that night before resting his tired head upon it, he decided he would go and see that Miss Lanford possessed no magical charm.

* * *

"Here it ees, madame. Jacques has made an identical paste copy of your pink tourmaline ring," Felice stated, setting two small boxes side by side on the toilet table in Lady Fuddlesby's bedchamber. Glancing down with a look of distaste at Knight, who was watching the proceedings, Felice opened each box and exclaimed, "Voilà! No one can tell the deeference, but you know the genuine ees in the black velvet box and the fake ees in the blue satin."

Attired in a pink wrapper and prepared for bed, Lady Fuddlesby stared down at the identical-looking rings lying on their sides in the boxes. She picked up the paste copy and examined the stone set in the heavy, intricate setting carefully. "Oh, indeed, the rings appear just alike. I confess I feel quite clever having thought of this way of meeting my financial needs and satisfying my sentimental memories of dear Viscount Fuddlesby. This ring will serve its purpose admirably. I shall pretend to myself it is the original one."

Felice smiled at her mistress. "It ees noble of you, madame, to make this sacrifice for the young lady."

"Nonsense!" Lady Fuddlesby replied mistily, placing the ring back in its box. She picked up a sealed letter. "Felice, I have written a note to Lord Mawbly telling him he may come around tomorrow and collect the ring. See that a footman delivers it this night."

Lady Fuddlesby handed the missive to her maid. "Now I will have the necessary funds and can put everything in motion regarding Henrietta's ball. No expense shall be spared! I will tell the dear girl all about my plans tomorrow after Lord Mawbly leaves."

"She ees sure to be thrilled, madame," Felice declared before leaving the room to find a footman.

Lady Fuddlesby bent to scratch behind Knight's ears. "Why, my darling boy, your fur is raised! Whatever is the matter? Goodness, you will do yourself a mischief!"

Her ladyship continued to stroke her cat's ruffled fur. He is probably upset because I am selling the ring to the Mawblys, Lady Fuddlesby thought. Knight is such a high stickler! I know he cannot have forgotten the atrocious insult Hester Mawbly uttered the other day in the park.

Lady Fuddlesby's mind ran over the events. She had taken the cat out for an airing on the warm spring day. He sat tall and proud on the seat beside her in the open carriage, green eyes in his black mask taking in the Mayfair sights. She noticed, with affection, his nose and whiskers twitched in obvious interest at the varied odors carried by the breeze.

Lady Mawbly's carriage had drawn up beside them during a pause in the drive. The ladies exchanged greetings, but then Lady Mawbly had pointed her fan at Knight with a screech, exclaiming, "I must drive on, Clara. I detest cats."

Now Lady Fuddlesby clucked her tongue remembering Knight's outraged feline expression. She soothed, "Calm down, dear boy, and come to bed. It is late and I find generosity can be quite tiring. You must forget that ninnyhammer Hester Mawbly. She lacks good breeding."

Her ladyship climbed into bed and drew the pink coverlet up around her snugly. Knight settled down at the foot of the bed, a stubborn expression on his face.

Soon her ladyship's gentle snore could be heard

in the darkened room. The black and white cat cast a quick look at his mistress before jumping down from the bed and slinking over to the toilet table. Despite his weight, he hopped up onto the surface silently, his paws landing expertly without disturbing anything.

He appeared to study the boxes containing the rings lying open in front of him, his head tilted speculatively. Suddenly a paw, with claws extended, reached in the black velvet box and removed the genuine ring. Knight dropped it aside, where it made a light metallic sound on the table's top. The cat turned his head sharply toward his mistress, but Lady Fuddlesby continued to snore.

Knight stretched his paw into the blue satin box, adroitly removed the paste copy, and dropped it into the black velvet box. The genuine ring was batted up and into the blue satin box, where the paste had rested a few moments before.

Apparently satisfied with this piece of chicanery, the rascal returned to the bed and fell instantly to sleep.

The next afternoon Lady Fuddlesby was none the wiser when she innocently turned the paste copy over to Lord Mawbly for a large sum of money.

Lord Mawbly, however, had acquired many jewels for his greedy wife over the years. He knew at once the ring was paste. Being a very timid man, he could not bring himself to confront Lady Fuddlesby with his knowledge. Instead, he pondered the problem during the carriage ride home. Luckily, he had not told Lady Mawbly he had been successful in striking a bargain with Lady Fuddlesby, so he would not have to deal with his wife right away.

But what was he going to do? His brow creased with concentration, until the solution struck him. The Duke of Winterton! He would turn the matter over to his daughter's beau. The man's godfather was on good terms with Lady Fuddlesby, and they were certain to know how to proceed. Tonight, at Lady Chatterton's musicale, he would tell the duke everything.

Chapter Nine

While Felice put the finishing touches to Henrietta's coiffure, a housemaid scratched at the door. Entering the room, she bobbed a curtsy and said, "Miss, her ladyship wishes to see you in her bedchamber when you're ready."

"Thank you, Sally." Henrietta dismissed the maid and turned to study Felice's face reflected in the cheval glass. The woman worked expertly with a length of amber-colored ribbon.

Since sleeping through Lord Baddick's attack, the Frenchwoman seemed in low spirits. Surmising the lady's maid felt guilty over her lack of assistance, Henrietta had tried to reassure her all had turned out well, but the woman's manner remained despondent.

Now Henrietta looked at the glossy curls Felice had coaxed, and complimented her. "As usual, you have worked wonders with my hair, Felice. You are a treasure."

Felice's lips stretched in a small smile. "Thank you, mees. You look beautiful in that amber gown. The color sets off your dark hair, and the cut shows your figure to advantage. Let me put these amber beads about your neck, and then you can go to her ladyship."

Henrietta smiled her thanks before rising, shaking out her skirts and making her way down to her aunt's bedchamber. She found the lady, attired in a raspberry silk gown, seated at a desk, writing out what looked to be some sort of list.

"Good evening, my lady. Sally said you wanted to see me before we leave for Lady Chatterton's musicale," Henrietta said, dropping a kiss on her aunt's rouged cheek.

She walked over to a pink chaise nearby the desk, where Knight stretched out languidly. Sitting down next to him, she stroked his white back, and the cat rewarded her with a throaty purr for her efforts.

Lady Fuddlesby put down her pen and gazed at her niece with an excited expression on her plump features. "Oh, my dear Henrietta. I have the most delightful news for you! You will be in transports when you hear it, just as I am."

Henrietta tilted her head in a questioning manner, a crease forming across her ivory brow. "What is it, Aunt? Is the Prince Regent to attend tonight's musicale?" she teased.

"What? Oh, my dear, you are bamming me," Lady Fuddlesby replied, and chuckled. Then, as a thought seemed to take hold in her ladyship's mind, she said, "Although now you have mentioned him, I wonder if I should include Prinny on the invitation list."

"Invitation list? Are we to have an entertainment of our own?"

"Yes." Lady Fuddlesby's pale blue eyes lit with anticipation. She clapped her hands with evident relish. "Henrietta, I am planning to hold a ball in your honor! All the best people will attend, we shall have champagne, perhaps flowing from a little fountain. Yes, that would be elegant, and oh, masses of hothouse flowers, and . . ."

Henrietta bit her lip in dismay. She contemplated whether or not she deserved such special treatment after her improper behavior since her arrival in Town, first at the Denbys' and then at Almack's. In addition, there had been the whole ill-judged relationship with Lord Baddick, and its shocking consequences. She did not think her performance in Town thus far merited such generosity.

She heard Lady Fuddlesby rambling on about Gunter's catering and their delicious lobster patties, and felt the cat's body underneath her hand heave a sigh. Henrietta began her protest, "I do not know—"

"Oh, indeed, dear, Gunter's is who everyone uses, and we could not expect Mrs. Pottsworth to prepare all the food that we shall require," Lady Fuddlesby argued, misunderstanding her niece's words.

Agitated, Henrietta rose and stepped over to stand in front of the desk. "No, it is not that, dear lady. While I appreciate your kindness, I am certain whatever Town parties we attend will serve the purpose of introducing me to eligible gentlemen. I simply feel a ball would be a great expense, and perhaps unnecessary."

Henrietta felt uncomfortable bringing up the matter of the cost, but knew from different incidents her aunt's pockets were not well lined. While Lady Fuddlesby was no lickpenny, Henrietta had noticed when her aunt had refused herself the purchase of a new bonnet, and had appeared worried after a mysterious visit from her solicitor.

But Lady Fuddlesby brushed the matter of expense aside in a curious way. "Nonsense, my dear. I just received that roll of soft from Lord—"

Here the lady interrupted herself and, with a fluttering of hands, rose from her seat and abruptly changed the course of the conversation. "Henrietta! What can you mean when you say a ball will be 'unnecessary'? Naturally, every young lady must have a ball in her honor. Why, I have been remiss in not planning one for you before now. All you need think of is what to wear. I believe the ball gown of white silk with the lace overdress Madame Dupre made up will serve. And since it will be a special occasion, I do not see where it would be improper for me to loan you a small diamond necklet."

Lady Fuddlesby chattered on, all the while gathering her reticule and a pretty Norwich shawl. Henrietta realized her aunt's mind was set on the subject of a ball, and she assumed an expression of enthusiasm far from her true feelings. Restraining a sigh, she allowed herself to be led downstairs to the drawing room.

Knight trailed the ladies downstairs, and when they entered the drawing room, he stared curiously at the stranger.

Mr. Edmund Shire rose from the brocade sofa and greeted them in his casual, unpretentious way. He wore a brown coat over tan breeches, and his cravat was tied in a simple style. Seeing the cat, he ventured a friendly "Here, kitty, kitty."

Knight promptly turned around and left the room. His abrupt departure indicated clearly he was uninterested in anyone who would address him in this inane manner.

Mr. Shire cleared his throat at the rebuff and said, "Ladies, if you are ready, let us return to my aunt's house. She wishes me at her side when the guests arrive."

Henrietta restrained a smile at the look of apprehension with which the country gentleman made this statement. He was clearly not the type of man who was comfortable with Society, or its diversions, unlike the Duke of Winterton, who was ever elegant. The duke was well bred enough never to show unease, or any other emotion for that matter.

Perhaps that was not quite true, she reflected during the drive to Lady Chatterton's. Mr. Shire monopolized a conversation with Lady Fuddlesby about a mutual acquaintance, leaving Henrietta to her musings. She remembered the duke had certainly forgotten himself the night at Almack's when he shouted "Minx" at her. And then, after rescuing her from Lord Baddick's perfidy, there had been that kiss. A kiss that had left a burning imprint on her.

She fell into reliving the experience once again, recalling the ecstasy of being held against his strong body. As the carriage rolled along, her longing to see the duke intensified. Gazing out at the London streets, she wondered if she would be able to determine if any clue was to be had regarding his sentiments about herself.

They were the first to arrive, Lady Chatterton meeting them in the hallway and indicating, in her whispery way, for them to go upstairs while she and her nephew received the other guests.

Entering the drawing room with Lady Fuddlesby, Henrietta stopped and blinked her eyes, attempting to adjust them to the dim lighting. Her previous assumption that Lady Chatterton held light in aversion was confirmed. The large drawing room with its dark, heavy furniture contained only a few branches of candles, casting most of the room in shadows. Evidently it was to be a small affair, since a mere six rows of chairs were set up in addition to the existing settees and wing chairs.

Soon other people were announced, and footmen circulated, passing glasses of ratafia and champagne. Absently accepting the ratafia, Henrietta looked up each time a new party arrived, hoping to see the duke.

She sensed her aunt waited for Colonel Colchester, and the two ladies talked lightly until the Duke of Winterton, his mother, and godfather walked in. They were followed by the Mawblys and Lady Clorinda.

Lady Fuddlesby started at the sight of her old rival, Matilda, conversing amiably with Colonel Colchester.

Seeing her dismay, Henrietta gently turned her aunt away, and said, "Come Aunt, let us take our seats. Lady Chatterton and Mr. Shire are here now, so the musicale will most likely begin."

Walking to the end of one row of chairs, they sat down, and it was not long before Colonel Colchester hurried over to sit on the other side of Lady Fuddlesby.

"Good evening, Miss Lanford," he said, and then immediately addressed her aunt. "Lady Fuddlesby, I must beg your forgiveness. I intended to ask to escort you this evening. Indeed, I have a treat at home for my brave soldier, Knight. But Giles invited Matilda to dine, and I felt it would be rude to leave them with just one another's company."

The tension drained from Lady Fuddlesby's face. "Oh, dear sir, 'tis of no consequence. Goodness, I must tell you our glad news. We are to hold a ball!"

Henrietta barely heard any of the conversation that followed between the two older people. Discreetly she watched the duke conversing with his mother and the Mawblys. How very agreeable he appeared in his slate-colored coat and black breeches. His dove-gray waistcoat must match his eyes, she believed, unable to see for certain in the room's low light.

Then her view of him was blocked by Lady Chatterton, who joined the group and appeared to be furiously whispering something to Lady Mawbly and Clorinda. Whatever it was resulted in an adorable case of dimpling on Lady Clorinda's part.

The duke strolled away from them, and he and the dowager came to sit on the other side of Colonel Colchester. Henrietta's gaze never left the duke when he paused before he sat down to rake her body with a knowing eye. "Your servant, Miss Lanford," he said in arctic tones.

Henrietta blushed scarlet and merely nodded to him. She was robbed of speech for the moment. How dare he speak to her in that cold way after the kiss they shared? And that look. She quite felt he knew exactly what she looked like without her clothes. And that was not possible from one embrace. Was it?

By the massive fireplace, Lady Chatterton attempted to quiet the room, without much success. Shocking the assembly, she finally shouted, "By God, be quiet, you great bunch of bacon-brained gudgeons!"

Barely concealed titters followed, as Society saved this *on dit* to be repeated over the teacups tomorrow. The beau monde loved being insulted, by one of their own, of course.

Henrietta noticed an indulgent smile on her aunt's face, but Mr. Shire had turned the same shade of purple Henrietta had heretofore only seen on Papa's face, when he was upset over his horses.

In her usual voice, Lady Chatterton announced, "The diva has not yet arrived, but I have persuaded Lady Clorinda Eden to sing for us."

A smattering of applause greeted Lady Clorinda, who stood in front of the gathering, lovely in a revealing peach gown decorated with blond lace. In a clear voice, she sang a haunting ballad of love.

As she performed the song, Clorinda's Venus-like body dipped and swayed gracefully. The gentlemen in the audience leaned forward as one in their seats, attempting to better view her magnificent bosom. Clorinda appeared to enjoy every moment of the attention she was receiving.

The Duke of Winterton sat with his arms folded across his chest and his lips pursed in a grim line. The girl was calling too much vulgar attention to herself, he decided. It would never do, if he decided to settle for Clorinda, for the future Duchess of Winterton to be the subject of distasteful notice.

Casually he glanced sidelong at Miss Lanford. The amber-colored gown she wore was vastly fetching. Her cheeks were rosy, and she appeared to be studying her gloved hands, which were folded in her lap. He reflected she had a certain quiet dignity about her.

Her innocence was unnerving. Without warning, his mind dragged him down into the memory of her sweet-tasting lips. The way her tiny hands had rested on his shoulders evoked a protective feeling in him no other lady had stirred.

He remembered with satisfaction that she had not pushed him away. On the contrary, Miss Lanford seemed to have savored the meeting of their lips as much as he.

Good God, he wanted her. It could not be denied.

A disdainful look crossed his aristocratic features.

Naturally, he could only have her in the marriage bed. In the past, when picturing his bride-to-be, she was always nameless and faceless, just a female form. Now, inexplicably, Miss Henrietta Lanford's demure countenance appeared in the vision. What would it be like to hold her naked body in his arms every night in their bed?

Giles forced his thoughts to those of a more practical matter. More to the point, what would it be like to converse with her during meals and at the end of every day? They seemed to come to cuffs frequently.

Would she be able to oversee the running of his households? He shrewdly guessed it was she who handled such things commendably at the squire's. But she would have no experience in dealing with a staff the size of his at Perrywood.

He had to admit, though, she had shown remarkable courage the night of Baddick's attack. Any other Society lady he knew would have swooned or had strong hysterics. Miss Lanford had been understandably overset, but still relatively in admirable control of herself.

His father's voice sounded in his brain, reminding him of his duty. Sighing, the duke asked himself about the undeniable fact that he owed more to his name than a mere squire's daughter.

On the subject of marriage, why had Miss Lanford agreed to marry a philandering miscreant like Baddick in the first place? This question had plagued him the most since the fateful night at the opera. Although he had not thought it at the time, he now wondered if she had loved the viscount before he had shown himself to be a blackguard.

A sensation of intense jealousy, normally an emotion foreign to him, swept over the duke. Frustrated, he ran a hand through his dark hair and ordered his mind to cease its haranguing inquisition. He was only able to do so after vowing to interrogate Miss Lanford at the first opportunity.

He had no chance to put this plan into action, however, as the diva arrived, and Lady Clorinda finished her song. Smiling angelically under hearty applause, she went to sit next to her parents, directly in front of him.

Lady Mawbly twisted around in her seat to face Winterton. The sudden bright light of her diamond brooch almost blinded him in the darkened room.

"Your Grace, has not my Clorinda the loveliest voice you have ever heard? Her stitchery is unequaled as well," Lady Mawbly began, and went on endlessly in a conversation that centered around her daughter's many accomplishments.

Lady Clorinda sat quietly by, giving him a view of her beautiful profile, as her mother shamelessly commended her, causing the duke to form the impression the girl thought the praise was her due.

Good manners, and the fact he was trapped in his seat since no one had risen in the interval between Clorinda's singing and the diva's appearance, prevented him from rudely telling Lady Mawbly to stubble it.

Fortunately, just when he reached the end of his tether, a hush fell over the room.

In front of the assembled guests, two pillars, formerly holding Grecian busts, now each held a branch of candles. The diva, a large, dark-haired woman in a severe black gown, stood between the columns and began her performance. Her wide mouth stretched open to the limit as she bellowed out an indecipherable aria.

The darkness of the room, combined with the

woman's black hair and clothing, resulted in only her white, lead-painted face being visible. Thus, a ghostlike head, seemingly suspended midair, roared out over the assembly.

Winterton's lips twitched at the sight, and he turned to see the expression on Miss Lanford's face. At that moment she looked his way, and he saw the laughter brimming in her eyes. They smiled at each other in silent communication.

After the singing, the duke rose, meaning to speak to Miss Lanford, but a hand on his arm stayed him. Lord Mawbly, his gaze darting nervously back and forth, said, "Your Grace, I beg a few minutes of your time."

Winterton stiffened. Could the man be impertinent enough to press him regarding Clorinda? His voice haughty, the duke inquired, "What is it, Mawbly?"

Glancing desperately at his wife, Lord Mawbly pleaded, "Over there, by the draperies, where we can be private."

Wary, the duke went along with the timid little man. When they were quite concealed in the shadows, Winterton demanded an explanation.

Lord Mawbly held a glass of wine in one hand, and he downed the contents before speaking. "Lady Mawbly insisted I approach Lady Fuddlesby about her pink tourmaline ring. Wants it. And let me tell you, Your Grace, Hester don't rest until she gets whatever jewel it is she desires."

"What is this to do with me, Mawbly?" Winterton responded impatiently.

Lord Mawbly went on with his story, without answering the duke's question. "Well, at first Lady Fuddlesby says no, she won't sell the ring. Put Hester in a terrible pucker when I finally told her.

For days she won't leave me alone in my library! Then I get a letter from Lady Fuddlesby saying she *will* sell the ring. I had to fork over a considerable amount of blunt, but anything's worth silencing Hester."

The duke frowned and said, "Are you telling me Lady Fuddlesby sold you a piece of her jewelry for a large sum of money?"

Lord Mawbly's left eye twitched nervously. "Yes. No. Well, not exactly. You see, her ladyship sold me a *paste* ring."

Winterton's eyebrows rose incredulously. "Paste?"

Lord Mawbly nodded his head up and down. "That's right. Paste. Now I don't know what to do. Thank God I never told Hester I struck a bargain with her ladyship, but mark my word, Hester will know at once that I have withdrawn money from the bank. Very close with the accounts, she is."

The duke shuddered inwardly at the picture the man painted of his marriage. "I shall take your word you are certain the ring is paste. After all the jewels you have, no doubt, acquired for Lady Mawbly over the years, you must know a fake when you see one. What do you plan to do about the situation?"

Darting an anxious look at where Lady Mawbly stood in conversation with the Dowager Duchess of Winterton, Lord Mawbly replied, "Thought as a friend of my family, you might help me."

Giles was taken aback. What could he do? He brought his hand up to stroke his chin thoughtfully. The timid little man in front of him might eventually spill the story to his odious wife, if she nagged him enough, which was frightfully probable. Poor Lady Fuddlesby would be the subject of a scandal. The duke knew neither he nor his god-father would tolerate that.

His brows came together. What could have possessed Lady Fuddlesby to have tried a trick like this? Hard on the heels of this question came the certain knowledge Lady Fuddlesby could not have known what she did. A genteel lady, she would never resort to fleecing anyone.

"Do you have the ring with you, Mawbly?"

Lord Mawbly gasped aloud. "Never! Hester would *smell* a piece of jewelry on me in a minute. It's hidden away in my books. Hester would never look at those."

The duke's eyes narrowed as he considered the man. "I shall investigate the matter, and you will hear from me in a day or two. Give me your word you will not tell any of this to another living soul."

"Yes, Your Grace. My word on it," Lord Mawbly replied, noticeably relieved.

The men shook hands and parted company, Lord Mawbly going over to stand furtively beside his wife, and the duke looked for his godfather. His gaze first sought Miss Lanford, however, and he found her sitting on a settee, talking with the cumbersome Mr. Shire.

Keeping an eye on her, lest she escape before he could speak to her, the duke drew the colonel aside, saying, "We have a mystery on our hands, sir."

"A mystery?" Colonel Colchester queried.

"Yes, and I am afraid it concerns Lady Fuddlesby."

The older gentleman snapped to attention. "What? Tell me at once!"

Giles proceeded to relate the disturbing story, ending with, "I wonder why Lady Fuddlesby would sell a piece of her jewelry to accommodate Lord

Mawbly. She does not seem overfond of Hester Mawbly."

Colonel Colchester's face was ashen. "'Tis of no significance why she did it. I confess I neither know nor care. We must give Lord Mawbly back whatever sum he paid Lady Fuddlesby for the ring. Clara must not be subjected to any unpleasantness, and the faster we end this matter, the better."

Knowing of the affection between the lady and his godfather, the duke spoke gently. "But, sir, that will not answer. Lady Mawbly has been hounding her husband for the ring and will most likely continue to do so. Eventually she might even approach Lady Fuddlesby herself. Then the fat would be in the fire! Lady Fuddlesby would declare she already sold the ring to Lord Mawbly. That man would no doubt meet his Maker within the hour when Lady Mawbly learns he has purchased *paste* for her."

The colonel made his hands into fists at his sides. "What do you propose we do, then?"

Giles's gaze once again fastened on Henrietta. He saw an expression of intense concentration was on her face while she listened to that country bumpkin, Mr. Shire. The sight made him strangely uncomfortable. "I believe I shall consult with Miss Lanford. Perhaps she can enlighten us as to Lady Fuddlesby's motives. The more information we have, the better decision we can reach about our next step."

Colonel Colchester took a deep breath and let it out slowly. "You have the right of it, my boy. But it will be deuced hard to do nothing in the meantime."

The duke looked at him sympathetically. "I know you are fond of the lady, sir, and I promise no harm will come to her."

The colonel's answer was gruff. "When my wife, Mary, died, I thought I would never care for another lady. I was wrong."

Giles grasped his godfather's shoulder. "Your wife would have wanted you to be happy again, sir. Lady Fuddlesby is a good woman, and quite . . . out of the common way."

"Quite," Colonel Colchester agreed, and smiled, a twinkle in his brown eyes. Then he added with a piercing look, "As is her niece, my boy. From the looks of things, Mr. Shire thinks so, too."

Winterton's hand dropped to his side. His voice grew chilly. "Mr. Shire, as a well-to-do landowner, would be a perfect match for Miss Lanford. They are of the same station in life, and if the rumors about the man are true, Mr. Shire's devotion to country ways and horses would delight Squire Lanford."

The colonel looked at his godson with irritation and said, "Balderdash! The man looks a great bore to me, and pretty Miss Lanford does not deserve that. I tell you she has a respectable birth and a fair-sized dowry. She is intelligent, spirited, and kind-natured. She merits a gentleman, *of any rank.*"

"You have persuaded me Miss Lanford is a veritable paragon, sir," the duke stated in a derisive tone.

"If only I had," Colonel Colchester said huffily, and walked away to join Lady Fuddlesby, leaving the duke to stand alone in brooding silence.

During this time over on the settee, Henrietta thought if Mr. Shire uttered another word about horses, she would surely scream. Had she not heard enough about the beasts all her life?

She pushed such uncharitable thoughts from her

mind. Mr. Shire possessed many fine qualities and would make a respectable, solid husband. And she could do worse. She knew that from her experience with Lord Baddick. If she only tried harder, a fondness for Edmund Shire might develop. Since she must marry, she really could not hope for more when considering a suitable gentleman.

Hard on the heels of these worthy thoughts, her treacherous gaze sought out the duke. He was in what looked to be a serious conversation with the colonel. She wished Winterton might come over and save her from Mr. Shire's company.

She desperately wanted to speak to the duke. The exchange of looks between herself and His Grace during the diva's performance had caused her foolish heart to surge with excitement. Despite his bewildering and sometimes confusing manner toward her, he held her heart. He had, she realized, from the moment she met him at her parents' table.

As if Henrietta's fairy godmother had granted her wish, she saw the colonel move away from the conversation, and a few minutes later Winterton crossed the room purposefully to stand in front of her.

Mr. Shire rose. With a heart suddenly beating hard, Henrietta performed the introductions.

Unfortunately, just then Lady Fuddlesby walked up to her niece, remarking it was time they took their leave. Henrietta rose and cast her a speaking look, but the lady's attention was focused on Colonel Colchester, who stood next to her, and she missed the plea.

The colonel said, "My dear lady, you must allow me to see you and Miss Lanford home. Mr. Shire cannot want to leave his guests. I shall order a hackney at once."

Henrietta watched him go, biting her lip. Now there would be no opportunity to speak with the duke. Tears of frustration burned behind her eyes.

"Most kind of him," Mr. Shire stated gratefully. "I must not desert my aunt. Miss Lanford, may I hope you will join me tomorrow afternoon for a drive around the park? We can continue our important discussion about horse liniments."

"Miss Lanford is promised to me tomorrow, Shire. I, too, have an important matter to discuss with her," the duke said. He threw Henrietta a wicked grin that dared her to deny the truth of his statement.

How high-handed, Henrietta thought. Then this judgment was abruptly cut off when the words "an important matter to discuss with her" rang in her head. She felt a warm glow flow through her. What could he mean? She could not resist finding out.

"I am sorry, Mr. Shire. Perhaps you will ask me another time," she added, with a tug of guilt at the gentleman's disappointed expression.

"The next day, then," Mr. Shire persisted.

"I should like it above all things, sir," Henrietta dissembled. Glancing at the duke, she thought she detected a tightening in his jaw.

"I shall see you tomorrow at two, Miss Lanford." The duke bowed and half turned to leave. Then he faced Henrietta again, reached for her gloved hand, and placed a light kiss upon it.

Dazed, she watched as he walked over to his mother.

Neither Henrietta nor the duke noticed Lady Clorinda's green eyes narrow into jealous slits at that kiss.

On the ride home Henrietta's mind was far away. She left Lady Fuddlesby and Colonel Colchester over the tea tray, needing to sort through her thoughts.

Although her new maturity forbade her to do so, she indulged in a daydream in which, underneath a leafy tree in the park, the duke fell to one knee and begged for her hand in marriage.

She fell asleep smiling at the love reflected in his gray eyes.

Chapter Ten

It was not an expression of love, but one of impatience on the Duke of Winterton's haughty face when he arrived in Grosvenor Square the next afternoon. While Henrietta had spent a peaceful night, sleep had eluded Giles.

After enduring the evening ritual of a lecture from Sir Polly Grey, the duke lay awake with his fists clenched, listening to the sounds of the relaxed bird grinding his bill.

It wasn't long before Giles's brain insisted on repeating the nagging questions he had asked himself about Miss Lanford at the musicale. He had no answers when he finally drifted off, deciding only that he felt severely irked with the chit for being the sole cause of his not knowing his own mind.

This afternoon matters were complicated by the subject of his irritation's strikingly becoming appearance. She arrived breathlessly in the hall where he waited, clad in a sky-blue muslin gown, trimmed with lace, that flattered her bosom and shoulders. Its simple lines ended in three deep flounces and emphasized her doll-like features.

"Oh, Your Grace, I am sorry to be late," Henrietta said, tying the ribbons of her chip straw hat. "It is but a few minutes after two, so please do not be vexed with me."

"I assure you I am not vexed, Miss Lanford."

Henrietta tilted her head to look up at him. "But you have a terrible scowl on your face."

"I am not scowling," the duke ground out. "Let us take our leave before my tiger resorts to walking my cattle."

Stepping out into the sunny day, Henrietta smiled at the wizened little man holding the horses' heads. Her heart felt light. All that mattered was that she was in the duke's company, and he had said he had an important matter to speak about.

Just then his strong hand was at her elbow, assisting her into the open curricle. Henrietta experienced a sudden, dizzying desire to turn about in his arms and bring his handsome face to her lips.

Shocked at the terrible impropriety of these thoughts, she felt hot color burn her cheeks. Settling herself in her seat, she stole a glance at the duke, but he was busy gathering the reins and did not notice her mortification.

The tiger jumped onto the backstrap and they moved off toward Hyde Park. Henrietta admired the duke's high-mettled horses and the way he drove them to an inch.

"Papa would approve your prads, Your Grace."

"Thank you, Miss Lanford." Glancing at her, Winterton added, "One wonders if Mr. Edmund Shire would declare them first-rate. His estimable opinion of my horses would be a distinction almost as gratifying as your father's."

Henrietta detected a note of derision in the duke's voice. Feeling a need to defend the country gentleman, she replied, "Mr. Shire is a worthy man with a pleasing interest in horses."

The duke's mouth twisted in a half grin. "Pleasing? To whom? I recall your convictions regarding the animals to be 'nasty, smelly beasts,' " he reminded her.

Swiftly turning her angry gaze on him, she caught the mischievous twinkle in his gray eyes, which only served to heighten her indignation. "What concern are Mr. Shire's views to you, Your Grace? I doubt you judge a simple gentleman such as he a man of good taste, which is really too bad of you."

The duke's eyebrows rose. "Good taste? Miss Lanford, Mr. Shire is a prosy bore, and well you know it. But as you are drawn to him like a bear to the honeypot, I shall say no ill of him."

Although she privately agreed with Winterton's assessment of Mr. Shire, red flags of warning rose in Henrietta's cheeks over the implication she was enamored with Edmund Shire.

The duke continued on without caution. "At least he is a vast improvement over your last suitor. Why *did* you become betrothed to Baddick?"

Henrietta squared her shoulders. The correct answer to this impertinent question was that Lord Baddick had made his offer when she had been despondent and weak, having moments before heard Lady Clorinda's assertion that the Duke of Winterton was about to call on Lord Mawbly to ask for her hand in marriage.

Not about to tell the duke this truth, she glared at him, blue eyes flashing, and stated, "It appears, Your Grace, I am a poor judge of men. Only think, I was initially gulled into thinking *you* a well-bred man with agreeable manners and a superior intelligence. But I have come to find it is all a hum."

Unexpectedly, the duke threw his dark head back and let out a shout of laughter. "Come, Miss Lanford, let us cry friends. There is no need for you to comb my hair with a joint stool."

Henrietta's heart lurched in her chest in response to his merriment. How much more approachable he looked when relaxed, making her fingers long to touch him once again. She grasped the strings of her reticule tightly, willing her thoughts to focus on an appreciation of the sunny day.

The park was thin of people because it was not the fashionable hour. Still, it seemed everyone who was there wished to exchange a few words with the Duke of Winterton. The duke finally guided his team away from the main drive and situated them underneath a tree near the Serpentine River.

He addressed his tiger. "Jeffers, you may descend and enjoy the view. Do not go far."

When the little man had obeyed his master, Henrietta turned a questioning face to the duke. Unbidden, her dreams of receiving a proposal of marriage from him underneath a leafy tree sprang to her mind. Her foolish heart began its frantic beating anew.

"Miss Lanford, I did not want anyone to hear what I have to say to you," Winterton said, his expression abruptly serious.

"Y-Yes, Your Grace, wh-what is it?" Henrietta stammered, and swallowed hard.

"I am afraid I have an unpleasant matter to discuss with you. It concerns Lady Fuddlesby."

Henrietta's emotions quickly swung from disappointment at the fact the duke was obviously not about to discuss marriage, to anxiety for her aunt. Her voice was still unsteady as she urgently asked, "Lady Fuddlesby? Wh-what is amiss with my aunt?"

The duke held the reins in one hand and reached over to grasp Miss Lanford's gloved hand in the other. "Do not be upset. Together, we can contrive to avoid exposing Lady Fuddlesby to scandal."

Henrietta gazed down at their joined hands, feeling a burning sensation rising up her arm.

Apparently Winterton misunderstood the look to be one of reproach as he swiftly withdrew his hand.

This occurred over the course of a mere second, however, as Henrietta's chief concern at the moment was Lady Fuddlesby. "Scandal? Please, you must tell me what the difficulty is."

While he told Miss Lanford the story, the duke's voice was gentle. "Lord Mawbly approached me last evening at Lady Chatterton's musicale. It seems Lady Fuddlesby agreed to sell him her pink tourmaline ring for a large sum of money. When the lady turned the ring over to him, Lord Mawbly recognized at once it was not a genuine stone, but paste."

Henrietta's mouth dropped open. She blinked and then composed herself enough to utter faintly, "Paste?"

"Yes. We can be grateful Lord Mawbly came to me, as a friend of his family, to help sort through this dilemma."

Henrietta experienced a flash of displeasure at the mention of a close relationship between Winterton's family and Clorinda's. Hastily she brushed the thought aside. Now was not the time to be dwelling on such things. Her aunt had deceived a peer of the realm!

The duke interrupted her thoughts. "I have Lord Mawbly's promise not to repeat the tale to anyone, so on that head we may be easy. Colonel Colchester has been apprised of the matter and, naturally, is most anxious to set things right. I believe we might come to a resolution of the problem with your assistance, Miss Lanford."

Henrietta looked at him helplessly. "What can I do? I know the ring you are speaking of, but confess I am confused. Lady Fuddlesby once told me the story of the ring. Viscount Fuddlesby brought it back for her from Russia early in their marriage, and it was deemed quite valuable."

A breeze from the river ruffled the duke's dark hair. He was quiet for a moment, and when he spoke it was as if he was thinking out loud. "So Lady Fuddlesby decided to sell Lord Mawbly the ring for some unknown reason—money is the usual motivation for selling one's jewelry—perhaps believing her husband's assertion the ring was valuable, not knowing the stone was paste."

"Oh!" Henrietta said, and gasped, her blue eyes round with distress. Her thoughts chased after one another like kittens in a basket. "Your Grace, I believe it is all because of me that Lady Fuddlesby decided to sell her ring!"

The duke looked at her skeptically and said, "Because of you? Why?"

"You see, I have perceived Lady Fuddlesby is short of funds. Then, yesterday, she told me she plans to hold a ball in my honor. When I mentioned such an entertainment would be costly, she replied she had just received money from Lord . . . There she broke off and changed the conversation, but it is an easy deduction now to realize she was about to say Lord *Mawbly*."

Henrietta's eyes filled with tears as she thought of her aunt's sacrifice. She continued miserably, "That would explain why she did it. But she cannot have meant to sell Lord Mawbly anything but a genuine stone."

The duke removed a clean handkerchief from his coat pocket and handed it to the distressed girl. "You must not hold yourself responsible for what Lady Fuddlesby decides to do with her money, or in this case, about her lack of it. And I know your aunt would never do anything deliberately deceitful. It is a devil of a business, Miss Lanford, but we shall come about."

Henrietta dried her eyes and blew her nose, then looked at the ruined handkerchief ruefully. "I shall return this to you after it is laundered, Your Grace." She placed the handkerchief in her reticule. "In the meantime, I shall discreetly find out what I can."

"There!" he responded bracingly. "An excellent plan, my co-conspirator." The duke's expression betrayed a spark of mischief. "And while you feel you were hoaxed into thinking me a man with superior intelligence, I now *know* you to be a woman who could boast of that virtue."

A gurgle of laughter reluctantly escaped from Henrietta's lips. Pretending to have taken offense at his compliment, she retorted, "Oh, Your Grace! A lady is not supposed to be intelligent at all, no less boast of superiority of the attribute."

The Duke of Winterton chuckled appreciatively at this sally before calling to Jeffers. When the man took his position on the backstrap, the duke guided the carriage back through the park to Grosvenor Square.

During this time, he maintained a trivial conversation consisting of *bon mots* intended to soothe Miss Lanford's frayed nerves. All the while, he contemplated her pretty countenance.

Even with her nose pinkened from her earlier distress, she appealed to him as no other lady had. He'd felt ridiculously lighthearted when she had not proclaimed love as the reason for her betrothal to Lord Baddick.

He shifted uneasily. Witch! He was back under her magical spell. Then he thought with horror that he had not been out from under it since he'd tasted her lips. Fighting an overwhelming need to be close to her, he put as much distance as possible between them on the curricle seat.

Upon calmer reflection, he could not help but be impressed with Miss Lanford's sensible approach to her aunt's predicament. Once again, under adverse circumstances she had been overset, but had displayed a calm rationality instead of falling into strong convulsions.

Her concern for her aunt's feelings did her credit, and her distress over what she perceived to be her own part in the contretemps showed an unselfish nature. He could not deny she was everything she should be.

Except of his station in life.

The Duke of Winterton and Henrietta returned to Lady Fuddlesby's to find the house in an uproar.

Chuffley hastened them upstairs to the drawing room, muttering incoherently about kidnappers. He flung open the double doors, and a striking tableau met their eyes.

Lady Fuddlesby, reclining on the brocade sofa, sobbed into a lace handkerchief. Colonel Colchester stood over her, patting her hand ineffectively. Felice hovered nearby, holding a vinaigrette at the ready. To one side of the startling scene, Mrs. Pottsworth was delivering a blistering scold to a frightened maid who looked to be no more than four and ten.

"Good God! What is going on here?" the duke's voice exploded over the commotion.

As one, the gathering fell quiet and turned to look at him.

Lady Fuddlesby paused in her crying long enough to wail, "Henrietta, my dear, 'tis monstrous. Bless me! I shall soon be put to bed with a shovel."

Henrietta's hand went to her throat. Could the sale of the paste ring already have caused a scandal? Was that why her ladyship had fallen into a fit of the vapors? "Dearest Aunt, never say so. What can have occurred to cause you to feel near death?"

But Lady Fuddlesby's cries and moans gave no answer. Instead, the colonel straightened and, in a halting voice, addressed them. "Ahem, it seems our brave soldier has been . . . er . . . abducted."

Both the duke and Henrietta appeared thunder-struck.

"Soldier? What curst soldier?" the duke asked, exasperated.

"Was there ever a woman tormented so!" howled Lady Fuddlesby before anyone else could reply. She glared at the duke through tear-filled, swollen eyes and said, "My darling boy, Knight, of course."

A look of disgust crossed the duke's handsome features. "You mean all this racket is over a cat?"

Unfeeling man, Henrietta thought before she quickly stepped into the outraged silence this question produced. "My lady, do you mean to say someone has kidnapped Knight?" she asked with disbelief.

"Oh, my dear, precious boy. Gone in the hands of villains. Whatever am I to do?" her ladyship bemoaned. Her crying continued in earnest, and Felice hurried over to attend her mistress.

Colonel Colchester approached the duke and Henrietta. The gray-haired gentleman's face was lined with concern. He spoke in a low voice designed not to reach her ladyship's ears.

"Lady Fuddlesby and I were enjoying a comfortable cup of tea when Mrs. Pottsworth entered the room with the tweeny and told us the events which had transpired moments before. It seems they were in the kitchen going about their duties when there was a knock at the area door. The tweeny answered it, and says a burly man stood there with a child. He said his son had been bitten by a black and white cat, which had then raced down the stairs to this house."

Henrietta interrupted the colonel to exclaim, "But it could not have been Knight. He never goes out. Lady Fuddlesby is too afraid he will cross the street and be run over by a carriage."

The colonel nodded his head. "Yes, Miss Lanford. But the tweeny is probably ignorant of that fact, and I suspect too shy to question her elders. The man asked if a black and white cat lived here and, when the tweeny answered positively, demanded to see the animal so it could be identified as the culprit. Evidently Knight was in the kitchens at the time, and the tweeny easily coaxed him near the doorway with a bit of chicken. As soon as the cat was in sight, the man lunged forward and clamped a cloth over Knight's face. The animal instantly collapsed, and the villain scooped him up and stuffed him into a burlap sack. They ran off before the tweeny could even scream."

"Poor Knight. How frightened he must be," Henrietta said, horrified.

"This is preposterous," the duke protested. "Why would anyone want to steal a cat? There are hundreds of them to be had wandering the streets."

Henrietta's eyes widened when a frightening thought struck her. She wrung her hands together and said, "They wanted Knight specifically. Someone must want to hurt him. Who would be cruel enough to want to harm an innocent cat?"

The Duke of Winterton's expression turned cold and calculating. "I can think of someone cruel, and more importantly, *cowardly* enough. And this person would perceive he has a grudge against the animal and you."

Henrietta started forward, clutching the duke's sleeve. "You cannot mean Lord Baddick," she whispered in a shaking voice.

The duke looked at her with admiration. "A superior intelligence, Miss Lanford," he murmured for her ears alone. Aloud he said, "As unimaginable as it seems, it could only be the viscount. I should guess he unwisely did not leave England as I instructed him, but has instead been spending his time brooding over his defeat at the hands ... or should I say paws, of Knight. Furthermore, the viscount must be aware of how much the cat is revered."

"What are you saying, Giles?" the colonel asked gruffly.

"Sir, Baddick thought of a petty means of revenge on this household. One that would not require his dirtying his own hands, but could be carried out by a servant. Before I arrived on the scene the night of his unwelcome advances toward Miss Lanford, Baddick's attempts had been waylaid by the cat. Indeed, the man's face, neck, and hands were badly scratched. I merely finished the job of trouncing the viscount that Knight began," the duke concluded.

The colonel was skeptical. "Lord Baddick would have to be a complete nodcock to employ such a scheme as kidnapping an animal for revenge."

"That is precisely what he is. That and more," Winterton added. "I agree the scheme is ridiculous, but it fits the viscount. And Miss Lanford is correct. Someone wished to hurt Knight in particular, not just any cat. Since we cannot think of any other suspects, the conclusion must be the villain is Lord Baddick. When I catch up with him, the viscount will find my threats are not to be taken lightly," he ended, his voice harsh with menace.

"Chuffley." The duke called the butler to his side. "Send a footman around to Viscount Baddick's town house and find out if he is in residence there, or at his estate in the country. Have the servant run. I need the answer immediately."

"Yes, Your Grace," the old butler answered, and scurried out of the room, obviously pleased to be of help.

The colonel rubbed the back of his neck with his hand. "What's your plan of action, Giles?"

"First, let us question the tweeny," the duke replied.

"Allow me, Your Grace," Henrietta begged. "She is young and overset. You might be too intimidating."

At the duke's nod, Henrietta walked over to the tweeny and spoke to her softly. She did not learn anything different from the colonel's report, but put an arm around the frightened girl and assured her she was not at fault. Mrs. Pottsworth appeared relieved at this and ceased her scolding.

From her position on the brocade sofa, Lady

Fuddlesby drew attention to herself. "I demand to know what you are all standing about discussing. We should be organizing a search party."

Once again, the duke took command. "Lady Fuddlesby, we have surmised that someone wanted to take Knight specifically. It was not just a random act."

Her ladyship gasped, and accepted a vinaigrette from Felice.

The tweeny threw her apron over her head and burst into fresh tears. Mrs. Pottsworth exclaimed, "Why would anyone steal Knight?"

"Why, indeed? It ees incomprehensible," Felice said with a moue of distaste.

Colonel Colchester walked over to Lady Fuddlesby's side and took her hand in his. "Take heart. We believe we know who the dastard is, and that will make our task more simple."

Lady Fuddlesby pushed herself up into a sitting position, a martial light coming into her pale blue eyes. "Who did it? Tell me at once."

"Lord Baddick," the colonel answered.

Lady Fuddlesby's hands flew to her chest. "What!"

The duke said, "We believe Lord Baddick would be small-minded enough to find kidnapping a cat a measure of revenge after his foiled plans for your niece."

Henrietta hung her head in shame.

Lady Fuddlesby whimpered, "But that evil man will have drowned poor Knight by now."

Winterton's mouth pursed into a thin line. "I think the viscount too shrewd to have one of his servants destroy the animal in Town, where he might be observed, and the deed traced back to Baddick. Through riding with you in the park,

Lady Fuddlesby, Knight is rather well known. The man most likely has orders to merely bring the cat to Baddick, then the viscount will have another servant who does not know where the cat came from dispose of it. But not if I can help it," he added quickly at Lady Fuddlesby's choked sob.

Henrietta's chin came up. "And I." At the duke's raised eyebrow she asserted with conviction, "You cannot think I mean to be left out of this."

The duke eyed her as if she were a tiresome child. "Don't be silly, Miss Lanford. The colonel and I shall go after Baddick and the cat."

His godfather cut off this line of thinking at once. After glancing at Lady Fuddlesby meaningfully, the colonel turned back to the duke and said, "I am needed here, Giles. You will be able to handle the matter." A wily look came into the older man's eyes. "And I believe you will need Miss Lanford's aid once you catch up with Knight. She should go with you."

Winterton was unconvinced. "I fail to see what Miss Lanford can do but slow me down."

Henrietta's eyes flashed fire, and she glared at the duke. "When we find him, Knight will certainly not come to you, Your Grace, but he will come to me." Her voice took on a sarcastic tone. "How do you propose to wrestle an unwilling feline from his captors?"

The duke had no answer, so he glared back frostily at the girl.

Lady Fuddlesby held up her hands. "Stop this arguing. You have your tiger with you, do you not, Your Grace? So the proprieties can be satisfied. Only bring back my darling boy to his home where he belongs!"

At that moment Chuffley entered the room after

a brief knock. "Your Grace, the footman has returned from Viscount Baddick's town house. He received the intelligence his lordship is at his estate."

"Excellent work, Chuffley," the duke said tersely.

Colonel Colchester queried, "Giles, won't the viscount's servants ride ahead and warn him you have inquired into his whereabouts? I would think, after you threatened his life, the man would leave instructions to be notified at once of any questions posed by you or Lady Fuddlesby."

"You most likely have the right of it, sir. But it can make no difference to our plans. If you are ready, Miss Lanford?"

"I am," Henrietta responded firmly. She rushed across to her aunt's side. "Dear Aunt, please try to calm yourself. We will leave no stone unturned to retrieve Knight. And perhaps Lord Baddick does not mean to harm Knight, only take him away from us."

Lady Fuddlesby shook her head slightly.

"Good luck to the both of you," the colonel said in farewell.

Kissing her aunt's cheek, Henrietta turned with a swirl of blue muslin skirts, and was out the door and down the front steps before the duke.

Winterton hurried after her and reached her side in time to assist her into the curricle. Shooting her a look that plainly spoke his displeasure at having her along on such a mission, he climbed up beside her and said, "You had best hold on, Miss Lanford. I intend to travel at a pace somewhat faster than our drive in the park."

"Do not concern yourself with my comfort, Your Grace. It is Knight that you should be thinking of," Henrietta said piously, wounded that he did not desire, nor think necessary, her company.

The duke gritted his teeth and they set off at a smart pace.

They were out of Town, and into the countryside, after driving for over an hour in maddening silence. Henrietta determined she would rather be the first to offer the olive branch than continue on in this manner. "Your Grace, when do you feel we should stop and inquire after them?"

Winterton twisted his lips in a cynical smile. "Tired and wishing for some refreshment already, Miss Lanford?"

Henrietta's good intentions fled. "I most certainly am not! I merely thought it would be prudent to ask if anyone had noticed a burly man carrying a sack."

"I have not stopped so far because they have had at least an hour and a half's start on us. We do not know if they broke their journey. More likely, the man is driving directly to Baddick's estate." The duke's tone was once again that of one addressing a recalcitrant child.

Henrietta shifted in her seat away from the infuriating duke to prevent her temper snapping. She recalled occasions in the past when she had let her emotions get the better of her, acting childishly and then later regretting it. She told herself she had matured beyond such behavior.

Henrietta praised herself again, a few minutes later, when she resisted the urge to make a scornful comment when the duke followed her suggestion and pulled into an inn yard.

He threw the reins to Jeffers and hurried inside without Henrietta to question the landlord. A bare minute passed before he returned. "They have seen nothing," he informed her.

She nodded her head in response and the pattern was repeated at four more inns along the road.

Three quarters of an hour later, Henrietta felt she must get down at the next inn and take care of an urgent personal need. In addition, something to drink would be welcome after all the dust from the road, but she would allow her tongue to swell up and turn black before admitting it to the stuffy duke. It was bad enough he would probably realize why she needed to go inside at the next stop, she thought, and blushed.

This stop proved to be a small hedge-tavern called the Nose of the Dog. Happily, Henrietta was spared embarrassment when the duke said, "We will partake of something to drink before moving on. I only hope the man who took Knight has not already reached Baddick's estate."

They walked inside the small establishment, and Henrietta immediately excused herself. When she returned a few minutes later, she found the duke seated at a table drinking wine. He stood at her appearance, and helped her to a seat.

"No luck, Miss Lanford. They have not seen them here either." He motioned to a serving woman carrying a jug of lemonade.

Henrietta bent her head, covering her eyes with her hands, and using the tips of her fingers to massage her forehead. She felt like crying. Her voice trembled when she said, "Oh, he is just a poor cat far from home, Your Grace. I fear he will not survive."

The serving woman finished pouring the drink and lowered the jug to the table. "You missin' a kitty? I seen a lost cat here, just a little while ago. Came to the back door and meowed like a banshee."

Henrietta dropped her hands and exclaimed, "Pray, what did he look like?"

"Big, 'e was, and strange lookin', too. 'Is face was masked, like some evil creature." The country woman shuddered and then continued, "I crossed myself before I threw 'im a fish 'ead."

The duke's commanding voice rang out in the small room, "Where is the animal now?"

The serving woman shrugged and picked up the jug. "Can't say, Your 'Onor. 'E gobbled up that fish 'ead and off 'e went down the London Road about a quarter of an hour ago."

Winterton threw some coins on the table, and Henrietta called out their thanks before they hurried out the door. Jeffers, lounging by a tree, saw them coming and ran to take his place behind them.

They drove down the road they had just come from. After about ten minutes the duke stopped the curricle and instructed the tiger to walk alongside the road and scan the bushes for any sign of the missing cat.

The little man jumped down. Winterton put the curricle in motion at a very slow pace and said crossly, "We probably passed the devil on the way somewhere. Knowing that cat, he probably grinned when he saw us go by."

Relief at the prospect of recovering Knight, as well as amusement at the duke's words, caused Henrietta to laugh out loud. "Oh, Your Grace, surely not. Knight would have welcomed a ride!" She chuckled and said, "Poor thing, having to resort to eating a fish head. I assure you he would not touch one at home."

"I believe you, Miss Lanford. I am familiar with the animal's penchant for culinary delights. Since we heard he was abducted in a burlap sack, I have frequently pitied the man who had to haul the obese monster away," Winterton said with a wry grin.

Henrietta gave him a look of mock reproach but giggled nonetheless.

Winterton stopped the curricle and gave a long-suffering sigh. "I see no sign of the animal. It might be best if I got down as well and walked. That way I can cover the other side of the road from Jeffers."

"What a good idea," Henrietta approved. "I shall drive while you and Jeffers walk."

Winterton eyed her skeptically. He inquired, "Do you know how to drive, Miss Lanford? Those are not ordinary country horses, as you rightly noted earlier today."

Affronted, Henrietta said curtly, "I admit I led a lonely childhood and that my parents largely ignored me. But my father did take the time to teach me how to handle the ribbons."

Passing her the reins, the duke studied her intently. He remembered the Lanfords' lack of interest in their daughter. Observing her stormy face, he said, "Miss Lanford, I, too, know what it is like to endure a solitary childhood. When I was growing up, no one besides my tutor had much time for me. My parents, especially my father, were cold, unfeeling people, terribly conscious of their great wealth and consequence."

Cross from the long drive and the duke's unloverlike treatment of her, Henrietta gazed directly into his gray eyes and said tartly, "Then you mean they are rather like yourself, Your Grace."

The truth always hurts. Surely for the first time in his life, the Duke of Winterton was struck speechless.

He sat there tall and angry. His features hardened, and his voice, when he finally spoke, was quiet and menacing. "You think me cold, do you?"

Before Henrietta knew what he was about, Winterton closed his fingers around her chin in a firm grasp. She stared into his furious eyes and her heart lurched madly.

Chapter Eleven

Swiftly he lowered his head. The kiss began as a warm persuasion, but rapidly progressed into an expression of passion long held in check.

Henrietta felt a surge of excitement. Winterton's firm mouth sent shivers through her, demanding a response, and she eagerly returned the pressure of his lips. Her gloved hand reached up tentatively to wind around the back of his neck, and her fingers caressed him, eliciting a low moan from the duke.

Jeffers's sharp cry interrupted the couple. "Your Grace! I've found the cat. He's hiding here underneath the hedgerow."

Winterton raised his head. For a long moment he stared bemusedly down into Miss Lanford's wide eyes, noting her sweetly curved lips were still moist from his kiss.

A gentleman did not kiss a gently bred miss unless his intentions were honorable. Severely chastising himself for his folly, he snatched his hand away from her chin. While he was no rake, Winterton knew his plans for the future could not include the squire's daughter, no matter how tempting the little baggage was. He was behaving abominably by kissing her.

The realization left him feeling decidedly blue-deviled. Placing the reins into her hands, he jumped down from the curricle, muttering, "Devil take all women . . . and cats."

Henrietta watched the duke stride up the dusty road toward Jeffers, who was kneeling before the tall hedgerow. She sat shaken for a moment. The numb feeling gradually crystallized into mortification when she thought about her wanton response to the duke's kiss. Surely no lady behaved thus.

But how like him not to proclaim any affection for her, she fumed silently. Her brows drew together. Perhaps his condemnation stemmed from her bold return of his kiss. She considered the matter and decided the man had no finer feelings. She had been correct in her assessment of his character when she compared him to the parents he described as cold. The wretch!

Bringing herself back to the matter at hand, Henrietta urged the horses down the lane a short ways to where the duke stood next to his tiger, peering into the bushes. "Where is Knight, Jeffers?" she addressed the servant, ignoring Winterton.

" 'E's crouched in 'ere, miss, and won't come out."

"Come here then and take the reins so I can fetch him," Henrietta responded.

Winterton turned an icy gaze on her. "I do not need your help, Miss Lanford. The animal is merely stubborn, but I shall prevail."

"Being more stubborn yourself," Henrietta said softly.

"What did you say?" the duke asked her, his eyes narrowed.

"Nothing, Your Grace," she replied demurely. Raising her voice, she called, "Knight, come along now, and we will go home."

There was no response from the hedgerow.

"I'll go in and get 'im, Your Grace," Jeffers offered.

"By the heavens, you will not," the duke stated grimly. "See to the horses. I shall retrieve the feline beast myself."

He stripped off his acorn-brown coat and handed it, along with his hat, to the tiger. Pulling on his York tan driving gloves, the duke bent and again peered into the recesses of the hedgerow.

Knight sat hunched, wide-eyed and alert to his strange surroundings. Winterton moved forward, reaching for the cat. Knight shrank back out of his reach. The duke lunged for him, muttering curses, and the cat turned, scurried through the bush, and ran out into a farmer's field, much to the surprise of a grazing cow.

"Knight!" Henrietta cried, half standing in the curricle in an effort to see over the hedgerow.

Perceiving a gap in the bushes, the duke pressed his way through and into the field, dislodging a blackbird who shrieked in protest.

A few minutes later, like a ball being shot out of a cannon, Knight careened through the same gap, ran down the lane, and with a flying leap, landed on the floor of the curricle. He hopped up on the seat beside Henrietta and, scarcely taking a minute to catch his breath, began washing his paws with his pink tongue, his attitude one of total nonchalance.

Henrietta hugged him close for a moment, then petted his white back, removing a small leaf stuck to his fur.

"All's right and tight now, miss," Jeffers ventured, and chuckled. Abruptly he fell silent, and his face became wooden.

Looking up to see the cause of the little man's discomfort, Henrietta could only stare.

The proud Duke of Winterton stood outside the hedgerow, gazing wrathfully down his nose at the occupants of the curricle. His fine cambric shirt had numerous small tears in it, as did his buff pantaloons, from the spiny shoots and thorns of the hawthorn. His cravat was half-untied. Dust and scratches covered his normally gleaming Hessian boots. A lone white flower hung from his dark hair over one ear.

From the glowering expression on his face, Henrietta knew she must not laugh. A choking sound escaped from her, and she struggled for control.

Jeffers wordlessly handed his master his coat and hat.

The picture the duke presented shrugging on the immaculate coat over his disheveled clothing was almost Henrietta's undoing. The hat dislodged the flower, and it floated to the ground mercifully unnoticed by Winterton when he climbed up into the curricle.

Taking up the reins, the duke looked thoughtfully into the distance. A moment passed and then he said, "I should like to make for Baddick's estate, but regretfully such a course would prove futile. Odds are, the viscount has been warned of our questions by his London servants, if the man who took Knight has not already given Baddick the news of the cat's escape."

"This time he will leave the country, will he not, Your Grace?" Henrietta asked hopefully.

"Yes. Baddick cannot be cork-brained enough to stay in England now." With a flick of the ribbons, the duke put the horses in motion.

Knight curled up on the seat between them and fell asleep.

Seeing the picture the girl and the animal presented, the duke decided they were a witch and a cat. With frustration in his voice, he said, "Much as I should relish making Baddick wish he had obeyed me before, I am not at liberty to pursue him at the moment. Rest assured, however, I shall make inquiries on the morrow to be certain he is gone."

Henrietta frowned. "Why do you say we are not at liberty to go after him now? I confess I should find Lord Baddick's humiliation gratifying after the misery he has caused my aunt this day."

"Bloodthirsty, Miss Lanford? I should like to see Viscount Baddick upon six men's shoulders myself, but I am afraid I cannot give in to such desires. No, I must escort you home before it grows dark and your reputation suffers," he informed her imperiously.

Insufferable man! "It is not my reputation you are troubled about, Your Grace," she told him briskly. "You are so accustomed to ladies throwing themselves at you, you fear a bride behind every tree! But you need not distress yourself on my account. I have no wish to be compromised by you, and pray you will convey Knight and me back to Grosvenor Square with all speed."

"An excellent plan, Miss Lanford."

Henrietta folded her hands together primly in her lap where they could not find their way about the duke's throat, and turned her gaze to the beauty of the English countryside.

At Viscount Baddick's estate, his lordship was in his bedchamber enjoying the charms of his latest ladybird.

After a while, his butler was finally able to impart the information a man waited downstairs to see him. Attired in a paisley dressing gown, Lord Baddick strolled into the hall where the burly man stood.

"Well, where's the blasted cat, McGrath?" Lord Baddick demanded.

"See 'ere, milord, you didn't say the cat was a wild animal. I gots 'im in the sack easy enough after I drugged 'im. But soon as 'e woke up there was a terrible yowling, then 'e started jumpin' around inside and rippin' the bag with them needlelike claws."

"Yes. His claws are sharp," the viscount murmured, one finger tracing a long scar running down the side of his face.

"I'm sorry to tell you, 'e got away," McGrath said nervously. When the master only nodded his head in dismissal, the man left the house quickly, happy to escape without punishment.

Lord Baddick shrugged the matter off. The cat's kidnapping and eventual death had only been a whim.

Intending to return to Lily's willing body, he began climbing the stairs, but was stopped by his butler. The servant's message caused the viscount's face to whiten around the red scar.

After giving lengthy instructions, Baddick returned to his bedchamber, flung open the door, and said, "Lily, my love, we are going to Paris!"

Knight's arrival home brought loud exclamations of joy from everyone, with the exception of Felice, who, while she was sorry her mistress had been made unhappy, had secretly looked forward to having her ladyship's clothing free of cat hair.

Lady Fuddlesby, holding Knight tightly in her arms, ordered Mrs. Pottsworth to prepare the cat a welcoming meal. "For he must have been too frightened to find anything to eat during his horrible ordeal, poor dear. Perhaps we can tempt him with a turbot and a dish of cream."

"Yes, milady. Come along, Knight," Mrs. Pottsworth called when Lady Fuddlesby released the cat onto the floor.

With amusement Henrietta noticed the cat's jaunty walk when he followed the cook out of the hall in the direction of the kitchens. For Knight's sake she decided it would not be prudent to mention the fish head he had devoured at the Nose of the Dog.

No one braved a remark on the Duke of Winterton's astonishing appearance. Instead, over a refreshing cup of tea in the drawing room, Lady Fuddlesby and Colonel Colchester listened without interrupting while the duke and Henrietta told the story of how they had found Knight.

Sitting on the brocade sofa, Henrietta sipped her tea gratefully. They had left the tavern before she had had time to drink her lemonade, and her throat felt parched.

Lady Fuddlesby and Colonel Colchester expressed their relief at having Knight home again. They praised Giles and Henrietta for their actions, both privately hoping the incident had served to bring the young people closer together.

The colonel was hard-pressed to restrain his amusement at the thought of his austere godson searching the hedgerows for a cat. It seemed the spirited Miss Lanford possessed the power to make Giles behave quite out of character. All to the good. When he had first arrived in London, the colonel

thought his godson seemed so stiff, he feared someone would mistake him for a corpse and bury him.

Having exhausted the discussion on Knight's return, the duke concluded by saying, "You may be
easy, Lady Fuddlesby, in that I shall be certain this
time Baddick has left the country."

"Oh, I do so thank you, Your Grace. I confess I
shall be very careful with Knight in the meantime.
Do you think I would be wise to hire a guard?"

Henrietta noted the duke's lips twitched before
he made his reply.

"I do not think you will be troubled again, my
lady. Now I must take my leave. I apologize for
staying as long as I have in all my dirt."

Colonel Colchester smiled warmly at Lady
Fuddlesby. "I should leave as well. May I call on
you tomorrow to see how you are faring?"

"You know you may, dear Colonel," Lady
Fuddlesby said as everyone rose. "Will we be seeing
you, Your Grace, before Henrietta's ball next week?
I daresay it will be the most grand affair of the
Season thus far. I have spared no expense."

Henrietta's startled gaze flew to the duke. Mention of the ball reminded her forcibly of the contretemps over the pink tourmaline ring. Surely the
duke had not forgotten they were to try to uncover
the truth and save Lady Fuddlesby from scandal.

His next words reassured her. "Actually, I hope
you and Miss Lanford will attend a small dinner
party I am holding in three days' time. I know it is
short notice, but pray you forgive me since the
gathering is impromptu."

Winterton's gaze found Henrietta's, and a silent
communication passed between them. She knew
the reason for the duke's invitation was so she

might share whatever information she learned regarding the ring.

Despite the long and harrowing day, Lady Fuddlesby beamed happily. "How delightful, Your Grace. Henrietta and I would be most pleased, will we not, my dear?"

Henrietta curtsied low, saying, "Yes, thank you, Your Grace. I shall look forward to speaking to you then."

The duke bowed, indicating with a slight nod he took Henrietta's meaning, and he and his godfather took their leave.

Afterward Lady Fuddlesby cried, "Oh, the duke is a genuine hero, rescuing Knight as he did." Her expression coy, Lady Fuddlesby declared, "He would make a splendid husband, dear."

Henrietta stared at her aunt, annoyed that the lady gave all the credit for Knight's return to the duke, ignoring her niece's contribution to the salvation of the cat.

"Who do you mean would make a splendid husband, my lady? The duke or Knight?" she retorted mockingly before excusing herself and sweeping from the room, leaving Lady Fuddlesby to chuckle at her niece's wit.

The next day, Henrietta endured her promised drive with Mr. Shire with a grim determination. The duke was correct, she judged when the country gentleman pontificated on the subject of the proper care of a mare ready to foal. Mr. Shire was a dull dog. Still, dullness might be preferable to stuffiness.

Trying to spare her maidenly ears any breeding terms resulted in a garbled conversation filled with significant pauses, while Mr. Shire unsuccessfully struggled to find an inoffensive word to replace the one he really needed for clarity.

Pulling the carriage to a halt outside the town house in Grosvenor Square, Mr. Shire surprised her by saying, "I shall be out of Town for a few days on a personal matter, Miss Lanford. Perhaps you might guess the nature of my task."

At Henrietta's blank countenance, he continued in his unexceptional way. "Well, my purpose will become clear to you at your ball. Lady Fuddlesby has been kind enough to extend me an invitation, and I am anxious to attend."

Henrietta could not take the time now to try to fathom Mr. Shire's words. The mystery of her aunt's ring demanded her attention.

Making her escape as quickly as possible, Henrietta entered the house. Seeing Chuffley in the hall, she asked, "Where is my aunt, Chuffley?"

The butler responded, "Her ladyship has gone out on calls, miss."

"Did she take Felice with her?"

"No, miss, Sally went along. I believe Felice is working on her ladyship's ball gown."

Thanking him, Henrietta ran up the stairs to her bedchamber. Quickly removing her hat and gloves, she hurried down to Lady Fuddlesby's apartments. Felice was just the person to help her find out about the pink tourmaline ring, and this was a perfect opportunity to question her since Lady Fuddlesby was out.

Henrietta found the abigail in Lady Fuddlesby's sitting room repairing a tear in the lace of a pale pink ball gown. Knight was curled up on a velvet cushion near the fireplace, apparently placed there for his use. Henrietta's eyebrows rose when she saw Felice and Knight in the same room. Since Knight usually left any room Felice occupied, Henrietta could only judge Knight's harrowing experience had left him a more tolerant cat.

Seeing her, the maid started to rise, but Henrietta said, "There is no need to get up, Felice."

"Her ladyship ees not here, mees," the Frenchwoman stated, sitting down and resuming her sewing.

Henrietta casually walked into the room to stand by the fireplace. "Is that the gown my aunt plans to wear for my ball?"

"Yes, mees."

"La, I would have thought she would commission Madame Dupre to make up a new gown," Henrietta said carelessly, hoping Felice might let slip some information about her ladyship's finances. Not that she considered Felice would be privy to details, but perhaps Lady Fuddlesby had muttered an aside in front of the maid about not being able to afford a new gown.

Felice pursed her lips and did not look up. "Thees gown will be as good as new once I have repaired the lace, mees, and looks very fine on her ladyship."

Henrietta frowned. Well, at least she knew Felice was not one for servants' gossip. Maybe a more direct approach was needed. Surely Felice knew the pink tourmaline ring was gone, since it would be her responsibility to maintain an account of Lady Fuddlesby's jewelry, as well as keeping the various items clean.

"I suppose Lady Fuddlesby will wear the pink tourmaline ring the late Viscount Fuddlesby gave her. It would be ideal with that gown," Henrietta said, watching Felice's reaction closely.

Felice sat very still for a moment, then shifted the gown and began setting tiny stitches on another part of the lace. "I do not know, mees. It ees possible."

Henrietta knew it was not possible since Lord Mawbly had the ring. Frustrated, she blurted, "Possible? Felice, I would like to examine the pink tourmaline ring, please. It . . . it fascinates me."

Felice glanced up, her sharp black eyes staring thoughtfully into Henrietta's face. Henrietta shrank back under the scrutiny, but to her amazement, the maid rose, put the dress aside, and moved over to Lady Fuddlesby's jewel case. She extracted a blue satin box and handed it to her.

Henrietta opened the case, and the pink stone winked in the afternoon sunlight. Disbelieving her own eyes, she stammered, "But this cannot be. . . . The duke said . . . Oh, I am confused."

The maid stood with her hands folded across her chest. "Mees Lanford, it ees time you, how do you say it? Ah, yes, cut line. What do you know about thees ring?"

It was obvious to Henrietta Felice knew more than she did, and would not divulge any information unless she was told the whole story. She believed the maid could be trusted, so she explained the duke's account of Lady Fuddlesby's sale of the ring to Lord Mawbly, and his lordship's assertion the stone was paste.

At the conclusion of the tale, Felice's sallow skin took on a ghostly shade, and she paced the room, muttering fearfully, *"Je ne sais quoi!* It ees all over now. To the gallows, they will take us. The hangman, the noose—"

Henrietta grabbed the woman by the shoulders and gave her a little shake. "Felice! Calm yourself and help me untangle this muddle. How can Lord

Mawbly have the pink tourmaline ring when I hold it in my hand?"

"A copy. Her ladyship charged me with obtaining a paste copy. My friend Monsieur Jacques made it. He did superb work." At Henrietta's look of confusion Felice explained, "You see, Lord Mawbly, he wants to buy the ring. But Lady Fuddlesby did not wish to sell it. Her husband had given it to her. So her ladyship decides she wants a paste copy she can keep to remember him. She sells the real ring because she needs the money for your ball—"

Felice stopped, hearing Henrietta's sharply indrawn breath. "*S'il vous plaît,* I should not have told you," the maid said anxiously.

"No, it is all right. I suspected Lady Fuddlesby sold the ring to pay for my ball." Henrietta bit her lip to keep from crying. That her aunt should make such a sacrifice for her! Her own parents would never forfeit anything they treasured to benefit their daughter.

She rubbed her hand across her forehead. "Felice, the only explanation is that somehow her ladyship switched the rings by accident."

Knight's head popped up from the cushion, his green eyes suddenly alert.

Henrietta paced the room, still holding the ring in her hand. "This must be the genuine stone since Lord Mawbly has the paste."

"But how could such a theeng happen? Her ladyship knew which ring was which. They were in deeferent-colored boxes," Felice exclaimed.

Knight slinked out of the room guiltily.

Henrietta distractedly noticed him go, then turned her attention to the maid. She shook her head dismissively. "It does not matter. We must contrive to switch the rings again, so that Lord

Mawbly ends with the genuine stone as he was meant to. I shall take this with me the night of the Duke of Winterton's dinner party. He can then make things right with Lord Mawbly."

Felice's dark eyes narrowed into a knowing look. "Ah, the duke ees to help you. He ees a virile man, no?"

Henrietta felt hot color rise to her cheeks. Ignoring the maid's remark, she said, "Bring the ring to me the evening of the dinner. I dare not keep it now, because my aunt might miss it. Should her ladyship notice its disappearance after the dinner before the duke and I can replace it, will you be able to give her some excuse?"

Felice frowned for a moment, then said, "Yes, mees. I can tell her Monsieur Jacques wanted to assure himself the stone was secure, or some such excuse. But do not worry. Lady Fuddlesby will not wear the fake in company, and I do not believe she ees taking the ring out every day."

Henrietta sighed with satisfaction. "Very well then." Looking closely at the abigail, she continued, "I know I can trust you not to repeat any of this, Felice."

The maid's back was ramrod-straight. "Yes, Mees Lanford."

"Thank you. As I have told you before, Felice, you are a treasure. And if you wish to please me, you will cease scolding yourself because you were sleeping the night of the unfortunate incident with Lord Baddick. It is in the past, and I assure you, I never think of it."

"You are very good, mees," Felice responded with open admiration for the girl.

Henrietta handed her the pink tourmaline ring and returned to her bedchamber. She wondered how the duke would react to the news of the ring switch. She allowed herself to picture his handsome face regarding her with high esteem when she presented her discovery and the genuine ring to him. Smiling, she found herself hardly able to wait for the days to pass so she could see him again, and they could solve Lady Fuddlesby's mishap with none being the wiser.

In the duke's bedchamber the evening of the dinner party, Tyler, very stiffly on his stiffs because of the appalling condition of the duke's clothing after his adventures in the countryside, helped his master into an evening coat of darkest blue.

In a corner of the room, Sir Polly Grey gnawed with contentment on a branch placed inside his cage for this purpose. He paused in his task to mutter in the seventh Duke of Winterton's voice, "Giles. An heir. Marriage."

Tyler pursed his lips at the parrot, and asked the duke in an oppressive tone, "What shall we wear in our cravat this evening, Your Grace? The ruby or the diamond?"

"You decide, Tyler. I shall be eclipsed by Lady Mawbly whatever I wear." The duke knew there was nothing that brought more satisfaction to the valet than when he deferred to his opinion on dress. It was the least Giles could do after the valet had fallen into a near faint at the sight of his soiled and scratched Hessians.

After selecting a large ruby pin and placing it artfully in the folds of the duke's cravat, Tyler took advantage of his master's complacent mood to offer another opinion. "I hear Lady Mawbly's daughter, Lady Clorinda, is a suitable girl. Will she be one of the party this evening?"

Sir Polly Grey's beak stilled. Black eyes alert, he cocked his head to one side in a listening manner.

The duke was not prepared to discuss the ladies of his acquaintance. "Yes, Lady Clorinda will be here with her parents. Where is the matching ruby ring, Tyler?"

While Tyler fussed with finishing touches, Winterton's thoughts turned to Miss Henrietta Lanford. He hoped she had gained useful information. Lord Mawbly, still in possession of the paste ring with his wife none the wiser, grew more anxious by the day. Giles had seen him at White's and had delivered his invitation to dine. The timid man had accepted, and beseeched him to bring the matter of the ring to a close before Lady Mawbly became suspicious.

Accepting a bottle of spicy scent from Tyler, the duke applied the lotion sparingly, then left the room to descend the stairs.

Arriving in the drawing room, he reflected the tedium he had experienced upon his arrival in Town had somehow vanished. He wondered what had occurred to bring new sparkle to his life, then brushed the puzzle aside.

His hand reached out to a bowl of red roses adorning a Chippendale table. Feeling a soft petal, Giles looked forward to crossing swords with the intriguing Miss Lanford.

He did not connect his acquaintance with the girl to the disappearance of his boredom.

Chapter Twelve

The first of the guests to arrive at the Duke of Winterton's dinner party were the Mawblys. Lady Mawbly, diamond and gold necklaces flashing against a bronze-colored dress, ushered her daughter into the drawing room.

The duke's eyebrows rose at the sight of Lady Clorinda, dressed in virginal white. The neckline of the girl's crepe gown rose to her throat. Her only jewelry was a proper set of pearl earbobs that peeked out from behind the demure golden curls arranged charmingly around her face.

Perhaps he had been too hasty in his conclusion that the lady was forward. Recalling his manners, Winterton greeted his guests while a footman offered glasses of wine. "Lady Mawbly, Lady Clorinda, I am happy to have you here this evening."

Lady Clorinda sank into a smooth curtsy. "Thank you, Your Grace. I am honored to be invited and must compliment you on your exquisitely tasteful home."

"Indeed, Your Grace. Everything is as it should be," interposed Lady Mawbly, her rabbity face fairly twitching with curiosity while she examined the costly contents of the drawing room.

The duke suppressed a grimace. Lady Mawbly

was an odious woman, but one he would have to tolerate if he wed her daughter. Clorinda's father, on the other hand, was a good sort of fellow, but in the duke's opinion needed to assert himself with his wife.

"Ah, Lord Mawbly, for a moment I thought the ladies had arrived without you."

Lord Mawbly trailed into the room looking hot and uncomfortable. "Good evening, Your Grace. If you please, I must speak—"

"Giles!" Matilda, Dowager Duchess of Winterton, interrupted, sailing into the room with Colonel Colchester. Dressed in regal purple, she served as the duke's hostess for the evening. "I captured Owen coming downstairs from his apartments, and tried to scold him for his tardiness in welcoming our guests. But the maddening man pointed out I was equally at fault."

The dowager duchess smiled teasingly at the handsome military man. Matilda had observed, with displeasure, the way the colonel had positively fawned over Clara Fuddlesby at Lady Chatterton's musicale. She considered the colonel her own territory because he had been a close friend of her husband for many years. A strong competitive nature made her determine to redirect the colonel's attention toward herself.

The colonel appeared puzzled over the lady's flirtatious manner, but indulgently played along.

Winterton strolled over to her side, raised her gloved hand, and gave it a brief kiss. "You look attractive in purple, Mother. It suits you. Good evening, Colonel."

"Going to be a deuced fine party, my boy. Hope we get that information we need," his godfather responded with a significant look at his godson.

Matilda rapped the colonel's arm with her fan. "Information? Pshaw! You gentlemen and your business dealings. This is a party. Remember we are here to enjoy ourselves."

The duke's elderly butler, Prestwich, shuffled into the room and announced in a feeble voice, "Lord Sebastian and Sir Thomas Martin."

"Hallo, everyone," the affable Sir Tommy called out. He bowed to the ladies, allowing them a view of his balding head.

The duke gave a brief nod to Lord Sebastian, who moved away to greet the dowager. Winterton shook hands with his friend Sir Tommy, giving him a reproachful glance over his arrival with the aging dandy, Lord Sebastian. "Tommy, I have not had the pleasure of seeing you since Almack's opening night."

Sir Tommy looked rueful. In low voice he said, "Sorry, old fellow, but your mother needed another gentleman to make up the numbers, and told me to bring a friend. Sebbie was the best I could do on short notice, especially when there's a cyprians' ball tonight."

The duke chuckled. "Forgive me, Tommy, for keeping you from choosing your next *chère amie*."

Ignoring the taunt, Sir Tommy said, "Don't get on your high ropes over Sebbie. He may be a rattle, but he's inoffensive enough, and besides, he's togged out to the nines."

Turning to Lord Sebastian, the duke saw he wore an exceptionally well cut cornflower-blue coat. The gentleman appeared acquainted with the Mawblys, and they had moved over by the fireplace and were chatting amiably.

Out of the corner of his eye Winterton thought he saw Lord Mawbly signal to him, but at that moment Prestwich announced, "Lady Fuddlesby and Miss Henrietta Lanford."

All eyes turned to the new arrivals. Lady Fuddlesby, in burgundy silk, nodded to the company and made as if to join the colonel, who had smiled at her entrance.

Standing beside the colonel, Matilda gave Clara a chilly nod, then laid a possessive hand on the military man's arm and resumed their conversation as if Lady Fuddlesby did not exist.

Lady Fuddlesby stopped short, a crestfallen expression on her round face. Perturbed at Matilda's slight and hurt by the colonel's seeming unconcern, her ladyship remained where she was, at her niece's side.

Henrietta was dressed in an ivory satin gown trimmed with violets. White gloves covered her arms to just below the puffed sleeves of the gown. Silk violets adorned her dark, glossy curls, and a dainty necklace of amethysts circled her slim neck.

Henrietta hoped she was not staring. The duke's town house was the epitome of elegance, the classically inspired furnishings done in blue and gold understated in their resplendence. The grandeur overwhelmed and intimidated Henrietta, but she squared her shoulders against the prying eyes of the gathering.

The duke excused himself to Sir Tommy and crossed the room to the ladies, unaware of Clorinda's jealous gaze boring into his back. "Lady Fuddlesby, Miss Lanford, you both look lovely this evening."

Dropping a deep curtsy, Henrietta said, "Thank you, Your Grace. My aunt and I are delighted to be your guests." Surely she imagined that he held her hand overlong when she rose from her curtsy.

The duke led them over to Sir Tommy and performed the introductions.

Lady Fuddlesby nodded at the young man distractedly, her attention riveted by the disgraceful way her old rival, Matilda, was flirting with the colonel.

Sir Tommy ran his gaze over Henrietta. "By Jupiter, Miss Lanford, I am pleased to meet you. Remember you from the opening night at Almack's. Prettiest gel there in your silver gown. Wanted an introduction, but had to toddle off early."

Henrietta liked the tall, friendly Sir Tommy at once, although the mention of Almack's brought a blush to her cheeks because she remembered her embarrassing behavior that night. She was sure the congenial young man could have no notion her vouchers to Almack's had been withdrawn after that night. "You are kind, Sir Tommy."

Turning her head so she might address a remark to the duke, Henrietta was taken aback by the look of warning Winterton was giving his friend. Almost as if he thought Sir Tommy's comments toward her overwarm. Looking back at Sir Tommy, Henrietta was further perplexed when she caught a wide, knowing grin on the gentleman's face.

She had no time to contemplate the strange exchange between the men, for just then a footman opened one of the drawing room's double doors holding a tray of glasses in his hand. Henrietta watched, astonished, when Sir Polly Grey flew over the servant's head, into the room, to land on a Greek bust from where he peered at the company curiously.

"Giles!" Matilda shrieked, causing instant silence in the room. "Get that creature out of here at once."

Lady Fuddlesby bristled. "Oh, Matilda, you always were a silly creature. 'Tis just the duke's jolly little parrot, not a dragon come to breathe fire on you until you are burnt to ashes."

Henrietta's eyes opened wide at her aunt's harsh statement, which almost sounded like her ladyship wished the dragon might appear. With a sniff, the dowager duchess ignored Lady Fuddlesby's remarks, turning to the colonel for support.

Colonel Colchester spoke to Matilda quietly, further infuriating Lady Fuddlesby, who picked up a glass of wine from the tray and drank its contents in one gulp.

A rather stout man with graying brown hair and numerous fobs hanging from his waistcoat rose from his seat by the fire and said, "I'faith, Duke, does the bird speak? If so, mayhaps it could tell me who the charming ladies are at your side."

Henrietta detected the duke's hesitation before he spoke. "Lord Sebastian, may I present Lady Fuddlesby and Miss Henrietta Lanford?"

Henrietta curtsied to a smiling Lord Sebastian, and acknowledged the Mawblys, who had also risen.

Lord Sebastian raised his quizzing glass and eyed both ladies appreciatively.

Next to Lord Sebastian, Lady Clorinda and Lady Mawbly had identical looks of distaste. Lady Mawbly whined, "Your Grace, can you please have that bird removed before my nerves become overset?"

The footman had set his tray down and was trying to capture Sir Polly Grey. When the servant pounced on him, the bird panicked and flew to the other side of the room, causing more uneasiness among the ladies. A stray feather floated down to land in Lady Mawbly's wine, causing the woman to let out an ear-piercing shriek before the footman rushed to replace the glass.

The duke walked determinedly toward where Sir Polly Grey had landed on the back of a blue satin settee. "Sir Polly, come here at once."

Winterton held out his hand in the manner of a perch, but the parrot disregarded the command. Instead, his black eyes fixed on Henrietta.

Henrietta moved to stand next to the duke. "La, Sir Polly Grey, how wonderful to see you again. However do you manage to get out of your cage? You must be the most intelligent bird I have ever known."

Sir Polly Grey left the settee to fly in Henrietta's direction. Quickly she placed her reticule on a table and raised her gloved hand. The parrot landed on it with a happy squawk.

Matilda said derisively, "Miss Lanford, how fortunate we are that despicable bird is attracted to you. Since you have been clever enough to charm him, now he can be returned to his cage without delay."

But when the duke reached for Sir Polly, intending to take him upstairs, the bird shrank away from him, fluttering its wings as if it would fly away at the duke's touch.

Winterton heaved an exasperated sigh. "Very well, Sir Polly, Miss Lanford will take you upstairs. You do not mind, do you, Miss Lanford? Prestwich, escort Miss Lanford to Sir Polly Grey's cage."

Perceiving an opportunity to speak to the duke privately about Lady Fuddlesby's ring, Henrietta said, "Your Grace, will you accompany the butler and me? I fear Sir Polly may prove troublesome on the stairs, and I would be glad of your assistance."

Lord Mawbly startled the company by hurriedly saying, "I shall join you."

His wife's incredulous expression and words stopped him. "Silias! Don't be nonsensical. The duke and Miss Lanford will be chaperoned by his butler. They do not require your presence."

Lord Mawbly sat miserably on a gold and blue striped chair.

Henrietta, talking softly to Sir Polly, left the room with Winterton and the butler.

As she looked after them, Lady Clorinda's lips formed into a petulant pout. Here she was, dressed in a gown that looked as if it belonged to a Methodist, and the first thing Winterton did was leave the room with that country nobody.

When her more revealing ensembles had failed to bring the duke up to scratch, she had felt a change in tactics was in order. Encouraged by his invitation to dine, which she felt indicated the duke's desire for her to approve his home, she and her mama had concocted the plan of covering her voluptuous assets. Their hope was that, denied the pleasure of viewing her charms, the duke would offer for Lady Clorinda in order to obtain them.

Clorinda's green eyes narrowed in rage while she remembered how the duke had kissed Henrietta's hand at the musicale. Heaven only knew what they were doing upstairs. Dismissing the thought, she decided that it was all for the best if the duke wanted to carry on a last flirtation before they were married.

Tugging irritably at the dress's high bodice, Clorinda went to sit next to her mother, giving the lady a sharp set-down for her stupid advice regarding her dress.

Now seated on a gold satin settee, Matilda continued to monopolize the colonel, leaving him no chance to associate with Lady Fuddlesby.

Her ladyship was consuming large quantities of wine. Lord Sebastian approached her and flirted expertly. "Are you bringing Miss Lanford out this Season, Lady Fuddlesby?"

Smiling at him coyly, all the while sneaking glances at the colonel to see his reaction to her new courtier, Lady Fuddlesby answered, "Why, yes, I am. We have been run ragged with entertainments these past weeks."

"It must be a difficult task for you when the two of you are so close in age. I cannot imagine a lady as beautiful as yourself sitting with the chaperons," Lord Sebastian replied gallantly.

Lady Fuddlesby ignored the suspicion Lord Sebastian, or Sebbie as he begged her to call him, resorted to the paint pot, and flirted with him over her fan.

Upstairs, Henrietta and the duke entered his bedchamber. Prestwich stood at attention in the doorway.

Winterton hurried ahead of her, opening the door to a large cage standing in one corner. Henrietta scratched Sir Polly Grey's head, much to the bird's contentment, and popped him into his cage without any trouble.

Jumping from perch to perch, Sir Polly proclaimed gleefully in the seventh Duke of Winterton's voice, "Giles. A suitable gel."

Henrietta's mouth dropped open in an unladylike manner. "He spoke! Sir Polly Grey can talk!"

The duke smiled grimly. "Yes, much as I wish he could not."

"But what did he mean? And that cultured voice. It sounded like that of a grand old man." She turned to gaze at the amazing parrot.

The bird fell mercifully silent and began eating seeds like an ordinary member of the avian family.

The duke fingered the ruby pin nestled in his cravat. "Er, never mind, Miss Lanford. Tell me, have you learned anything about the ring?"

"Oh, you could never imagine it, Your Grace," Henrietta began eagerly. "Lady Fuddlesby had a paste *copy* made of her pink tourmaline ring. She intended to keep it for sentimental reasons, selling the genuine ring, which is quite valuable, I suppose, to Lord Mawbly."

"Good God," uttered the duke. "How did you find this out?"

"Her ladyship's maid, Felice, had the copy made, and she told me everything. Somehow, before Lady Fuddlesby turned the ring over to Lord Mawbly, the paste and the genuine rings were switched." Henrietta lowered her head. "My assumption her ladyship sold the ring in order to pay for my ball proved to be correct."

The duke reached out a hand, and his fingers raised her chin. "Remember, it was Lady Fuddlesby's decision. She obviously cares for you a great deal and will enjoy holding the entertainment in your honor."

Henrietta looked up at him uncertainly. "I guess you are right, but I cannot help feeling as though I do not deserve such a sacrifice on Lady Fuddlesby's part. She has been so kind to me already."

"It is not for you to determine whether or not you deserve it, Miss Lanford." Dropping his hand to his side, the duke said, "Come, every pretty young miss must have her own ball. Now all we must do is contrive to end this muddle with the rings by switching them back again."

Henrietta reached for her reticule, saying, "I

brought the genuine ring with me. Oh, goodness, I left it in my reticule downstairs."

"No matter. Lord Mawbly will have to bring me the paste before we can carry out the switch," the duke pronounced.

Disappointed, Henrietta cried, "I thought Lord Mawbly had already given it to you and we could make the exchange tonight. I dare not leave the genuine ring with you, lest Lady Fuddlesby notice its disappearance before I can replace it with the paste."

The duke ran a hand through his dark hair. "In that case, you must keep the real stone until I can secure the paste from Mawbly. I shall call on you when I have it. We must return downstairs before our lengthy absence causes comment."

Henrietta suddenly became acutely aware of where she was. Before, her concentration had been on Sir Polly, and then the contretemps with the ring. Now the massive bed with its dark red velvet hangings loomed in front of her. Unbidden, an image of the duke reclining on the velvet bedspread with his arms outstretched to her appeared in her imagination. She felt intense heat rush to her cheeks at the improper vision.

The duke took her arm, and Henrietta was half-disappointed when he led her toward the door. They walked with Prestwich downstairs to the drawing room.

Entering the room, Henrietta noticed her aunt flirting with Lord Sebastian. Upon closer inspection of the scene, she decided Lady Fuddlesby's face looked flushed, and she was giggling like a young girl.

Frowning, Henrietta started to cross the room to

her aunt's side when dinner was announced. Sir Tommy appeared at her side to lead her in.

"Not the thing for me to say, Miss Lanford, but you look a caring sort of person. Appears your aunt is a trifle foxed. Been tippling the wine while you were upstairs with Winterton. No need to become alarmed, though, she's safe with Sebbie. Cares too much for his clothes, Sebbie does, but he's a right 'un."

"Thank you, Sir Tommy. My aunt does not usually take more than a glass of wine. I fear she is upset this evening, and I appreciate your concern."

Henrietta thought the dining room a miracle of gleaming wood, hothouse flowers, crystal chandeliers, and luxurious plate. Sections had been taken out of a table she imagined could fill the large room, but now seated the ten people comfortably.

Sir Tommy held out a chair, and Henrietta seated herself. An impressive silver epergne depicting cherubs holding fruits stood in the middle of the table, partially blocking Henrietta's view of the other guests down the table.

Lord Sebastian sat on her right and Sir Tommy on her left. She noticed the duke sat at one end of the table and Matilda at the other. Happily, Lady Fuddlesby sat on the duke's left, with the colonel beside her. Perhaps the colonel would have an opportunity to redeem himself.

Footmen stood behind each guest's chair, the duke not following the trend in some houses for the dishes to be placed upon the table, and passed from person to person. Henrietta quietly thanked a footman who served her with turtle soup and filled her wineglass.

She heard her aunt's voice, louder than usual, addressing the duke. "Thank you, Your Grace,

Knight has indeed recovered from his ordeal. I have been thinking how wonderful it would be to commission Thomas Lawrence to paint the little dear's portrait. You know I dote on Knight more than any *male* in the world."

Lady Fuddlesby had partially turned her back to the colonel, sitting next to her, but this remark was obviously intended for his ears. The military man shifted in his chair, ill at ease.

Henrietta could not hear what the duke replied to her ladyship's declaration.

Lady Clorinda, sitting across from Henrietta, shot her a nasty look while she said to Colonel Colchester, "I am afraid I cannot admire cats, sir, although I believe Lady Fuddlesby's animal must be superior."

The colonel paid her no heed since he was busy trying to get Lady Fuddlesby's attention. Her ladyship refused to acknowledge him.

Clorinda turned away to speak to her father, seated at her left. Lord Mawbly's brow was damp and his face flushed. Every few moments he glanced down the table to where his wife sat next to the duke.

Henrietta decided she was neglecting her own table partners, and turned to Lord Sebastian on her right. "My lord, your coat is a handsome shade of blue."

Lord Sebastian's face brightened. Compliments on his dress were sure to endear the speaker to him. "Devilish good of you to say so, Miss Lanford, and while I agree with you, I must tell you the shade is not nearly as ravishing as the blue of your eyes."

Henrietta stiffened, then chided herself for her reaction. Lord Sebastian's comment was surely a harmless flirtation. She was just not the sort who could play the coquette, and her experience with Lord Baddick's practiced phrases had left her wary.

After a moment she was able to reply calmly, "Thank you, my lord. Are you in Town for the Season or do you reside in London year round?"

They conversed amiably about the merits of Town life, and Henrietta discovered Lord Sebastian was the rare dandy who also enjoyed spending time in the country. During their talk, she found her gaze drifting frequently to his lordship's cravat where an unusually ugly pin rested in the snowy folds. It was fashioned to depict a peacock displaying its full colors, and was comprised of a riot of garish, multicolored stones. Henrietta longed to ask him about it, but felt by doing so she would be expected to compliment him on it, which she could not. The thought crossed her mind the pin was an allusion to dandyism, and she hastily turned a giggle into a muffled cough.

The meal lasted quite two hours, and when the covers were being removed, the dowager duchess said, "I know we ladies are supposed to leave the gentlemen to their port, but since we are a small party I insist we abandon the custom and retire to the drawing room as a group."

Lord Mawbly made a choking sound, casting a desperate glance at the duke, but Winterton's attentions were focused on helping an unsteady Lady Fuddlesby rise from her chair. She required assistance from the room, but refused the colonel's arm, taking the duke's instead.

Matilda placed her hand on the colonel's arm, saying, "You may escort me, Owen."

Colonel Colchester, frustrated with what he thought was Lady Fuddlesby's unreasonable behavior in the face of what was, for his part, only good manners to an old friend, gruffly replied, "Yes, I shall, Matilda."

Glancing triumphantly at Clara Fuddlesby, Matilda turned to the colonel. "Owen, after all these years, one would think you would call me Tilly."

As he observed the tension between his godfather and Lady Fuddlesby, Winterton's eyes met Henrietta's and they exchanged a grieved look. Henrietta took Lord Sebastian's arm since Lady Clorinda had claimed Sir Tommy.

Lady Mawbly did not put the same strictures on herself regarding the niceties of conversation as Henrietta did. While everyone was leaving the room, she advanced on Lord Sebastian and said, "My lord, sitting across from you during dinner, I could not help but notice your pin. Wherever did you find such a thing?"

Taking the lady's interest as flattery, Lord Sebastian proudly explained, "My manor house is called Peacock Hall. I commissioned Rundell and Bridge to make this pin in its honor."

Lady Mawbly crinkled her nose in obvious distaste. "Rundell and Bridge made that?"

The insult hit its intended target. Red-faced with anger, Lord Sebastian drew himself up to his full height and escorted Henrietta from the room.

Lord Mawbly groaned aloud at his wife's farouche behavior.

Once again in the drawing room, the dowager duchess claimed everyone's attention. "We have an accomplished singer here among us this evening. Lady Clorinda has graciously agreed to perform a ballad, and Lady Mawbly will accompany her on the pianoforte."

"Lud, not again," slurred Lady Fuddlesby before

she sank down onto a settee. Henrietta hurried to sit beside her.

Matilda and the colonel sat on the settee opposite them.

Sir Tommy, quite used to listening to young misses sing, assumed an expression of polite attention.

Lord Sebastian, still embittered over Lady Mawbly's crass remark, crossed his arms across his chest and sat back, resigned, in his chair.

The duke leaned negligently against the fireplace.

Lord Mawbly quickly traversed the room and was almost at the duke's side when his wife's voice stopped him midstride. "Silias! You may turn the pages for me."

Trembling, Lord Mawbly ventured, "Must I, Lady Mawbly? I wish to speak with the duke."

Hester stood before the pianoforte glaring at her husband. "You cannot wish to speak while our daughter is singing. Come here at once."

Like a whipped dog, Lord Mawbly obeyed.

Lady Mawbly sat down at the pianoforte and removed her gloves.

She began to play, and Lady Clorinda stood bashfully by, eyes downcast, singing a sweet ballad. None of her posturing at Lady Chatterton's musicale was present tonight.

The duke's mind was on Miss Lanford. How luminous her ivory skin appeared against the shining satin of her gown. When she had arrived this evening, he detected an apprehensive air about her. But after the adventure with Sir Polly Grey, she had relaxed and conversed easily with the other guests.

Clearly his mother held the girl in dislike, but

Giles found, to his surprise, he did not care. Instead, he wondered about the uncomfortable twist in his stomach when he saw Miss Lanford seated at the table between Lord Sebastian and Sir Tommy. Seeing her give her attention to the gentlemen had caused him to lose his appetite, partaking of little of the food painstakingly prepared, an act that had, no doubt, angered his French cook.

These musings were abruptly cut off by Lord Mawbly's sudden throat-clearing. The duke looked up and found the heavily perspiring man darting his gaze back and forth from his wife's hand to the duke's face.

Curiously Winterton looked at Lady Mawbly's hand. The paste copy of Lady Fuddlesby's pink tourmaline ring winked at him in the candlelight.

Good God! At once he realized what Lord Mawbly had been trying to tell him all evening, but had not been given the opportunity. He wondered fleetingly how Lady Mawbly had found it. Shifting his gaze to Lord Mawbly, he nodded at his lordship, indicating he realized the complication to an already delicate situation.

Deuce take it, what a coil. He ran his hand through his dark hair. He must tell Miss Lanford of Lady Mawbly's possession of the ring, and they would have to alter their plans.

After applauding Lady Clorinda's singing, the duke said, "Thank you, Lady Clorinda. Miss Lanford, if you will follow me to the library, I will give you that copy of Scott's *Lady of the Lake* you wanted."

Not waiting for anyone's reaction to this statement, the duke held out his arm for an obviously confused Miss Lanford, and they left the room together.

Walking down the corridor at his side with only the sound of her skirts swishing in the quiet, Henrietta asked, "Your Grace, what is it? You know I did not ask for any book, although I confess I would like to read *Lady of the Lake*. But I did not desire to leave my aunt. She looks about to swoon from too much wine."

Opening the library door, the duke guided her inside the dimly lit room. When he turned to face her, Henrietta saw his expression was grim. "I did not want to tell you until we were private, fearing *you* would swoon."

"Me? I hardly drank any wine at all," she protested.

"You may want a glass when you hear Lady Mawbly is wearing the paste pink tourmaline ring," the duke told her.

"What! But I thought Lord Mawbly was not going to give it to her," Henrietta exclaimed, reaching out to clutch his sleeve.

"My guess is she must have located it herself. Lord Mawbly would never have given it to her, because he feared with her knowledge of jewels, she would recognize it as paste."

The color drained from Henrietta's face. She felt tears of frustration form behind her eyes. "Oh, no, what are we to do? We must switch the rings before Lady Mawbly realizes the truth and a scandal breaks upon our heads."

"Exactly. Give me the genuine ring now. I shall give it to Lord Mawbly. He will have to be the one to switch the rings when Lady Mawbly removes the paste copy from her finger."

"Yes, it is the only way." Henrietta fumbled in her reticule for the ring box. The tears she tried to hold back began to fall down her cheeks and she brushed them away impatiently.

Pulling the ring box out of the ivory satin bag, Henrietta gazed unswervingly up at Winterton. Her voice shaking with emotion, she said, "Thank you for helping me with this terrible predicament. I know I can trust you to see us safely out of the difficulty."

Gazing down at her sweet and vulnerable expression, the duke had to forcibly stop himself from crushing her in his arms. He took a step closer to her and grasped the hand holding the ring box. Instead of taking the box, he pulled her arm to him. Slowly he rolled the top of her white glove down just past her elbow. Lowering his dark head, he placed a warm kiss inside the crease of her arm.

"Your Grace ..." Henrietta whispered, wishing he would kiss her again.

Outside in the hall, Lady Clorinda seethed with humiliation and fury. She was correct. Winterton did mean to set Henrietta Lanford up as his mistress. Why else would she be holding a jewel box while he kissed her arm in that lustful way? At least she had not witnessed any further intimacies between the two.

Her expression thunderous, Clorinda barely noticed in time the couple were turning to leave the room by the very doorway she hid beside. As she hurried back toward the drawing room, her thoughts raced dangerously. How Society would laugh at her, once she and the duke were betrothed, when it became known Winterton had set up a mistress at the very time of his engagement.

Her lips thinned with anger, Clorinda formed a plan.

Chapter Thirteen

The next day Henrietta rose at nine to a gray London morning. She'd spent a fitful night, waking frequently, and worrying Lady Mawbly would realize her new ring was paste.

She was equally concerned about the rift between Lady Fuddlesby and the colonel, and was anxious to see how her aunt fared this morning after all the wine the lady had consumed the evening before. Realizing Lady Fuddlesby would probably benefit most from sleeping late, she vowed to visit her bedchamber later in the day.

After breakfasting, Henrietta spent the remainder of the morning curled up in a window seat in the drawing room, reading the copy of *Lady of the Lake* Winterton had been obliged to give her.

Chuffley surprised her by announcing she had a caller.

"Who is it, Chuffley?" Henrietta asked eagerly, hoping it might be the duke with news of the ring.

"Lady Clorinda Eden, miss."

Lady Clorinda! Why would she be calling? They were hardly first oars with one another. "Show her in, please, Chuffley."

Henrietta seated herself on the brocade sofa, and smoothed the skirts of her powder-blue morning gown.

Lady Clorinda walked into the room, a vision in a red and white striped gown with a matching red spencer. "Miss Lanford, how good you are to receive me."

"Please sit down, Lady Clorinda. Shall I ring for tea?"

Lady Clorinda sat in a chair opposite the sofa, and lowered her gaze to the carpet. She spoke in a quiet voice. "No, I don't think I could swallow anything just now."

Henrietta felt her body tense at the strained tone of Clorinda's voice. "Is there something wrong?"

Clorinda's emerald eyes filled with tears. She produced a dainty lace handkerchief from her reticule and dabbed at the wetness. "Yes, there is something dreadfully wrong, Miss Lanford. May I call you Henrietta?"

At Henrietta's nod she went on. "I hardly know how to approach you about such a delicate matter, so you must forgive me if I am forthright."

Henrietta's heart starting beating hard. She did not know what it was Lady Clorinda was about to say, but felt a sudden acute sense of dread. "I believe in plain speaking, Lady Clorinda, and pray you come to the point."

"Very well. I was on my way to the ladies' withdrawing room last evening at the Duke of Winterton's town house and passed by the library. The door stood open and I . . . I saw you and the duke—"

A sob escaped Lady Clorinda's lips and it took her a moment to regain her composure.

Henrietta sat very still.

"Henrietta, I saw you holding a jewel box. I saw the duke kiss you in the crease of your arm. Oh, fie, I wish I had never witnessed anything," Clorinda exclaimed. She flung out her hands in a display of despair.

Two crimson stains appeared on Henrietta's cheeks. "Go on."

"I know what that jewel box contains," Clorinda asserted.

A new anguish seared Henrietta's heart. Not only had an intimate moment between her and the duke been observed, but Lady Clorinda knew of the pink tourmaline ring. Was that why she was here? To tell her she would inform Lady Mawbly of Lady Fuddlesby's folly?

Henrietta opened her mouth to beg for Lady Clorinda's discretion, but the lady's next words caused the sentiment to die unspoken on her lips.

"An expensive piece of jewelry often precedes a . . . er, business arrangement between a gentleman and a female."

Henrietta's eyes opened wide and Clorinda rushed on. "A life as a mistress is not a happy one, dear Henrietta. It may seem attractive now, while you are young, and of course, the duke is a handsome, wealthy gentleman. No doubt he would satisfy your every desire, for a while."

Henrietta listened with bewilderment. She struggled to comprehend Clorinda's words. "You think the Duke of Winterton means to set me up as his m-mistress?"

Clorinda's eyes held an understanding warmth. "It is only natural to deny it, but you won't be able to keep the secret long."

Henrietta hesitated, unable to speak, torn by conflicting emotions. Lady Clorinda did not know about the ring being paste, and for that she must be grateful. But Clorinda's assumption that she would consent to being the duke's light-skirt filled her with an anger that took her breath away in its intensity. She sat mute, struggling to control her emotions.

Clorinda spoke softly, in a pitying voice. "I can only imagine how painful it must be, Henrietta. I feel sure you are in love with the duke, because you are not the type of girl to accept the fate of a member of the Fashionable Impure. Why, I'm certain there are any number of gentlemen in the landed gentry or the clergy, even a wealthy gentleman of the merchant class, who would be proud to call you wife."

A heated denial of the accusation rose to Henrietta's lips. And what was all this talk of clergymen and merchants? She would ring for Chuffley and have the woman thrown out for her insolence.

But what explanation would she give for the scene Lady Clorinda witnessed? To speak the truth about the jewel case Lady Clorinda saw would expose Lady Fuddlesby to the very scandal Henrietta was trying to avoid. With a quiet dignity she said, "Thank you for your concern, Lady Clorinda, and now I must ask you to leave."

Lady Clorinda reached a hand out to touch Henrietta's arm, but immediately drew it back at Henrietta's look of distaste.

Her voice pleading, Lady Clorinda begged, "Do not think my coming here was motivated by selfishness, I beseech you. Naturally, as Winterton's chosen bride, I do not care to begin my marriage knowing my husband has recently acquired a new mistress."

Henrietta quickly dropped her gaze to the floor, concealing her reaction to this statement. Her head ached with pain. So the duke was to wed another after all that had passed between herself and

Winterton. After the kiss they shared the night of Lord Baddick's attack. After that burning embrace in his curricle when they were out in the country looking for Knight. After the way he had pulled her glove down, just last evening, kissing her arm in such a way as to cause her to feel a yearning need she could not even define.

Then, through her distress, a little voice inside her head reminded her no notice of the engagement had appeared in the newspaper. No mention of any betrothal had ever been made by the duke. Only Lady Clorinda had said it was so. Maybe Clorinda was lying.

Rising shakily to her feet, Henrietta said, "Good day to you, Lady Clorinda."

Clorinda rose. "I am thinking of your welfare as well, I assure you. Just because Winterton cannot marry you does not mean you will remain unwed should you resist the duke's offer of protection."

A furrow appeared between Henrietta's brows. "What do you mean Winterton cannot marry me?"

Clorinda stared at her. "Are you so innocent of the ways of Society? Gentlemen of Winterton's wealth and rank *never* marry beneath them. If he had lost his fortune and you were a wealthy heiress, then he might consider lowering himself to align his name with that of a squire's daughter. But such is not the case."

Studying Henrietta's stricken face, Lady Clorinda nodded and said, "Ask anyone, and they will tell you what I have said is true. Think of your future, Henrietta."

With those words, Lady Clorinda took her leave in a flurry of silks.

She walked down the steps of the town house, maintaining a rigid composure. She allowed a footman to assist her inside her carriage and they pulled away. Only then did she give way to gales of laughter. Eventually a stitch formed in her side, forcing her to wipe her streaming eyes and content herself with a smug smile.

Back inside Lady Fuddlesby's town house, Henrietta was far from amused. She stood in the drawing room, her mind reeling. Her initial distress regarding Clorinda's claim the duke meant to make her his mistress faded away, in light of the lady's statement that someone like the duke would never marry beneath him in Society. Clorinda had said she might ask anyone and her beliefs would be confirmed.

Henrietta glanced at the clock on the mantel and saw it was one of the clock. Lady Fuddlesby might be awake. If anyone would tell her the truth, surely it would be her aunt. Besides, Henrietta was concerned about the rift between Lady Fuddlesby and the colonel and was anxious to see how the lady had fared this morning.

In the hall outside Lady Fuddlesby's bedchamber, Henrietta met Felice. "Good morning, mees. I hope you are feeling better than her ladyship today."

In a low voice Henrietta asked, "Is her ladyship poorly?"

Felice's lips folded into a disapproving line before she said, "Yes, mees. She ees suffering from the effects of too much wine. If you weesh to speak to her, you will have to get past her guard."

Henrietta looked after the maid's retreating back and frowned. Guard? What guard? She knocked softly and opened the door.

The curtains were drawn tightly closed against the gray light of day. It was too warm for a fire, and no candles were lit. Henrietta heard moans coming from the bed and walked forward toward the bedside.

Knight appeared out of the darkness in front of her as if to block her way. Even though they had long ago cried friends, his twitching tail and unblinking stare plainly told her she was not wanted at the moment.

She hesitated, venturing a quiet "Aunt, are you all right?"

Lady Fuddlesby called out, "Oh, my dear Henrietta, I fancy the grapes were sour. Knight! Let Henrietta pass. You must forgive my darling boy, he is only being protective."

Henrietta reached down to scratch behind Knight's ears before coming to stand at her aunt's bedside. "I know he is. You are looking sadly pulled, my lady. May I get you anything? Some tea, perhaps?"

Lady Fuddlesby pressed a hand to her stomach and grimaced. "No, thank you, dear. I had a cup already."

She looked at Henrietta through tear-filled eyes. "It has happened again. All these years later. Matilda has taken my beau away from me. You might well stare. You see, I was being courted by the seventh Duke of Winterton before Matilda set her cap for him. He chose her, rather than me, because she was an earl's daughter and I was only a miss."

Henrietta froze. As casually as she could she asked, "Is rank so important then?"

Lady Fuddlesby wiped her eyes. Her expression stiffened and she spoke with a hint of bitterness. "Oh, yes, dear. Very important. A man of high rank would have to be deeply in love, indeed, to marry a lady not of his station. Even then, he might not do so out of respect to his name and consequence."

A flash of wild grief tore at Henrietta's heart. Clorinda had spoken the truth. The duke would never marry her. She marveled at her own arrogance in thinking he would. Other than his kisses, he had given her no indication he held her in affection, no less that he loved her. And kisses were easily given, she thought with newfound cynicism.

Trying to swallow the lump that lingered in her throat, Henrietta turned her attention to her aunt's feelings. "My lady, I do not know about the previous Duke of Winterton, but you are wrong about Colonel Colchester. The gentleman cares for you deeply. It is plain to anyone who knows the two of you. I am certain last night was simply a misunderstanding, one that will be cleared when next you meet."

Lady Fuddlesby's mouth was set in a stubborn line. She reached out and patted Henrietta's hand. "No, dear, I fear not. Besides, my unladylike behavior was probably enough in itself to give him a disgust of me."

When Henrietta might have protested, her aunt stopped her before she could begin. Pressing her fingers to her temples, Lady Fuddlesby moaned, "Please leave me now, dear. My head aches dreadfully."

"If there is anything I can do for you, my lady, you have only to let me know," Henrietta assured her. She squeezed her aunt's hand, and turned and fled the room for the sanctuary of her own bedchamber.

Closing the door, she went to stand in front of one of the tall windows in the room. Pulling the curtain aside, she looked out over the Mayfair scene, and remembered the dreams she had the snowy afternoon she had arrived in London.

Well, she had matured since that day, she believed. Certainly she'd had the veils of illusion stripped from her eyes. First by Lord Baddick, and now by the conventions of a Society that considered it wrong to marry beneath one's social rank.

Turning away from the window, Henrietta's gaze fell on the handkerchief the duke had lent her that day in the park when she had first learned of the misfortune with Lady Fuddlesby's ring. Freshly laundered, it lay on her dressing table, ready to be returned to its owner.

Picking up the square of fine lawn, she carried it with her to the bed. She lay down, holding it to her cheek. Feeling as if she were bleeding from every pore, she stared at the bed hangings dry-eyed. Her sense of loss was beyond tears.

The three days before the ball were spent in despondency by both women. Colonel Colchester called on Lady Fuddlesby late in the day after the duke's dinner party. Feeling she could not face him, her ladyship had instructed a surprised Chuffley she was not at home to callers.

This insult exasperated the colonel enough to keep him away until the very day of the ball. It also left him time to reflect on his relationship with the lady, and to pay a call at Rundell and Bridge.

At approximately four of the clock on the day of the ball, Lady Fuddlesby was supervising the placement of flowers about the ballroom when Chuffley came into the room holding a card on a silver tray.

Her ladyship picked it up and peered at it inquisitively. Mr. Edmund Shire, it read, and one corner was bent down, indicating Mr. Shire was calling in person. What could he have to say that could not wait until this evening? Lady Fuddlesby wondered. "Tell him I am busy, but will spare him ten minutes. Show him to the drawing room."

In the drawing room a few minutes later, Mr. Shire appeared in the doorway clad in a walnut-colored coat and buckskins. He bowed before Lady Fuddlesby, who sat on the brocade sofa. "My lady, thank you for seeing me. Forgive me for calling on the day of your ball, but I felt it fitting you should know my plans."

Lady Fuddlesby eyed him curiously. "Sit down, Mr. Shire. May I offer you tea?"

Settling into a chair, Mr. Shire said, "No, I'll come right to the point. I've been out to Hamilton Cross to see Squire Lanford. By George, he's got a stable full of pretty fillies out there."

Puzzled, Lady Fuddlesby said, "Really, Mr. Shire, Henrietta is an only child."

Mr. Shire guffawed. "I meant mares, my lady. And three of them recently foaled. If I weren't forking out the blunt on putting in a new fountain at my country house, I'd be sorely tempted to strike a bargain with the squire. As it is, I've reached another sort of agreement with Squire Lanford."

Lady Fuddlesby's expression remained blank. Mr. Shire beamed and explained. "I have the squire's permission to ask Miss Lanford to marry me. He's no end of a good fellow. Agreed right off when I told him about my estates. We talked horses mostly."

Mr. Shire rose. "I won't keep you. Just thought it proper to let you know I'd be putting the question to Miss Lanford tonight. She'll probably want to announce the betrothal at the ball. I have a mind to arrive early to settle everything, if it's all the same to you."

"Yes, yes, of course you may," Lady Fuddlesby replied faintly. Mr. Shire took his leave, and her lady-ship sat thinking.

Edmund Shire was all that was suitable. He was a wealthy landowner and had a mild-mannered personality. Life with him for Henrietta would be comfortable and predictable.

Lady Fuddlesby's mouth turned down at the corners. Henrietta would be bored with the country gentleman in a week. The girl was too high-spirited to settle for such a colorless man. More important, she was sure her niece was in love with the Duke of Winterton.

Her ladyship was so lost in thought, a growing noise outside the doorway startled her into rising to her feet. Recognition of the owners of the voices caused her heart to pound.

"I tell you, Chuffley, I shall see her. Go back downstairs and leave us alone," Colonel Colchester ordered sharply. He entered the drawing room and closed the double doors in Chuffley's dismayed face with a snap.

Lady Fuddlesby stared at the military man's determined face. Finding her voice, she uttered, "Good afternoon, Colonel. What brings you here before the ball?"

Colonel Colchester came to her side, pulling her down to sit next to him on the sofa. "This damned quarrel between us brought me here. I apologize for letting Matilda play her tricks the other night. Should have sent her on her way with a flea in her ear. But for God's sake, Clara, I thought you trusted me."

Lady Fuddlesby's face brightened when she looked into the colonel's dear brown eyes. She reached over and clasped his hand warmly. "Oh, Owen, can you forgive me for being so silly? I let an incident from my youth cloud my judgment. Of course I trust you."

The colonel continued to hold her hand while dropping neatly to one knee on the floor in front of her. "Clara, you must know what is in my heart. I love you. Will you do me the honor of being my wife? Er, with Knight's permission, of course," he added with a tender smile.

Lady Fuddlesby's mouth dropped open. Then tears of joy formed in her eyes. Her lips curved into a wide grin. "Yes, Owen. Oh, yes, I shall, and Knight will not have anything to say about it."

A smile broke out on the colonel's face, and he rose from his kneeling position to press his lips to Lady Fuddlesby's. Drawing back a minute later, he reached into his pocket and withdrew a small jewel box.

Lady Fuddlesby gasped aloud at the sight of the ruby surrounded by diamonds sparkling up at her. "How lovely," she breathed, when the colonel slipped the ring onto her finger.

The colonel proceeded to show her how lovely he thought *she* was, which took up quite a quarter of an hour. By the time the colonel left to go home to change for the ball, Lady Fuddlesby's head was in such a whirl of happiness, she had entirely forgotten about Mr. Shire's plans to offer for her niece.

Henrietta, sitting listlessly while Felice fussed over a few finishing touches to her hair, was therefore surprised when Sally entered the room saying, "Mr. Edmund Shire is in the drawin' room wantin' to see you, miss."

"Thank you, Sally." Henrietta dismissed the housemaid, thinking Mr. Shire wanted a few minutes before the ball to tell her about his trip to the country. "I believe I must be ready, Felice."

Felice's gaze ran over her. With a nod she said, "Yes, mees. You will break the gentlemen's hearts tonight."

Impulsively Henrietta gave the Frenchwoman a quick hug. "Thank you, Felice. Hopefully, by the end of the evening we will have the paste ring in Lady Fuddlesby's jewel box and the real stone on Lady Mawbly's hand."

Henrietta hurried down the stairs without another glance at her reflection, not wanting to see if the lack of sleep over the past few nights had resulted in shadows under her eyes.

She did not know the faint shadows only added to the ethereal sight she presented. She wore a white silk gown with a white lace overdress. The bodice of the dress was low, and trimmed with pearls. Pearls marched up the front closure of the short puffed sleeves, beneath which her arms were encased in long white kid gloves. Lady Fuddlesby had been true to her word and had sent Felice to Henrietta's room with a delicate diamond necklet and matching earbobs that twinkled in the candlelight.

Henrietta entered the drawing room, properly leaving the door open behind her. Mr. Shire, dressed in a sadly out-of-fashion evening coat of a mustard color, rose from his seat, a smile of greeting on his face. "You look well, Miss Lanford, if a trifle pale."

Ignoring this dubious flattery, Henrietta inquired politely, "How was your trip to the country, Mr. Shire?"

"Everything went just as I had hoped," he replied, his manner enigmatic.

Indicating that he should be seated, Henrietta thought it was unlike the open, friendly Mr. Shire to be mysterious. Her feelings heightened to nothing short of shock when she seated herself and found Mr. Shire on one knee in front of her.

"Miss Lanford, I have been to see your father, and he has given me his permission to ask for your hand in marriage. What do you say? Shall we announce the betrothal tonight?"

She merely stared at him, tongue-tied. He had taken her completely by surprise. That should not have been true, she considered, when many betrothals were announced by couples less acquainted. And Mr. Shire had shown her marked attention from the first time they'd met.

How happy Papa would be if she made a match of it with Mr. Shire. She could well imagine her father eagerly giving the country man his permission to ask for her hand. How disappointed Papa would be if she refused Mr. Shire's offer, and came home at the end of the Season unwed.

Pushing such thoughts from her mind, Henrietta said, "Please do get up, sir. It cannot be a comfortable position."

"That's one of the qualities I admire about you, Miss Lanford. You're so practical," he praised her.

Henrietta turned her head away, a sad smile on her lips. She did not want to be practical. She wanted her fantasies to come true. She wanted the duke.

Accept him, you silly gudgeon, screamed her brain. One more evening with the duke, demanded her heart.

At the moment she turned back to Mr. Shire and opened her mouth to speak, Lady Fuddlesby floated into the room on a cloud of happiness—pink no doubt, as was her gown.

Lady Fuddlesby held her breath for a moment, waiting for the couple to make an announcement, and when they didn't, let out a sigh of relief. Smiling broadly, she exclaimed, "Oh, my dear Henrietta, I have the most exciting news. You are to wish me happy. The colonel has proposed and I have accepted him."

Forgetting Mr. Shire, Henrietta rushed forward to embrace Lady Fuddlesby. "Aunt! I am so very pleased. Of course, I wish you many years of happiness together."

Mr. Shire glared at her ladyship over Henrietta's head, feeling Lady Fuddlesby should not have barged in on them, knowing the nature of their conversation. His annoyance only grew when he heard the lady's next statement.

"Come with me now, dear. The guests will be arriving at any moment, and you must be beside me to greet them. You will excuse us, Mr. Shire," she said, bustling Henrietta from the room.

When they were safely in the hall, Henrietta turned to her aunt, informing her, "My lady, you saved me from answering a proposal of marriage from Mr. Shire."

"Did I get there in time?"

"You knew then? He had asked me and I was about to give him an answer." Henrietta chuckled wryly. "What the answer was, I confess I do not know."

Lady Fuddlesby nodded wisely. "That is quite all right, my dear. Mr. Shire will keep while you mull the matter over. He came to me earlier in the day to tell me he had your father's permission to approach you, and in the joy of Owen's proposal, I forgot to tell you."

Her ladyship failed to mention how, when Felice had let fall the information that Mr. Shire was downstairs requesting an interview with Henrietta, the purpose of his visit came rushing back to her. She decided she would try to interrupt the proceedings before her niece could accept or refuse the man. That way, her ladyship reasoned, she could put it about at the ball her niece had received an offer but had not yet accepted. Tongues would wag, and the Duke of Winterton would be certain to hear of it. Perhaps the information would jar the impossible duke into coming up to scratch. Oftentimes men had to be prodded a bit before they knew what was right in front of them.

The two ladies made their way to the hall, where they spent the next half hour greeting the guests. Henrietta stiffened when Lady Clorinda arrived with Lord and Lady Mawbly.

"Good evening, Henrietta," Clorinda said in a condescending sort of way.

Henrietta raised her chin. She reflected Lady Clorinda was the one who looked like Haymarket Ware in her gown of seafoam-green gauze. The bodice was designed in such a way as to give the appearance the gown might fall from the lady's shoulder at the least provocation. A diamond necklace of considerable worth circled Clorinda's neck, making the one Henrietta wore appear an ornament for a child.

Returning Clorinda's superior gaze, Henrietta asked sweetly, "Lady Clorinda, it appears you have forgotten your shawl. May I have a servant fetch one for you?"

Clorinda glared at her, then flounced away without answering. At least we are open about our animosity, Henrietta thought.

Finally the moment she had unconsciously been waiting for was upon her. The Duke of Winterton arrived with his godfather. Henrietta thought no matter what happened in her life, she would never forget a single detail of the duke's magnificent, aristocratic face.

Her heart pounded in her chest when his tall figure, faultlessly dressed in Spanish blue, turned away from Lady Fuddlesby and strolled to her side. There was a spark of some indefinable emotion in his gray eyes while his gaze took in her ensemble. "Miss Lanford, no angel can be as divine as you appear this evening," he said smoothly, raising her gloved hand to his lips.

Henrietta's bearing was stiff and proud, but her spirit was in chaos. Somehow she must contrive not to let him know the effect he had on her. She had to conquer her involuntary reactions to that captivating look of his.

Curtsying, Henrietta managed to smile brightly. "If anyone is of the cosmos this evening, it is surely my aunt. She has been in heaven since she and the colonel decided their future."

Glancing toward where his godfather and the lady stood with their heads together, the duke nodded with satisfaction. "I am happy for them. They are well suited."

Unlike the two of us, a nasty voice sneered in Henrietta's head.

The duke lowered his voice for just her ears. "Speaking of Lady Fuddlesby, I must tell you Lord Mawbly has been unsuccessful in obtaining the paste ring."

Henrietta nodded her head. "I surmised as much

when Lord Mawbly arrived earlier. It seems as if his nerves can no longer stand the strain."

"You may very well be right. Lord Mawbly even bribed his wife's abigail attempting to retrieve the ring, but according to the woman, Lady Mawbly has not once removed the blasted thing from her finger."

"What are we going to do?" Henrietta asked, her ivory brow creased with concern.

The duke inclined his head at Sir Tommy and Lord Sebastian, who had appeared in the doorway, waiting their turn to go through the line. "We will contrive something, Miss Lanford. Promise me a waltz?"

"Yes, Your Grace."

He made his way up the stairs, leaving Henrietta to stare after him sadly. A waltz. It would most likely be their last. If she married Mr. Shire, she doubted they would be likely to come to Town often. And if she returned home unwed, her father would not give her another Season.

Pinning a welcoming smile on her face, Henrietta greeted Sir Tommy and Lord Sebastian, a heaviness centered in her chest.

Chapter Fourteen

Upstairs, the ballroom looked a confection with its pink silk hangings. Hothouse flowers perfumed the air, and a breeze fluttered through the room from the windows open to the evening air, making the candles flicker.

Lady Fuddlesby had carried through her plans for fountains of champagne, and a table of delicacies was set up at the far end of the large room. An orchestra, hired for the occasion, was tuning its instruments, waiting for a signal from her ladyship to begin the ball.

Colonel Colchester stepped over to the leader and exchanged a few words with him. The colonel motioned for Lady Fuddlesby to join him, and with the commanding air of a man who'd led troops into war, gained the attention of the room.

"Ladies and gentlemen. Before we begin dancing, I have an announcement to make. You may congratulate me. Lady Fuddlesby has graciously consented to be my wife."

Amidst applause and well-wishers, the colonel signaled the orchestra and led his lady out onto the floor for the waltz. They made a handsome couple, the colonel in a pebble-gray evening coat that went well with his gray hair, and Lady Fuddlesby in her customary pink, her round cheeks rosy with happiness.

Standing next to her son, Matilda shrugged in mock resignation. "I was never serious about Owen. If I had been, I would have won him just as I did your father all those years ago."

Studying his mother's hard face, the duke experienced a qualm of displeasure. "If you will excuse me, Mother, I wish to dance with Miss Lanford."

"You are too late, Giles. Mr. Shire has claimed her hand. I should not be surprised by an announcement from that quarter. Lady Chatterton was telling all who would listen her nephew meant to offer for the chit."

The duke's dark brows drew together and he stood scowling in the couple's direction.

Matilda nudged him with her fan and said, "Lady Clorinda is in looks tonight."

As he tore his gaze away from Miss Lanford, the duke's eyebrows shot up in surprise when he took in Lady Clorinda's provocative gown. He thought she looked more beautiful, and more exposed, than ever. Noticing his interest, the lady pointed her bosom in his direction, a smile of welcome on her face.

"Excuse me, Mother," the duke said. He crossed to a delighted Lady Clorinda's side, and swept her onto the dance floor.

Being dragged about the floor by a clumsy Mr. Shire, Henrietta noted the duo and heaved a sigh. At least the two had not announced their engagement at her ball. If they were engaged. She had serious doubts about the matter, but reflected, if not Clorinda, then some other pampered daughter of the nobility would claim the duke.

They were promenading about the room when

Henrietta realized she was behaving decidedly rag-mannered toward Mr. Shire. He was pontificating on her father's stables again, and as usual, horse talk prompted her mind to wander.

With a start, Henrietta heard Mr. Shire's next words. "I should like to announce our betrothal to-night at your ball, Miss Lanford. That is why I hur-ried back to Town from the squire's hospitality."

"Miss Lanford, you're looking frightfully flushed," Sir Tommy interrupted, suddenly standing in front of them. "Come with me and we'll find out if it's true champagne flowing from a fountain is usually flat. Excuse us, Shire."

Henrietta saw Mr. Shire's frustrated face before Sir Tommy whisked her away. Accepting a glass from Sir Tommy, she drank deeply, unaware her throat had tightened during her conversation with Mr. Shire.

"Here, now, Miss Lanford. You're not going to fol-low your aunt's unhappy propensity to wine, are you?"

A giggle escaped her, before she assumed an ex-pression of mock severity. "My aunt never allows herself to become bosky. The other night was an ex-ception. It was a lover's quarrel which led her to the wine bottle, and as you heard, all has been re-solved."

Sir Tommy's lip curled in derision. "Ah, yes, love. Never get involved in it myself. Unless, of course, it's to wager on an upcoming betrothal. Which re-minds me, you wouldn't want to increase the weight of my purse by letting me know in advance about you and Edmund Shire, would you?"

Henrietta was spared from answering this imper-tinent question by the arrival of Lord Sebastian. Bowing before her, he took her empty glass and shoved it in Sir Tommy's hands. "May I have the honor of leading you in the set of country dances forming, Miss Lanford?"

Nodding her assent, she accepted Lord Sebastian's arm. The gentleman, dressed in a maroon evening coat, appeared pensive. "Hope Lady Fuddlesby will be content with a mere military man," his lordship commented when the steps of the dance brought them together.

Here was another example of someone considering rank as a factor in settling on a partner in marriage, Henrietta thought. How could she have been in London all these weeks and not been made aware of the enormous importance one's title possessed? She was bird-witted, she supposed. Aloud she said, "They love one another very much. Surely that must be the first consideration."

Lord Sebastian snorted. "A romantic, are you? I wouldn't have thought so with the rumors circulating about you and that bumpkin Shire. The man's coats are deplorable, Miss Lanford. I beg you to reconsider your decision."

"Indeed, my lord, I have no idea what my decision is, so how can I rethink it?" The steps of the dance separated them, and Lord Sebastian did not pursue the topic when they were brought together again.

Henrietta decided she must put a stop to the gossip about herself and Mr. Shire as soon as she could excuse herself from Lord Sebastian. As she promenaded after the dance with him, her gaze was caught by the pin his lordship chose to wear in his cravat this evening. Several marquise-shaped stones of a dark pink color surrounded a round golden topaz. The whole combined to make a flower. The pink stones reminded her of Lady

Fuddlesby's ring, although the stones in his lordship's pin were of a darker, almost purplish hue.

Glancing up from her study of the pin, she saw the Duke of Winterton approaching with long, purposeful strides. "Miss Lanford, our dance, I believe."

Henrietta could hear the opening strains of the waltz while the duke escorted her out onto the floor. She felt her pulse pound with excitement. He placed his arm firmly about her waist, his hand scorching her back. His other hand came up to clasp hers, and they began to move about the floor.

Like the first evening she had waltzed with him, at the Denbys' ball, a riot of sensations rushed through her body. Her gaze dropped from his silvery eyes to his mouth. Memories of the way his lips felt against hers caused a bittersweet pain. She would never experience those feelings again.

Suddenly she felt him pull her closer than the regulation twelve inches apart demanded. She leaned her head back to see up into his face, several inches above her petite stature. He was watching her intently.

"Rumors are flying about you, Miss Lanford. It seems you have enslaved poor Mr. Shire. Some are saying he has already offered for you," he murmured.

Henrietta could not meet his gaze any longer. She lowered her lashes and stared at the top button of his white waistcoat. She wanted to cry out that she could never marry Edmund Shire because she loved another. Instead, she remained silent.

The duke's grasp tightened, wringing a gasp from her. "Never say it is true," he growled.

"Your Grace," she said to the button, "you should

not be holding me quite so tightly unless you want to occasion gossip yourself."

Because she was looking down, Henrietta missed the arrested expression that came over the Duke of Winterton's face. He gazed off into the distance above her head, seemingly unaware of his surroundings for a minute. His jaw tightened in a determined fashion.

Then his heavy lids dropped down and he thrust her away from him. Looking down his nose at her, he stated coldly, "I have formed a plan with Lord Mawbly to switch the rings."

Henrietta's head came up. "How will you do it?"

"Mere child's play. I shall inform Lady Mawbly that I understand she owns a pink tourmaline stone, and that I wish to view it. When she takes off her glove, I shall ask her to remove the ring from her hand. Lord Mawbly will be standing by, and when he sees that I hold the paste ring in my hand, will cause a diversion, during which time I shall slip the genuine stone from my pocket and return it to Lady Mawbly."

Henrietta eyed him skeptically. "And you think this a simple scheme to carry out?"

He raised his eyebrows cynically. "Have you a better idea?"

"No, Your Grace."

His long fingers dug into the soft flesh of the hand he held. "I promise not to do anything harebrained. Do you promise the same?"

The smoldering flame she saw in his eyes startled her. "Of course," she whispered, all the while wondering what she had agreed to.

The dance ended. The duke bowed and left her to cross the room to Colonel Colchester. Henrietta believed he meant to inform his godfather of his plan to switch the ring. She knew she must seek out Mr. Shire and disabuse him of the notion she would marry him.

She found him by the refreshment table, frowning into a glass of wine. He looked up with a show of relief at her appearance. "Mr. Shire, I have something to say to you. Let us move away from here to behind those potted plants."

"Yes, yes, an excellent idea."

When they had secured a measure of privacy, Henrietta said in a rush, "While I am aware of the great honor you do me, I am afraid I must decline your kind offer, sir. You are a truthful man, and deserve an honest answer. I cannot marry you because my affections are otherwise engaged."

Mr. Shire shifted uncomfortably, but said, "Watching you this evening, I gathered as much. It is all right, Miss Lanford. Let us part friends."

Henrietta felt a surge of gratitude toward the country gentleman. "Sir, you are understanding—"

"Paste!" Lady Mawbly howled.

Henrietta picked up her skirts and hurried back to the dance floor.

A shocking sight met her eyes.

At Lady Mawbly's scream, the music had stopped. Everyone formed a circle around where the lady stood glaring daggers at Lord Sebastian, who was holding the pink tourmaline ring under his quizzing glass.

He said, "You tell me the stones in my pin are not pink tourmalines, and I take leave to inform you neither is this ring you are showing me. It is naught but paste."

Fans fluttered and whispers hissed across the room.

Henrietta edged her way to the front of the circle,

and her panicked gaze sought the duke. He was standing next to the colonel and Lady Fuddlesby. Lady Clorinda and Lord Mawbly were with them.

"You!" Lady Mawbly said with loathing, pointing at Lady Fuddlesby. "You tricked my husband. You sold him a paste stone."

Another round of whispering raced around the room at this scandalous statement.

Lady Fuddlesby's face was ashen. In a voice trembling with outrage, she exclaimed, "How dare you, Hester? That ring is more genuine than your teeth."

Matilda said snidely, "I always thought you had windmills in your head, Clara."

Colonel Colchester turned on her angrily. "Hold your tongue for once in your life, Matilda."

Gasping in outrage, the dowager duchess turned to her son, but she got no help from him.

The duke strode to the center of the room. Holding the genuine ring hidden in his hand, he snatched the paste from Lord Sebastian's fingers. With a sleight of hand a magician would have been proud of, he switched the rings.

Holding the genuine ring under his own quizzing glass, he declared, "I must contradict you, Sebbie. Perhaps your glass needs cleaning. Wipe it off and look again."

He handed the genuine stone to Lord Sebastian.

All eyes were riveted on the scene while Lord Sebastian pulled a handkerchief out of his pocket with a flourish, wiped his quizzing glass, and re-examined the stone.

A second later he reported with some heat, "This is not the same ring I saw a moment ago. I know jewelry. What sort of game are you playing here?"

Lady Mawbly grabbed the ring from his fingers.

Once again, the duke commanded the room's attention. "This is something Lady Fuddlesby and the Mawblys can settle in private. In my opinion, it is a simple misunderstanding, easily righted. I am surprised you are all so interested in such a trivial matter, when I am about to announce my engagement," he ended haughtily.

Silence reigned in the room. No one cared about the ring any longer. Everyone wanted to hear what the Duke of Winterton had to say.

Standing several feet away, Henrietta felt her blood run cold. Oh, no, he was going to announce his betrothal to Lady Clorinda. She prayed she would not disgrace herself by bursting into tears.

"Ladies and gentlemen, may I present the future Duchess of Winterton."

All held their breath.

Lady Clorinda's face broke into a brilliant smile.

"Miss Henrietta Lanford," the duke intoned.

A collective gasp sounded.

Winterton walked unerringly to Henrietta's side and raised her hand to his lips.

For Henrietta, the minutes passed as if in a dream. She was vaguely aware of Clorinda's strangled scream of fury, and the surge of excited talk about the room. It seemed the duke's mother had fainted.

The music began again, sounding far away. All she was really conscious of was the sound of the duke's voice saying her name over and over again in her brain.

Then Lady Fuddlesby and the colonel were at her side. The duke's arm steadied her while they all walked to the library, the Mawbly's, minus Lady Clorinda, trailing behind.

Henrietta felt in a daze. She looked up at the

duke, and he pressed his gloved fingers against her lips. "First we must settle the situation with the rings, then we can talk."

The door to the library stood ajar. Pushing it open, the duke entered the room, and the company turned as one to look at the large desk at one side of the room.

Sitting upon the far corner of its gleaming surface, a startled Knight stared back at them, a large lobster patty clamped in his jaws. The cat quickly began devouring the treat as if someone would take it from him at any moment.

Lady Mawbly began her tirade. "I demand to be told what is going on here. I tell you, Clara Fuddlesby, I shall have you in court if you think you can hoodwink me."

"Shut up, Hester," Lord Mawbly bellowed at his wife, shocking her as well as the rest of the gathering.

"Silias," Lady Mawbly said awfully. "How dare you speak to me in that tone?"

"I am your husband, damme! It's high time I took you in hand." Ignoring his wife's mutinous face, he proclaimed, "You've caused all of us a deal of trouble with your greed, but it ends here. It's true the ring you had was paste, but the stone you now hold is genuine."

Lady Fuddlesby paled. "Oh, dear, oh dear, how can this have happened?"

Standing next to the desk, the duke held up the paste copy. "The rings were somehow switched, my lady. You inadvertently sold the paste copy to Lord Mawbly." He turned and placed the paste copy on the desk.

The colonel supported Lady Fuddlesby when she swayed under the weight of this information.

The duke continued the story. "Lord Mawbly came to me with the problem, and with Miss Lanford's help, I was about to make things right this evening when Lord Sebastian unfortunately discovered the truth about the paste ring."

Henrietta found her voice. "I daresay he would not have been so vehement about his findings had you not been so cruel about his peacock pin the other night, Lady Mawbly."

"Well, I only wish to take my ring and leave this house at once," Lady Mawbly declared with a sniff.

Colonel Colchester said, "I'm afraid that won't be possible. Lady Fuddlesby agreed to sell her ring under duress. Now that she is to be my wife, she will not be selling the ring. I shall give you a draft on my account to return your money, Lord Mawbly."

"Oh, Owen, you are generous," Lady Fuddlesby chirped.

Lord Mawbly seized the genuine ring from a groaning Lady Mawbly and handed it to Colonel Colchester, saying, "An excellent plan, sir."

Colonel Colchester took the ring and laid it on the desk next to the paste copy. "I shall give you my vowel—"

"No, indeed, Colonel. You are a gentlemen of your word. It is not necessary," Lord Mawbly assured him. "Come along, Hester. We're going home. And when we get there I'll have something to say to Clorinda about her gowns as well."

They left the room, Lady Mawbly accompanying her husband with an unaccustomed meekness.

Lady Fuddlesby pressed her fingers to her temples. "Oh, I do not know what I would have done without you tonight, Owen. And you as well, Your Grace."

Colonel Colchester placed an arm about Lady

Fuddlesby and gave her a squeeze. "I'll always be there for you," he told her gruffly.

Abruptly everyone's attention was drawn to the desk. With a devious look on his masked face, Knight pushed the rings about the desk with a clever paw.

Henrietta's gaze flew to the duke's. A gurgle of laughter escaped her lips.

With a gasp, Lady Fuddlesby hurried over to the desk and collected her rings. She spoke sternly to her pet. "Knight, you never did such a thing. I will not believe it of you."

Knight looked up at his mistress, the picture of innocence.

"Clara," the colonel said, and cleared his throat. "I believe we should leave the newly betrothed pair alone for a few minutes."

Henrietta twisted her hands together in front of her.

Lady Fuddlesby came to her side with a swirl of pink skirts. "Oh, my dear, I do wish you happy. And now that you will spend at least part of the year in London, we shall see one another often."

"Thank you, Aunt," Henrietta managed.

"Come along, my brave soldier," the colonel called to the cat from the doorway. "Let's see if we can find you another lobster patty."

Knight sprang from the desk and bounded out the door. He had his priorities in order.

While the colonel closed the door, Lady Fuddlesby could be heard admonishing him. "Owen, the way you spoil dear Knight, I daresay he will be the size of a cow within three months of our marriage."

Alone with the duke, Henrietta felt her heart lurch madly. "I . . . I understand you only announced our betrothal in order to direct attention away from the contretemps with the ring—"

Henrietta broke off when the duke reached out and pulled her into his arms. In a deep voice he muttered, "If you believe that, I must recant what I said about your superior intelligence."

Staring up into his silvery eyes, Henrietta dared to hope.

The duke traced his finger down her cheek. "I love you, Henrietta. I know I made a mull of it earlier, but I am asking you now to be my wife." His steady gaze bored into hers in silent expectation.

"Oh, yes, Giles, please," Henrietta cried just before he crushed his lips to hers.

Raising his dark head a few minutes later he murmured, "You do love me, Henrietta? I could not bear it if you did not."

Staring up at him dizzily, she said, "I love you very much, Giles. But what of the difference in our stations?"

The Duke of Winterton used his lips to show her how little the matter meant to him.

After a grand wedding at St. George's, the newly wed couple returned to the town house in Park Lane. Carrying his wife into his bedchamber, the duke placed Henrietta across the red velvet bedspread and lovingly began removing her clothes.

From the corner of the room, Sir Polly Grey spoke in the seventh Duke of Winterton's voice. "Giles. Marriage."

The duke turned his head toward the bird and shouted, "I am married, you fool, and all I want is to bed my wife."

In *Giles's* voice Sir Polly Grey repeated gleefully, "All I want is to bed my wife."

But the two on the bed paid no attention.